Sacrificed

The Ignited Series
Book Two

Desni Dantone

Sacrificed

This is a work of fiction. Names, characters, and incidents are either the product of the author's imagination or are used fictitiously. Any resemblance to actual persons, living or dead, or events is entirely coincidental.

The scanning, uploading, and distribution of this book via the Internet or via any other means without the permission of the author is illegal and punishable by law. Please purchase only authorized electronic editions, and do not participate in or encourage electronic piracy of copyrighted materials. Your support of the author's rights is appreciated.

Cover design by Georgina Gibson, www.georginagibson.com

Printed in the United States of America

All rights reserved. Copyright © 2014 Desni Dantone

Published 2014 by Laine D. Publishing

ISBN 13: 978-0989509022

The Ignited Series:

Ignited

Sacrificed

Salvaged Soul (Coming Soon)

Avenging Heart (Coming 2015)

CHAPTER 1

The chill in the air contrasted sharply with the blue sky and warm sun. Days like today were teasers, early peeks of the quickly approaching spring. For once, I wasn't looking forward to it. To me, it meant time was moving forward. Time was my enemy. Only the hawk circling above seemed to understand my peril as it swooped closer—as if sensing my impending doom as an easy meal.

I tried not to think about the fact that I was doomed. That wasn't easy, considering I was reminded of it every day. That was why we were here, in Smithfield, West Virginia, after all. We'd followed the Skotadi here, in hopes that they had the answers to preventing my inevitable fall into darkness.

We had found them, too, after a great deal of searching. If the little town in which our shabby hotel was located was isolated, the warehouse the Skotadi worked out of was off the radar. Literally. Located twenty minutes outside of town, no GPS could have found the place. It had taken us a while to pin it down.

I had to give it to them—the Skotadi were smart. They knew how to hide.

But then, so did we. Snuggled amongst the trees and large

boulders on a high ridge overlooking their warehouse below, we had an unobstructed view of them, and they were none the wiser. Problem was, despite having a great surveillance set-up, we still didn't have a clue as to what the Skotadi were doing. With black out windows on all sides of the warehouse, we couldn't watch them on the inside. All we got was the occasional Skotadi coming and going through the day. To where, we didn't know.

Ultimately, we needed to find a way inside, though that wasn't a part of our immediate plans. We weren't about to bulldoze our way in there, guns blazing, and take on a small army of Skotadi by ourselves. There were only four of us and, while we were eager, we weren't stupid. Figuring out what was going on in that warehouse was going to require a well-calculated plan and a whole hell of a lot of preparation. And luck.

In the meantime, we have been monitoring their activities, looking for patterns and signs of weakness, and keeping a list of the Skotadi we saw as a way of determining how many we were dealing with. So far, we had a list of about twenty with our own weird names like *Skull Tattoo*, *Nerd Glasses*, and *Big Ugly Moose*. We had to have fun with the names, because otherwise, we would be bored out of our minds.

We *were* bored out of our minds.

Currently, my best friend Callie Sanders—and the only human involved in the circus show that was my life—was busy doodling sketches of the four of us on the notebook as I watched over her shoulder. I was impressed with how accurately she portrayed each of us, right down to the ornery twinkle in Alec's eyes and the determinedness of Nathan's. I, of course, had a bright smile on my face, which was where her accuracy dwindled.

When she realized I was watching, she glanced up at me with a smile. "Think I have a chance at art school?"

I returned her smile despite the dull ache in my chest.

While her parents thought she was on some once-in-a-lifetime trip to Italy to study art for the remainder of our senior year, she has chosen instead to stick by me. Though she was here with me now, she had the opportunity to go home, and she had a family to go home to. Callie had the opportunity to think about her future, what school she wanted to attend after graduation, and where she would be next year. Not me. All I could think about was staying alive and not becoming a monster.

I used to be a normal teenage girl, or so I had thought. That all changed a few months ago, when I learned there was a whole other world out there—a world in which gods and goddesses, good and evil, and the supernatural existed—and I was a part of it. Actually, I was a big part of it. Sort of *The One*, if you will. Only, not in a good way. More like in an *I could bring upon a wrath of evil the world has never seen* kind of way.

It wasn't until recently that I learned I was destined to side with the forces of evil, the Skotadi. The moment I'd learned of my fate, I'd set out to alter it. But then, the Kala—the good guys at war with the Skotadi—were just as intent on stopping me.

Except for Nathan. He was a Kala, but unlike the rest of them, he wanted to protect me, to help me. He'd been doing it all my life, since I was three years old, so he had gotten good at it. The fact that he had recently admitted to having feelings for me only seemed to strengthen his resolve to see me through this mess.

He was so determined he even agreed to work with Alec Sierra—super-hybrid of the Skotadi like me, reluctant to accept his fate like me, and the first boy I'd ever kissed. To say that things were strained between Nathan and Alec was an understatement. Somehow, they had not only managed to not kill each other, but it was the two of them, working together, that had discovered the location of the Skotadi's hideout.

It was because of them and their freakishly similar methods of torture and interrogation that we were here. Granted, we were in the middle of nowhere, and so far had nothing to do but stare at a crummy old warehouse. Still, we were taking steps in the right direction.

I nodded at Callie's sketch. "Send this along with your applications. Art school will be a sure thing."

She giggled, and my smile widened, morphing into a real one. Alec perked up at the sounds of a good time and leaned over Callie's shoulder to see what we were up to. He cocked his head to the side as he surveyed the drawing.

"I'm not hot enough," he commented.

Callie and I shared a look. We started to laugh, until we saw Alec's face. He was serious.

"No, really," he continued. "I'm not hot enough. My face isn't chiseled enough. My hair has never been that…neat, and don't even get me started on how much broader *his* stick shoulders are than mine."

From behind me, I heard Nathan chime in, "Looks accurate to me."

Glancing over my shoulder, I was the only one to see the dimple in Nathan's cheek. His eyes flicked to mine quickly, before lowering to the one-man tic-tac-toe game he was playing in the dirt.

"No," Alec insisted, and grabbed the notebook from Callie. "Let me see this thing."

She protested as he attempted to correct her mistakes and, as they fell into their usual friendly banter, I turned my attention to Nathan.

"Who's winning?"

His dimple reappeared, and I barely avoided embarrassing myself by dipping my finger into it. It was just so darn cute. Who knew? I was a sucker for dimples.

"Tied." He wiped the dirt surface clear and started a new game with a strategically placed X. He looked up at me, silently inviting me into his sad, but seriously adorable, attempt to thwart the boredom. I placed a circle, and we continued back and forth until we ended in a draw. Again. And again.

It wasn't exactly fun, especially when neither of us won, but I enjoyed it because of how close I had to lean toward him to mark my squares. I was very aware of my forearm every time it brushed against his, and I had to admit, I had never played a more sexually charged game of tic-tac-toe.

I made a circle, and was pretty sure I would have him up against a wall after my next move. I waited anxiously for him to put an X in the square I hoped for, but it never came. I glanced up at him, and followed his gaze to what had caught his attention.

In the distance, visible through the trees thanks to the dirt cloud left in its wake, a fast moving vehicle approached the warehouse. It wasn't the first one we had seen coming and going but, as always, it was something we needed to pay attention to.

"Alec."

The sharpness of Nathan's voice brought Callie and Alec's play-fighting to an abrupt stop. They both looked up as a blue van made a fast turn into the warehouse parking lot. A little faster than it probably should have.

We all watched eagerly. The warehouse had been quiet all morning, so the appearance of any activity had us all on edge, if not a little excited. I wasn't the only one who desperately wanted *something* to happen.

Though this wasn't what I'd had in mind.

The van pulled to a stop alongside the warehouse's rear entrance and two Skotadi exited the vehicle. They walked to the back of the van and opened the door, where two more emerged, carrying a woman. One had her by the shoulders, while the other held her ankles. Even from the distance, I could see her legs bucking and arms straining as she struggled against them.

Nathan lifted the binoculars to get a better look, and I asked him, "Who is it?"

He shook his head and passed the binoculars to me. Through the lens, I could see that her mouth was covered with duct tape so we couldn't hear her screams. Her eyes were wide with fear, but even with the close up view, I couldn't tell if they were human eyes or hybrid eyes.

Kala had silver rings around their irises, Skotadi had gold, and developing hybrids, like myself and Alec, had black. Skotadi eyes were easy to pick out; Kala's a little less obvious. The black rings were almost impossible to spot unless you were looking for them.

She wasn't a Skotadi, that much was certain. And she was terrified. For good reason. I'd only seen a little of what the Skotadi were capable of, and that had been enough. I knew that whatever they had in store for this woman couldn't be good.

I passed the binoculars to Callie, and she passed them on to Alec without looking through them. She still hadn't gotten used to this alternate life of mine. Not that I have, but Callie was even more freaked out than I was when it came to stuff like this. I gave her a sympathetic smile as she tried to look everywhere but at the scene unfolding before us.

"I don't think she's a Kala," Alec observed. "Maybe developing?"

"What about the Skotadi?" Nathan questioned. "Have we accounted for those four?"

I took the notebook from Callie and scanned over the list of ridiculous names.

"We've seen that big guy a few times," Alec said. "*The Hulk.*"

"The scrawny driver," Callie added. "He drives all the time."

I found the names *The Hulk* and *Chauffeur*. I was pretty sure the other two were named *Pinnocchio* and *Shaggy*, and everyone agreed with me. At least we didn't have four more Skotadi to add to our already long list. There were already too many of them for us to take on. At this rate, we'd never figure out what was going on in that warehouse, let alone save the poor woman they had dragged inside.

"Who was she?" Callie whispered from beside me. No one responded. The only question more difficult to answer was Callie's next one. "What are they doing to her?"

If either Nathan or Alec had a guess, neither of them voiced it. Instead, Callie's question hung up in the air around us, blanketing us. I had never felt more helpless.

Movement to my right distracted me from my overactive imagination. I cast a glance over my shoulder as Alec slinked by us, moving in a crouched position. With one look at his face, I knew that he was up to something. And, knowing Alec, it probably wasn't anything good.

Before anyone could ask, he whispered, "I'll be right back," and continued crawling toward the cluster of trees to our left.

"Where are you going?" Nathan whispered harshly after him.

Alec stopped behind the cover of a large boulder. "To try to see what they're doing," he said over his shoulder.

The three of us were all in such states of disbelief that all we managed were grumbled, unintelligible arguments. They fell on deaf ears anyway since Alec didn't wait to hear what any of us had to say. He disappeared down the side of the embankment.

"Better hope he doesn't get caught," Nathan scoffed. Translation: *I'm not going to bail his ass out if he gets caught.*

I slanted my eyes at Nathan and wiped the knowing smile from my face before he saw it. Sure, he played tough, and sure, he detested Alec. But if Alec got caught, I knew Nathan wouldn't stand idly back and do nothing. Nathan was too good of a guy to turn his back, even on Alec. Even if he would never admit it.

Rather than say anything remotely like that to Nathan, I said instead, "He won't get caught."

Nathan grunted, clearly not as optimistic as I was. I had to be optimistic. If I let myself worry about Alec, about myself, and this predicament we were both in, I would only drive myself crazy. Not dwelling on the inevitable every second of every day was the only way I knew how to do that.

Nathan did enough worrying for the two of us. He remained tense at my side as he stared down at the warehouse, his jaw clenched tight. I suspected that he was contemplating his options: leave Alec to his fate, leave Callie and I to go drag Alec back, or wait and cause Alec severe pain when he returned. *If* he returned.

No, no. Of course, he would return. It was Alec. He was smarter than he might lead others to believe. Sure, he was a little overeager, but I could hardly blame him. He was in the same boat as me, only he had a six month head start. He was just as determined as me. As Nathan. He wanted to fix this just as badly as the rest of us, if not more so.

Alec wouldn't do anything stupid. He would be fine.

I opened my mouth to reassure Nathan, but the words froze in my throat at the same time the tiny hairs on the back of my neck stood on end. When Nathan's eyes turned to mine, I knew that he sensed them too.

And I knew that all hell was about to break loose.

CHAPTER 2

Nathan exploded to his feet so fast that even the Skotadi sneaking up on us were startled. With a quick glance over my shoulder, I saw that there were three of them. One lifted a radio to his mouth. Nathan took him out first, cutting off the Skotadi's call for reinforcements with a strategically placed, diamond-coated knife to the chest. As the body dissipated, Nathan stepped in front of Callie and me, putting himself between us and the two remaining Skotadi.

On one hand, I was grateful for his protection. On the other hand, I hated it. Ever since his brush with death last month, when I realized that he wasn't invincible, I have feared for his safety as much as my own. The thought of ever losing him had become my newest nightmare. So, even if he was determined to do whatever was necessary to keep me safe, I was just as determined to do the same for him.

Besides, the Skotadi wanted *me* alive.

I had barely scrambled to my feet when Nathan shoved me back and to the side, out of the way, as if anticipating my heroic intentions. I collided with Callie and the two of us toppled over in a heap of arms and legs. Before I could jump up again, Callie grabbed my arm, holding me back and leaving me to watch helplessly as Nathan clashed with the two Skotadi.

I reminded myself that this was Nathan. And Nathan was a fighter. Except for that one close call, he had always managed to come out of these situations okay. It was more than luck. It was talent. He was good at what he did.

But that didn't mean he couldn't make a mistake. And what if he did? How long could he go on with his near perfect record before slipping up? It would only take a second, one misplaced step, and he would be lost forever.

I could never let that happen.

When four more Skotadi charged from the tree line, my worst fear became a tangible possibility. One that I refused to accept.

He could defeat two Skotadi without breaking a sweat—but six?

I *had* to do something. I looked around for the best weapon I could find, and wound up with a rock the size of a softball. It was heavy and pointy…it would at least stun a Skotadi long enough for Nathan to finish him off. As I stood with the rock raised above my head, two Kala emerged from the tree line. Their eyes glimmered with flashes of silver as they surveyed the scene.

Oh, this keeps getting better and better, I grumbled to myself.

It wasn't looking good, for any of us. My stomach dropped when I remembered Callie, an innocent, but guilty by association. I had to fight for her too. I knew Nathan wouldn't go down without a fight—and neither would I. At least if we all died, we died fighting.

I took a step forward, and Callie grabbed my leg. I shook her off easily, but didn't get far before she grabbed me around the waist and pulled me back with unyielding force. I turned to her—to tell her to run, because I wasn't leaving Nathan.

It wasn't Callie that had grabbed me.

It was a boy. A boy that I knew, even if I didn't know I did until I looked into his eyes. I recognized the black hair that curled under his ears, the slope of his shoulders, his tall lean frame.

I've seen him nearly every night for months. In my dreams. The Boy-in-White—only dressed in faded jeans and a black hoodie. As if seeing his face for the first time now, in the flesh rather than in a dream, wasn't enough, I found myself lost in his eyes—such a pure green that they redefined the color.

He held my gaze as firmly as he gripped my waist, and I got the impression he was just as stunned as I was. He recovered first, grabbing Callie with one hand, and quickly steered both of us behind the cover of a large boulder several yards away.

The only reason I let him was because I was in shock.

A shriek of horrendous pain behind me snapped me out of it, and I remembered what I had been doing before the boy grabbed me.

Nathan needed my help.

As if sensing my intentions, the boy pushed me down behind the boulder, beside Callie, before I could slip out of his grasp. He dropped to a knee in front of me and brought a finger to his lips, instructing us to be quiet.

Then he finally spoke, and his familiar voice was like a lullaby to my ears. "Stay right here. Let the pros handle this," he said. He froze me with a quick wink, and then he was gone, heading straight for the fight.

I crawled around the boulder after him. I had always sensed that he meant no harm to me, and I was still sure of that now…but Nathan? I didn't know what he intended for Nathan.

And then, there were the other Kala to worry about.

At least, from what I could see, Nathan was okay. Another Skotadi had been dissipated while I'd been in la-la land with the Boy-in-White. The two Kala had joined Nathan in fighting the remaining five Skotadi. That was reassuring, but still, I had a brief pang of concern as the mystery boy from my dreams drew closer to him.

The Skotadi saw the boy and faltered. Enough for Nathan and the other two Kala to quickly finish off their immediate threats. As three bodies evaporated, the boy produced two shiny objects, seemingly from nowhere, and with two snaps of his wrists, dispatched them into the chests of the two remaining Skotadi as they stared at him. They both dissipated, probably before they even knew what hit them.

In a matter of seconds, nothing remained of the Skotadi.

There was a beat of awed silence as the two Kala and Nathan surveyed each other, then all at one, all three raised their guns. Two pointed at Nathan; one pointed at the Boy-in-White.

The Kala shifted anxiously once they realized where Nathan's gun was aimed. Nathan didn't flinch. He might not have known what I knew, but he wasn't stupid. He knew this boy was someone important. And having a gun pointed at his head gave Nathan the upper hand.

If only Nathan knew what I knew. It was quite possible that

the fate of humanity rested on this kid's shoulders. But Nathan only had one thing on his mind. As disturbing as it was, I found it flattering.

"Where's Kris?" he demanded of the boy. When a response apparently didn't come fast enough for his satisfaction, he added, "I will shoot you."

That threat—because I knew it wasn't an empty one—kicked my butt into gear, and I clambered to my feet quickly. "Nathan, I'm here," I called as I rounded the boulder.

His shoulders heaved in visible relief. A reassuring smile started to form on my lips, but the flash of metal to my left pulled it up short. I froze as the two guns pointed at Nathan turned to me.

Even more shocking than having two guns pulled on me one second was having someone throw themself in front of me the next. The only thing more shocking was *who*.

"No!" The Boy-in-White shouted as he moved to shield me.

Fortunately, no one had fired, so neither of us were shot. Not yet. It wasn't looking good for me as the two Kala shifted to get an angle around the boy.

"Gabby," the boy said sharply, "we talked about this. She's off limits. Richie?"

Gabby and Richie, was it? I supposed it was nice to know the names of the people about to kill me. And from the hateful scowls on both of their faces, they were dead-set on ensuring it.

When they didn't lower their weapons, the boy pulled me snugly behind him, guarding me fully with his body. "Stay behind me," he whispered to me, then he raised his voice to the Kala,

"Put the guns down, guys, or so help me, I will do *nothing* to help you assholes."

Risking a peek over the kid's shoulder, I watched as the girl—Gabby—swatted a strand of curly brown hair out of her eyes, which remained coolly fixed on me, along with her gun. Though his gun also remained trained on me, the guy named Richie slanted his eyes uneasily to Nathan.

And for good reason. A confident and pissed off Nathan could intimidate anyone. Only I saw the glimmer of fear in his eyes when they met mine. I desperately wanted to run to his side, but the kid was holding me back. I figured that sticking by him was probably best for me at the moment anyway, as far as expanding my life expectancy was concerned.

"Put the guns down," the boy pleaded with them again. "It's alright. Look at her. Does she look dangerous to you?"

They glanced at each other, but neither looked ready to waver.

Suddenly, I heard the cocking of a gun beside me, close to my ear, but it wasn't my head it was pressed to.

"Do as he says, or I'll blow his brains out," Alec announced his stealthy return. He stepped beside me, his eyes trained on the two Kala, and gun pressed to the Boy-In-White's head. Though he never looked directly at me, I swore I saw a faint glow in his eyes. A flash of gold.

That wasn't good.

Maybe the Kala saw the glint in his eyes, or maybe it was the tone of his voice that told them he wasn't bluffing. Whatever it was, it worked. They lowered their weapons, reluctantly.

"Throw them on the ground," Nathan ordered.

They did as they were told, and only then did Alec turn to me. His eyes weren't glowing gold anymore, and I wondered if I had really seen it at all, or if I had imagined it.

"Go to Nathan," Alec told me. Shocked to hear those words come out of his mouth, I faltered. He lifted an amused eyebrow. "Go on."

Nathan watched me carefully as I scurried toward him. Satisfied that I was in one piece, he returned his attention to the Boy-in-White, who he still had his gun trained on. As did Alec.

I wanted to tell them both to ease up. I knew the boy wasn't a danger. Hell, he had nearly taken a bullet for me. I didn't know *why* he'd done it, but his actions alone spoke volumes.

That and I knew he could be trusted. From the dreams. But because I couldn't tell Nathan and Alec what I knew without telling them about the dreams, I bit my tongue and let them go about their own way of developing trust.

"Who are you?" Nathan asked the boy, and my ears perked up. I desperately needed a name, other than Boy-in-White.

His eyes fixated on me, as if I were the one who had asked him the question. "Micah," he said evenly despite having a gun pressed behind his ear. He nodded his head in the direction of the other two Kala. "That's Gabby and Richie."

From beside me, I heard a noise that sounded suspiciously like a growl. "What are you doing here?"

Micah's eyes narrowed on Nathan, and I realized I wasn't the only one who sensed Nathan's temper. I had to give it to him— the boy had balls, glaring at Nathan like that. "Same as you, watching the warehouse."

"Why?"

Micah glanced at me with a shrug. I could have been mistaken, but I swore I detected the hint of a grin on his face. "Why are you?"

Alec pressed the gun behind Micah's ear, forcing his head forward a fraction. "Answer the damn question!"

Micah definitely grinned now. I wondered if he was insane, because really, only a crazy person would be grinning with two guns pointed at his head. And then, Micah nodded at me. "Ask her."

My skin blanched as I felt everyone's eyes turn to me. "I...I don't know."

And I didn't. Not really. I assumed they were here because the Skotadi were here, but something about Micah's expression hinted at something more. Something I wasn't in on. I suspected there was another reason he had done his best to lure me here.

"Sure you do," he said confidently, and I silently prayed that he wasn't about to spill my secret about the dreams. He hesitated with an amused tilt of his head, his grin growing as he leveled his gaze on me. "Don't you know? I'm the one you were created to kill."

* * *

As it turned out, Gabby and Richie had a very good reason to pull their guns on me.

They knew exactly who I was—what I was. They knew how

dangerous I could eventually be. As did Micah. But for some reason, the kid insisted they keep their hands off of me.

And suggested that we join forces.

I suspected that they were only amusing Micah, but after a lot of coaxing and promises of peace, Nathan and Alec agreed to follow them back to their hideout. As we approached a large log house at the end of a long gravel driveway, I realized that they had been living much more luxuriously than we had.

The house was a rental property, most often used by large parties looking to enjoy the nearby ski resort. They assured us of its safety, and I didn't doubt them. They had been there for months already, and I doubted the Skotadi would have thought to look for a small group of Kala renting a house in the middle of ski country.

They filled us in on their plan to pick off the Skotadi at the warehouse little by little. They, too, had figured the Skotadi force too strong to take on with a single attack, but small raids on, say the vehicles coming and going, might weaken the Skotadi over time…and lead to some worthy intelligence.

Of course, if we agreed to work with them, there was a better chance of success. I saw it in both Nathan's and Alec's eyes. A partnership was our best shot.

Once a truce, overseen by Micah, had been established between all parties, Nathan and Alec had agreed to stay, at least for a little while. It only seemed right since we all had the common goal of snooping on the Skotadi. We could work together, help each other, get more accomplished in our pursuit of answers.

I knew it made sense for us to work together. But why exactly Micah, Gabby, and Richie were here in the first place remained a mystery. One that I intended to uncover soon.

Alec and Callie had gone back to the hotel to collect our stuff. That left me and a tightly wound Nathan alone with our new allies. It was he who whisked me down the hall into one of the bedrooms before I even knew who had ahold of my arm.

He shut the door softly behind us. As much as I would have liked to think he had brought me in there to do something fun, like make out, I knew that wasn't the case.

He had pulled me out of earshot of the others, simply to talk. And not about anything I really wanted to talk about. Not with him. Not since he'd made that ridiculous vow to not act on his feelings for me until we took some time thinking.

I'd gone along with his wishes at the time, but as the weeks went by, it became apparent that I didn't need to think about anything. I had feelings for him. Period. I used to have feelings for Alec. But what I'd once felt for Alec was now overshadowed by what I felt for Nathan. I knew that. I only wished he believed it.

But then, he had things to think about too—like his thought to be dead girlfriend, Lillian, waltzing back into his life as a Skotadi—and I didn't want to push him. I'd been a good girl, giving him his space, though it was a slow tortuous death for me. For the most part, I'd gotten good at pretending I wasn't an emotion wreck every time I was alone with Nathan. Now, I tried to downplay the turmoil churning my stomach by acting over-confident.

"What's up?"

He crossed the room to where I stood, and I allowed myself a brief daydream that he was coming over to sweep me off my feet and finally whisper to me the words I have been longing to hear from him for weeks, before kissing me madly.

Hey, a girl could dream.

"I don't know about this," he said instead. "Something doesn't feel right. I don't know if we can trust this kid."

"Nathan, it's fine," I insisted. "Don't ask me how I know. I just do."

He blinked slowly and waited. I wasn't surprised that he didn't get it. He didn't know about my dreams, and I intended to keep it that way. I had to convince him to trust Micah like I trusted Micah, without telling him *how* I knew to trust Micah.

"He's a part of this, Nathan. An important part. He might be the only one out there that can help me—really help me—and he wants to. I think we need to hear what he has to offer."

"If he's really *the one*, the Kala they created to bring an end to this war…" Nathan continued, and paused as if to be sure I completely understood the gravity of what he was about to say. "You do realize that you're the only one standing in his way? You're the one enemy he has, and you're standing here, in his house, telling me to trust him. You ever hear the saying, *keep your friends close, and your enemies closer*?"

When he put it that way, it didn't sound so smart. "Yeah, I know it looks bad. But, Nathan, I've got to trust my instincts on this one. I've got a good feeling about this."

There was more to it than us being born enemies. If it were

really that simple, why didn't he let Gabby and Richie shoot me? He'd had his chance to be rid of me…and he had protected me.

"You want me to trust him because you have a feeling?"

"A strong feeling, almost prophet-like," I explained. And who knew? Maybe I was a prophet.

Prophets had the ability to visit people in their dreams, as well as visualize the future, read people's intentions, and sometimes their minds. I sure couldn't read anyone's mind, but maybe I was picking up on Micah's intentions.

And they were good.

Nathan considered what I said. "You really think you might be a prophet?"

I shrugged. "I don't know. All I know is that I'm getting some good vibes from him." *In person as well as in my dreams.* "Just let me talk to him," I continued before Nathan formed another argument. "Alone."

"Alone?"

"Yes, alone. I don't want you to scare him."

He gave me one of his almost smiles, and I knew I was getting somewhere. I took the opportunity to edge past him before he thought of a reason to stop me. Honestly, I did want to talk to Micah. I really, really desperately *needed* to talk to him.

I only made it a few steps before Nathan grabbed ahold of my hand and spun me around. The motion brought us closer than he had probably intended, and I saw the argument he had formed fade, replaced by something else. Something I had been waiting weeks to see.

He still wanted me.

I didn't pull away from him. I didn't move a muscle. I waited for his next move, readied myself for it, whatever it may be.

It wasn't anything that I'd long hoped for. He dropped my hand and shifted, just enough to break the connection. And he was back in man-on-a-mission mode.

"Just don't let your guard down because you have a sense," he said gruffly, and I wondered if it was because of what had just happened or because his temper was rearing up. "If he's really who he says he is, we don't know what he might be capable of."

"Nathan, I've got it. I can do this." I placed a hand on his shoulder and tossed him a reassuring smile. "If it would make you feel better, you can hang out nearby, just in case I need you."

He nodded like that had been his plan all along, whether I'd asked or not. "Just be careful, alright?"

"I will," I said with a nod, and turned to find Micah.

It was my turn to get some answers.

CHAPTER 3

I found Micah on a bench swing, on the back patio, overlooking the snowcapped mountains. It was actually very pretty, and I took a moment to admire the view as I approached him. When I realized I was stalling, I zeroed in on Micah with a newfound determination.

I can do this.

He looked up as I drew near, and extended the bag of potato chips he was munching on. "Want some?"

I stopped in front of him, hands on hips. No time for small talk. "Who are you?"

He set the bag down with a shrug. "I'm Micah."

"I got that much. *Who are you?*"

The grin on his face begged for a bitch slap, but his next words held my hand in check. "What you mean to ask is, *why are you in my dreams*, right?"

I folded my arms over my chest, refusing to let him know how much his mention of the dreams unnerved me. On some level, I had hoped that they weren't real, that they were nothing more than a byproduct of my waning sanity. But he saw them, too. He'd just confirmed what I'd long suspected, but had never quite accepted.

The whole dream thing freaked me out.

Nathan had once told me that some prophets had the ability to visit people in their dreams, but he had made it sound like it wasn't something a lot of hybrids could do, and he'd never said anything about both people being aware of the dream. It was as if Micah and I *shared* our dreams. What could that mean? And why did it happen every night, regardless of whether I wanted it to or not?

In fact, I *didn't* want it to.

"Come sit down," Micah suggested softly, patting the spot beside him. "I won't bite. Maybe we can figure some of this out together."

I hesitated, but there was something in his eyes that reassured me. Though he was coming off as a little too cocky for my liking, I knew my instincts were right about him. They had to be. I'd dreamt it.

I had dreamt about him, and he was real. The rest had to be right, too.

I pretended to be enthralled with the view as I edged closer. Really, it was impressive, but my mind was roaming on everything but the scenery as I sat down beside Micah. None of those thoughts would form into words, however, and I sat there quietly, waiting for the right question to form.

So much for setting out in search of answers.

I felt Micah's eyes on me, watching me, and I stared straight ahead, pretending not to notice.

"You look different than I thought you would," he eventually said. His choice of words piqued my curiosity, and I finally turned to look at him as he continued. "I never saw your face. I imagined hundreds of different faces, but none of them were…you."

We stared at each other for what felt like an eternity before my thoughts formed into words. "Then how did you know it was me?"

He grinned. "I figured no one else would be stupid enough to be there, spying on the Skotadi, and when I got close enough, I just knew it was you."

Like I had known it was him? "How? How did you *know*?"

He shrugged. "I have good instincts. I can sense things about people."

"Are you a prophet?"

"It's my strongest specialty." He hesitated, looking at me as if he were looking inside me, searching for my deepest, most heavily guarded secrets. "I've known all along that you're not what you're supposed to be. I can sense it. Gabby and Richie weren't as trusting, so we hung back and watched you for a while."

"If they saw that I wasn't all…" I wiggled my fingers as if it were the international sign for evil, "then why did they nearly shoot me?"

"They're still a little skittish. They never agreed on my decision to find you, and they're afraid of something happening to me and screwing everything up."

His decision to find me? So, he had left the protection of the Kala base because of me? I'd suspected so. I just wished I knew why.

"Why did you want to find me?" I asked softly. *Please, don't let it be to kill me. Please.*

Please don't let Nathan be right, just this one time.

He turned to face me with eyes so penetrating I had to divert my gaze. I was really starting to hate the way he looked at me, like we were best friends after only just meeting.

"After our first dream together," he answered. "I had this pull to you, and this intense need to help you, even though I didn't know how. Or why. I still don't have those answers, but I do want to help."

I'd had a similar pull in my dreams. Only it wasn't to help him, but to *find* him. All along, I'd known that I was supposed to find him.

I stared down at my shoes, unwilling and unable to look at him. "What brought you here?"

"Another dream. A sort of vision. I knew something was here, and then we found the Skotadi's warehouse. We still don't know what they're doing there, but I imagine it's important or I wouldn't have had a vision of it."

"And you led me here?" I asked softly. In addition to Nathan and Alec uncovering the location of the warehouse by interrogating important Skotadi leaders, Micah had been speaking the name of this town to me in my dreams for weeks before we'd found it.

"Yes. There's something in that warehouse. We just have to find out what it is. And I knew you needed to be here."

I nibbled on my lip as I debated whether or not to tell Micah what I knew. Ultimately, I decided that he was legit, and that if he was going to help, he needed to know everything.

"They've been converting Kala to Skotadi out of that warehouse," I told him. "They've been doing it for years, apparently."

Micah was silent for so long I was forced to look up at him. And regretted it immediately.

Why did he have to look at me like that?

"We thought that if they could do that," I continued to fill in the awkward silence as Micah gawked at me, "then there might be a way to do the opposite, or maybe even prevent me from going Skotadi in the first place."

Micah nodded along in silence. He finally looked away from me and muttered more to himself than to me, "How can they do that?" Since I didn't have an answer for him, I said nothing. After a long stretch of silence, he added, "We'll figure it out. Somehow."

There was such determination in his voice, in his posture, in his eyes. I didn't doubt that he would do everything in his power to figure it out. Seeing all of that, I couldn't help but wonder why he was so determined.

My eyes narrowed instinctively. Turning to him with squared shoulders, I said, "You seem really motivated for someone who doesn't even know me."

"But I do know you," he returned automatically, and in a tone that sounded a little too intimate for my comfort. At least at this stage in our…friendship? It wasn't even that, not yet, but this kid talked like we'd been buddies for years. "I know you don't want this. I know there's too much good in you to succumb to your fate. I think you can fight it."

I jumped from my seat and paced the porch in front of Micah. For all he knew, I needed to stretch, or to walk off some steam brought upon by the heavy subject matter. Really, I needed some distance from him and his eyes. Sitting beside him on the bench had been too much. *He* was too much—the way he looked at me, the way he talked like we've known each other for years, the way he was so willing to help me…despite the risks to himself.

I remembered something that Nathan had pointed out, and only now realized how much sense he had made.

I spun to Micah like an attorney interrogating a witness. "Why would you want to gamble with your own life? We're supposed to be enemies. I was made to kill you. Wouldn't it just be easier to get rid of me now, than try to help me and it potentially backfire on you?"

"I don't agree with the Kala's decision to eliminate you," he said as if that explained everything.

I shook my head because…it didn't. Not even close. That was it? That was his reasoning? The look on my face must have portrayed my disbelief, because Micah held up his hands as if offering a truce.

"Alright. Think about this," he said. "If we can find a way to stop you from siding with the Skotadi—if you side with the Kala—there will be two of us. Two that the Skotadi can't touch. They won't have a chance at winning this war."

Now, that was the first thing he'd said all day that made any sense. And was something that I could believe. War tactics. That was something even Nathan could get on board with. And I knew Alec would be game.

"Actually, there will be three of us," I said, earning a raised eyebrow from Micah. "Alec's like me, sort of. They created him before me, a little differently, a little weaker than me, but he's a super-hybrid too."

"And Alec is…"

"Eyebrow ring, messy hair, green eyes." I snapped my fingers and pointed to Micah when the ultimate description hit me. "The one that pointed the gun to your head."

"Ah." Micah nodded as it clicked. "And he wants to fight back like you?"

"Yeah," I said. "Sometimes he says it's too late for him, that he's working on helping me now, but I know he doesn't want this either."

"Why does he think it's too late for him?"

I shrugged. "He started developing six months before me."

"Has he shown any signs of changing yet?"

I thought about the glimpse of gold I thought I'd seen in Alec's eyes earlier. Maybe I hadn't imagined it? Was it a sign that he was beyond help? If it had been real, it couldn't be a good sign.

"No," I said to Micah, and had to look away when he stared back, like he knew I was hiding something. I'd never been a good liar, but I wasn't exactly lying. I just didn't know. I needed to talk to Alec to be sure.

Fortunately, Micah didn't push, though I had the sense that he wanted to. Instead, he changed the subject. "Do you know what specialties you have? They start coming in yet?"

"No, not yet."

"Being a prophet, I have the ability to read people's specialties. I could do that for you, if you'd like," Micah suggested.

It was tempting. Really tempting. Waiting around for something to happen had me on edge ninety-nine percent of the time. Knowing what was coming might help alleviate some of the anxiety. That didn't mean I still wouldn't dread the moment they came in. Micah couldn't help me there. Or could he?

"Can you help me to…" I trailed off, unable to think of the right words to describe what I was afraid of.

"Control them?" he offered.

"Yes!" *Control* was the perfect word.

He nodded with a smile. "They're a little overwhelming at first, but I've had some practice. They're stronger for us when they come in than they are for the others. I can teach you some tricks I've learned along the way. No problem."

"Thanks," I said softly.

"We can start tomorrow," he finalized with a clap of his hands, as if he were actually looking forward to it.

And I suspected that he really was, though I had no idea why. He was really helpful. Far more than I had expected. Again, that little voice in my head wondered why he was so determined to help me, but I pushed it aside, because I did need his help.

Sure, I was a little suspicious. Either he was just a really good guy with a death wish, or he had an ulterior motive. Though I didn't necessarily think it was anything bad. Whatever it was, the fact remained that I needed his help. But I would be sure to keep an eye on him.

And go about the old-fashioned way of figuring out what he was hiding from me.

CHAPTER 4

When Alec and Callie returned with our bags, the fun of determining sleeping arrangements began. It really shouldn't have been as difficult as it ended up being. I found it ironic that guys often poked fun at girls for being difficult, because in this case, the guys were definitely the whinier of the two sexes.

Being that we were sharing a three bedroom house, some pairing up needed to be done. Fortunately, the owners were prepared to accommodate multiple guests. The obvious 'kid room' was furnished with two bunk beds while the room across the hall from it had two double beds. The master bedroom had only one king-sized bed, so the two people who took that room would have to get a little cozier than the others.

Richie suggested that the three girls share the master room and the guys split up into pairs. It seemed like a sensible arrangement, but when Richie added that he must room with Micah, that idea fell flat.

Nathan and Alec glanced at each other and both shook their heads in unison.

"We'll kill each other," Alec said. "Not that I would care, but…" He threw a thumb in my direction like everyone already knew I was the only reason they hadn't already killed each other.

"How about the two Skotadi rooming together?" Gabby suggested, eyeing both Alec and me with obvious distaste. I didn't doubt she'd prefer for us to sleep outside, under the porch like a couple of stray dogs.

"I'm cool with that," Alec said quickly at the same time Nathan answered with a resounding, "Not a chance."

A beat of silence followed, and I doubted I was the only one waiting for them to duke it out right then and there.

"Alright," I said before their tempers brewed any further. "Callie's not afraid to room with me, right?" I tossed a cold glare at Gabby before turning to Callie for confirmation.

As expected, she nodded.

"Richie, would you be okay if Micah roomed with Gabby?" I asked, biting back the sarcasm. Well, most of it.

His eyes widened and his lips curled in disgust, and the only explanation for his reaction that I could think of was that I had spoken to him directly, like he considered it an insult to be addressed by some lowly Skotadi. He turned his grey eyes away with a barely detectable nod of his head.

I ignored him and turned to Nathan. "I assume you would have no problem rooming with Richie?"

Nathan and Richie shared glances, and they both lifted their shoulders in acceptance.

I turned to Alec last.

"I'll take the couch," he volunteered quickly.

I had been about to suggest he take his pick of rooms. I hadn't even considered the couch, but he seemed to be happy with it.

In fact, Micah and Nathan were both looking at me like they couldn't believe I had managed to sort it out without someone being mauled in the process. I allowed myself a moment to bask in the glory before turning to Callie with a smile.

"Ready to move in?"

After Micah moved his belongings out of the master bedroom, I collected my bags from the Tahoe. I didn't know how I'd managed to obtain the biggest room in the house. I hadn't done it on purpose, but now that I had the room, I was going to enjoy it. I had so few things to look forward to these days that having a spacious bedroom with a king bed was the highlight of the year.

That was until I opened the door to find Nathan waiting for me in my room.

Then that became the highlight of my life.

I knew it wasn't a social call. For him, it was business as usual. But for me, well, my pulse raced erratically as I approached him where he sat on the edge of the bed.

Nathan. On my bed. It would have been a dream come true if I didn't know the reason for his visit. He didn't even need to ask.

I replayed my chat with Micah, minus any mention of the dreams and how we already knew each other. I stuck with a winning the war version of the conversation.

And he bought it. Convincingly so, which was a relief, because that meant I didn't have to plead with him to trust Micah like I trusted Micah. I didn't want to get into that conversation any more than I had to. Fortunately, when it came to war tactics,

Nathan was on board, just as I'd expected.

"Oh, and he's going to help me figure out my specialties and control them," I added.

Nathan nodded silently, and I couldn't help but wonder what was going on in that head of his. He seemed…off.

"He's a prophet," I continued to fill in the silence. "He said he'll try to read me, try to pick up on my specialties so that we know what we're dealing with."

"That's good," Nathan muttered. He flashed me a brief smile, but I knew him well enough to know it wasn't a real one. It was only a cover. Something was bothering him.

"What's wrong?" I asked.

Nathan's method of avoidance was to look at his shoes on the floor. Eventually, after he more than likely determined I wasn't going to let him off the hook, he answered, "He seems a little too willing to help you, and I can't figure out why."

I'd figured it was because of the dreams, and his feeling like he knew me so well because of them. But, Nathan was picking up on Micah's behavior too, and he didn't know about the dreams. So, what was it about Micah?

"I get the whole war thing," he continued, "but it's still a gamble for him if it doesn't work. I think he's got another motive. I just can't figure out what it is."

"I don't think it's anything bad, though," I said. And I believed that. Honestly. I just wished I knew how in the hell I knew.

For the first time ever, I saw a devious looking smirk on Nathan's face. "Depends on what you mean by *bad*."

"What do you mean by that?"

"Maybe he's into you," he murmured quietly, eyes dropped to the floor.

There it was. Jealousy. I'd come to recognize it, since we were around Nathan's primary source of jealousy twenty-four hours a day, Alec. But for Nathan to be jealous of Micah? That was unexpected.

Except, well, Nathan might not be that far off base. Micah did seem a little overeager. Perhaps that pull I felt toward him in the dreams was a byproduct of a crush he had developed on me. It wasn't hard to believe—not that I thought I should be desired by every guy, not even close—but when you're dreaming of the same person night after night, feelings could develop. They hadn't for me, but maybe they had for him.

And then there was the way I'd caught him looking at me a few times, like I was the girl of his dreams—and not just in the literal sense. Though I had my suspicions, I refused to let Nathan know he may be on to something. I would get to the bottom of Micah's intensity on my own, at another time. The last thing I needed was to give Nathan a reason to put up more walls between us. Alec had caused enough.

"No way," I said dismissively. I paused a beat and then, because my inner voice could not be quieted any longer, added, "Sounds to me like someone might be jealous."

The second I said the words, I regretted them. It wasn't like me to be that bold, and the few times I had confronted Nathan over the past few weeks about his feelings, he'd clammed up and avoided me for days after. Expecting the same now, I mirrored him by staring down at my feet as he was, and tried to read his reaction out of the corner of my eye. I thought maybe, just maybe, a small smile curved his lips. But no dimples.

There was a long stretch of silence, and I knew he was deliberating a response. I expected him to blow it off, and nearly fell over when he finally murmured, "Maybe I am."

More excruciating silence followed as I was rendered speechless. Had he really just admitted to being jealous? What did it mean? Did it mean *anything*? The fact that he hadn't already bolted from the room gave me the courage to dig deeper.

"Hey, Nathan..."

I lifted my head, but he continued to stare at his shoes, avoiding my eyes. From his posture and the rigidness of his shoulders, I figured that he already suspected where I was attempting to lead this conversation.

"Have you...?" I trailed off, suddenly afraid to ask. Deep down, I feared that I already knew the answer. I just didn't want to accept it.

There was a long silence, as I tried to gather the nerve to continue. Finally, Nathan broke it. His head lifted, and his eyes held mine. "Have you?"

What? I shook my head sharply. "I wasn't the one who needed time—"

"We both did, Kris. Remember?"

"Yeah, that's what we said, but...I mean, not really. Not me."

I thought he might have started to smile, but he was quick to recover, as usual. Then he was back to serious-mode. "You do,

Kris. You just don't really know it. Alec—"

"I used to have feelings for Alec. *Used to*. That was before you."

He made a face like he didn't really believe me, and I couldn't understand why. To me, it was easy. I didn't understand why he had to make this more difficult than it was.

"I know your feelings for me are real, Kris. So are mine. Trust me." He paused, his eyes pleading with me to understand. "But this thing with Alec isn't over. I know it's not."

"Really?" I stood and looked down at him where he sat on the bed. "Who gives a shit about what I say, right? What I say doesn't matter, huh?"

I didn't wait for a response. I'd heard enough—nothing had changed. Part of me had started to suspect that he was making this so difficult because he didn't want to be with me, but he didn't know how to tell me. As I turned to storm away, Nathan grabbed my hand to stop me.

"You're the one who needed time to figure things out, Nathan," I said as I spun on him, my voice rising. "Not me. You, because of Lillian. Stop trying to put it all on me."

He shook his head like he didn't understand what I was talking about. "Lillian? You think that's what this is all about?"

"You needed time to think," I reminded him. As if he had forgotten.

"Yeah." He said it like a question, prompting me to continue.

"Because your girlfriend just came back from the dead," I said. *And tortured me and threatened to kill you...*

He released my hand and made a face that looked surprisingly relieved. "I didn't need time to think because of Lillian. I don't know why you thought that. That was seven years ago."

"Right, but the only reason you weren't together is because you thought she *died*."

"Well, yeah, but a lot has changed since then. I've changed. And you…"

"What about me, Nathan? You still need to think about something. If it's not Lillian, then what is it?"

He lowered his face to his hands with a groan, avoiding my question. And my eyes.

"What is it?" I pressed, with a little more anger behind my tone than I had meant for. I stared at the top of his head as he rolled it back and forth. "Nathan?"

He peeked up at me through spread fingers. The look on his face was…unexpected. Open and vulnerable in a way I have never seen him before. It softened my anger, but not my defensiveness. I folded my arms to keep from wrapping them around him like I wanted to do. Not until he started talking.

"What about me?" I repeated.

His mouth opened, but he shut it again without a response. He'd always been so good at that—at thinking before speaking. Times like this, I wished he had a problem with word vomit like I was known to have from time to time. His ability to hold back his thoughts was frustrating.

"Nathan!"

He groaned. "You scare the shit out of me, okay?"

I froze, mouth agape and ready for another feisty argument, which had slipped away upon hearing his words. I supposed I shouldn't have been surprised that he was afraid of me, considering what I was destined to become. But Nathan had always told me that none of that mattered to him.

I didn't think that was what he was referring to now though, which meant that he was scared of me, the girl, not the monster. Though I had no idea why.

"You're the first girl since Lillian that I've felt any…" Uncertainty settled into his eyes as his teeth caught his lip. Finally, he said, "With you, it's different."

Entranced by his unexpected admission, I sat beside him as he continued.

"Lillian and I were young, we were having fun. Yeah, I loved her, but I was living in the moment. I never looked past the present…" He trailed off and I could tell that he was struggling to find the right words, or scared to say them. "You're the first girl I can see a future with. And that scares the shit out of me."

My heart did a little jig along with the *Lord of the Dance* going on in my stomach. Wow. That was so not what I had expected. And it filled me with hope—hope that he would forget about this *not acting on our feelings* thing he was hung up on. While hopeful, I knew he wasn't there yet. And I knew he had more to say. I just wanted it to be something promising, because I was so tired of not acting on *my* feelings.

"And you're only seventeen," he continued, sounding like it killed him to admit that. "You're young. You should be out there, exploring your options. Not moving into a relationship."

"What if that's what I want?"

"If that's really what you wanted, you wouldn't be so confused about Alec."

"I'm not—"

Finally, he lifted his head to look at me. "I can see it, Kris. I've seen the way you look at him sometimes. You started something with Alec that you never got to see through." He stopped and his jaw twitched before he muttered the next words. "Maybe you should have. Maybe you still should. I don't know, but what I do know is that you shouldn't be rushing into something with *anyone* before you've resolved what you started with Alec. Figure out what you feel, or don't feel, but *really* figure it out."

For one, Nathan wasn't just *anyone*. But his reasoning behind not wanting to rush into something before we were both sure actually made sense. Even though I wasn't exactly convinced that I was still hung up on Alec.

Sure, Alec had a way of getting to me—flustering me, exciting me—but he did that to every female he encountered. Yeah, he was hot. But so was Nathan. And yeah, Alec made me laugh like no one else could, but Nathan understood me like no one else could.

Nathan was my rock, and always would be.

No matter what he thought, I was convinced Nathan was the one I wanted. But I would also honor his request to get to the bottom of my 'unresolved' feelings for Alec. If that was what it would take to get what I knew in my heart I wanted.

"Nathan…" I scooted closer to him on the bed. He tensed

beside me, as if guessing my intentions. And he was correct, of course. "If I agree to resolve some issues, could you agree to kiss me from time to time, just to remind me why I'm going through all the trouble in the first place?"

His throat jumped before a small smile spread across his lips. I secretly loved the way I made him nervous sometimes—times like this. "From time to time, huh?" he said gruffly.

"That's all," I whispered, and waited.

I didn't know what I expected. Maybe, if I was lucky, for Nathan to actually agree to it. Maybe for him to finally give in, to finally act on the feelings he had for me. Or, maybe he would make another excuse and I would be left disappointed.

What I did not expect was for him to pull me to him and kiss the hell out of me.

While my hands lifted to the back of his head, as if trying to prevent him from fleeing, his gripped my waist like he might never let go. His lips meshed with mine eagerly, fiercely, like he had been waiting for this moment as much as I had. He controlled the speed with which we moved together, and it was slow and purposeful, like all the unspoken words he was too afraid to say could be expressed through his actions.

Knowing that he wanted me as badly as I wanted him fueled my desire. I've never been good at controlling my impulses, and this was no exception. Connected as we already were, it just wasn't enough. I needed—I wanted—so much more.

With a sudden burst of courage, I shifted to swing my leg over his. His hands remained on my waist, guiding me until I was straddling him. His lips slid from mine just long enough for a low guttural sound to slip between them, before crashing into mine again, claiming me, in that moment, as entirely his.

With the creaking of the door as it opened behind me, it all came to a sudden halt.

As I struggled to scamper off of Nathan's lap, he bolted to a stand, tossing me to the bed in the process. I flipped onto my back to see Callie standing in the open doorway, mouth agape.

"Uh..." she said as she backed out of the room. "I'll come back later."

She closed the door, shutting Nathan and me inside together. With the big pink elephant, sitting on my chest, making it impossible to breathe.

Or was it Nathan that had stolen my breath?

Damn, that boy could kiss.

His gaze shifted from the door to me, met mine briefly before skirting away. "Guess I'm not doing a good job of not acting on my feelings, huh?" he said quietly.

I scooted to the edge of the bed and sat up, placing my feet on the floor for stability. "I'm not complaining. In fact, I could do that again. If you wanted."

With his head dropped, I only knew that he was smiling from the dimples in his cheeks. After a moment, he looked up. His eyes were twinkling when they leveled on me, and oh, did I want to kiss him again.

I'm not sure what it was he saw when he looked at me, but his expression shifted into something resembling sadness. He dropped to a knee in front of me, his face level with mine. "Look, Kris..." His eyes were soft when they met mine. "We're here.

We're not going anywhere. We've got time to figure this out. Right?"

I shrugged and mumbled, "If I don't go all evil-Kris first."

"And that's not going to happen," he responded immediately. His hand brushed against the side of my cheek, and lingered there. "I won't let it."

He didn't give me a chance to respond, not that my brain could process actual words with the way he was touching and looking at me, before he stood again. He hesitated, then bent to kiss the top of my head before walking away.

I was left nearly hyperventilating when he paused in the doorway with a small grin on his face. "If anyone other than me or Callie tries to come in here, you let me know, okay?"

"And by *anyone*, you mean…"

"Alec," he answered automatically.

I nodded once. "Thought so." So figuring out my unsorted feelings for Alec did not include unchaperoned visits in my room. Good to know.

He started out the door, and paused again. "Same goes for Micah."

I smiled at his back as he shut the door behind him. Only then did the enormity of what had just happened hit me, and I collapsed onto the bed with a heavy sigh.

CHAPTER 5

It was Nathan that interrupted my sleep the next morning, and not in a good way.

As his obscenely loud thumps on my bedroom door startled me awake, I immediately regretted the moment I'd asked him to resume our training the night before. At the time, I'd meant it. I wanted to get stronger and better at fighting, especially since we would soon be going after the Skotadi.

Now, I would rather sleep in.

"Come on! Get up!" he called through the door.

"Oh, my God," Callie groaned as she rolled over beside me. "What is wrong with him? It's not even light outside."

"Go away!" I shouted at the door.

He banged harder, and louder, and it became apparent that he wasn't going to give up. I was just about to roll out of bed, grudgingly but ready to do whatever I had to do to shut him up, when the door swung open and Alec strolled in.

He might have been sleep-walking, it was hard to tell. His eyes were barely open slits, his hair more disheveled than usual, and his face lacked its usual devil-may-care grin. He crossed the room to where Callie and I lay in bed, watching him curiously. Wordlessly, he yanked the covers off of us.

His eyebrows shot up and his lips curled into a faint smile, and I knew that he was at least partially awake. He didn't even bother to hide the fact that he was checking both Callie and me, and our equally scarce sleeping attire, out. Just before it ventured into awkward territory, he turned and walked away.

He paused in the doorway, where Nathan stood watching, jaw slightly dropped. "You're welcome," Alec said to him before disappearing down the hall, probably back to the couch to sleep.

What I wished I could be doing.

I groaned as I reluctantly got to my feet. A sweatshirt lay on the floor next to the bed and I quickly threw it on over my camisole. It was big enough to cover more skin than the too-short-to-wear-anywhere-but-in-bed cotton shorts I was wearing. And that wasn't saying much.

If Nathan noticed, he didn't let on. His head had been turned over his shoulder as he watched Alec walk away. Now, he tipped it to me with a tight grin. "You're the one that wanted to start training again."

"Ugh. I'd forgotten how much I hated you before," I returned groggily. I nudged Callie, who had already pulled the covers back up and was burying her head into her pillow, preparing to go back to sleep. "Come on. This includes you, too."

She opened one eye. "What?"

"You need to know how to fight," I told her and nodded my head in Nathan's direction, "and he's the best one to show you how."

Callie glanced in Nathan's direction, and what she saw, I'm not sure, but her eyes widened in terror. "What in the hell did you sign me up for, Kris?"

"Torture," Nathan said lightly from the doorway before he turned away. I heard him chuckle as he headed down the hallway. "Lots and lots of torture."

He wasn't really leaving. He was simply giving us time to get dressed. I expected he would be waiting, somewhat impatiently, for us outside. If memory served me correctly, I knew that I'd better get my butt in gear, before I got a good dose of ass-kicking.

And Callie? I doubted she had much of a chance.

* * *

The others were all well-trained in weaponry and combat, something young hybrids were taught early on in their development. They were all soldiers of the Kala-Skotadi war. They didn't need the training Callie and I needed. Their entertainment for the morning consisted of watching us from the back porch.

Nathan used me to demonstrate a few beginner moves to Callie. I secretly reveled in the fact that he used me as an example of what to do. It made me feel better about the improvement I had made. Watching Callie, I wondered if I was as bad as she was when I'd first started. I sure hoped not.

After a few drills, it became clear that Callie was in desperate need of some one-on-one time. I thought that was why Nathan had suggested that I go work with Micah for a little while.

Or, it might have been the way that both of us had reacted

when sparring together, our bodies coming together on the few occasions I'd gotten close enough, or the couple of times I'd found myself restrained in his arms as he demonstrated something to Callie. Each time, there had been a hesitation just before he released me, and I knew that he, too, had been feeling the electricity between us.

The last time, I'd even seen it in his eyes—a sort of pain that he couldn't fix. That was when he'd suggested that I go do something else. Typical Nathan—the master of avoidance, his undocumented fifth specialty. No one could do it better than him.

Though he'd pretended nothing had happened, I hadn't been fooled. Nor had Callie. As I'd passed her when she stepped forward to take my place, she'd grabbed my arm and dropped her voice for my ears only.

"That was the hottest foreplay I've ever seen," she had said.

I'd smiled the whole way to the house to find Micah.

That was where I was now, with Micah, in the living room. The others were still on the porch, watching Nathan and Callie. Every now and again, I heard a laugh from one of them. Usually Alec. All they needed was some popcorn to make the experience complete.

I desperately wanted to watch, too. Actually, I'd rather be the one wrestling with Nathan, but if I couldn't do that, I'd rather watch Callie try to. It had to be more interesting than what Micah was trying to talk me into doing.

He tapped the open textbook in my lap, snapping my attention back to him. "Pay attention," he scolded me as he pointed at the book. *Hybrid's Guide to Learning Specialties.*

I still couldn't believe it. They actually had textbooks on this stuff. Granted, it was only available to the Kala community and wouldn't be found on *Amazon* anytime soon, but still, I found it hilarious.

Micah waved his hand over the page he had turned me to. "Do any of these sound familiar?"

Looking down at the page reluctantly, I studied the large chart that summarized the twelve specialties, with descriptions of the early signs of developing each one. Not one of the things listed there had happened to me yet.

"No," I replied automatically, then something caught my eye—once I was actually paying attention. "Well, actually, maybe the fighting thing."

Micah raised his eyebrows. "A fighter, huh?" He sounded skeptical.

My defenses immediately kicked in. "Even Nathan said I was getting the hang of it faster than he'd expected. And, well, I kind of enjoy it."

"Yeah, I wonder why," Micah muttered under his breath, but loud enough for me to hear.

I took that as a stab at my obvious attraction to Nathan, so I ignored him, and added confidently, "I think I have fighter blood."

Micah eyed me. "Want me to read you now?"

"Read me?"

"Read your specialties, like we talked about yesterday."

Oh, yeah. I'd been distracted by the combat drills and

laughter from the porch. But now that I remembered, I was curious to see what specialties I possessed. "Sure," I said. "How do you do it?"

He turned to face me on the couch and motioned for me to do the same. "It's a lot like meditation," he explained as he took my hands in his. "Close your eyes, relax, free your mind…"

I did as he said and tried to free my mind, whatever that meant. I supposed it meant not to think about anything. That was a lot harder to do than it sounded.

"Let me in," he added, his voice low and soft.

I opened one eye to look at him. With that one statement, things suddenly felt weird. The moment was instantly too intimate for my liking. Not to mention, I didn't really want him to 'see' certain things, and I knew some prophets were able to do that. Could he? Could he read anything he wanted? Everything?

"How good of a prophet are you?" I asked tentatively, withdrawing my hands from his.

"I'm okay."

"Can you read minds?"

He fixed me with a knowing smile. "Sometimes. When someone's emotions are very strong, it's impossible to avoid them. It's like they're shouting their thoughts at me. If they're holding their thoughts back, blocking them, I can't get through. Not yet, but I've been working on it."

"That's an invasion of privacy. Why would you want to do that?" Aside from the obvious voyeuristic reasons, of course.

"I'm not going to do it to everyone," Micah defended. "In the case of reading a Skotadi, it could be beneficial."

Well, I supposed in that sense it was okay. He made a good point. Still, it made me nervous. I would have to make sure to hold back my thoughts and emotions around him. That was going to be hard, considering I had a hard enough time biting my tongue most of the time.

And I was in a house with Nathan…and Alec. Yeah, I was going to have to concentrate hard on blocking Micah.

"What else are you practicing?" I asked.

"Other than mind reading? My dream communication has gotten better, don't you think?"

I nodded as I replayed his words in my head. "You've been practicing that?"

He nodded enthusiastically. "The first dream we shared, I barely saw anything. Now, we can actually talk, and your face almost came into focus last night. Of course, it's easier since I know what you look like now, so I'm not sure how much of that is from getting better at it, and how much is from knowing you."

I shifted uncomfortably in my seat. Discussing the dreams still made me uncomfortable, even with the only other person who understood them. Yet, he seemed to have no problem bringing them up.

"What else?" I asked to get him off the dream subject.

"Uh, well, I suck at element manipulation, so I've got to work on that a lot more," he said. "Healing diamond injury I was getting decent—"

"Whoa, wait," I interrupted. "Did you say diamond injury? That can be healed?"

"That's something the Kala had been working on with me

for months, before I left," he elaborated. "There are a few on the base who are very good earth manipulators, who claimed that certain elements have healing abilities, but they were coming up short when they tried to capitalize on it. They had me try it, since I'm so much more pureblooded than they are, gave me the elements to use, and it worked…sort of. I've been working on improving. It's exhausting, honestly."

"How could you practice? Who would you practice on?"

"Well, we kidnapped Skotadi," Micah said.

"That's kind of disturbing." Even if they were technically evil, and were probably doing far worse to the Kala in that warehouse.

It was pretty great though, too. Micah's ability to heal diamond injury could be a vital tool in the war and swing the favor to the Kala's side once and for all. This kid really *was* it.

I really, really hope I don't kill him.

Micah reached inside his shirt and withdrew a necklace with a small glass vial on the chain. "I carry the compounds with me. Just in case. Fortunately, Gabby and Richie haven't given me a reason to use them."

"Good to know we all have that extra security," I said lightly.

"Yeah, well, I'm not that good at it, so don't go getting careless with diamond," he said. "So, do you want me to read your specialties, or not? I promise not to read your mind, so long as you don't scream your thoughts at me."

"Okay, okay." I extended my arms, placing my hands in his once again.

"Close your eyes," he said gently, like I'd expect a therapist to talk to a patient about to be hypnotized. "Relax, and let's do this."

No sooner than I did as he instructed, I heard the patio door open and close behind me, followed by Callie's voice.

"Do what?"

My eyes snapped open and I saw Micah peering over my head. I knew, just knew, that Nathan was with Callie. I could feel his presence in the room. Realizing too late that my hands were still in Micah's, I snatched them out of his grip.

"I'm trying to read Kris's specialties," Micah said, his tone marked by a hint of defensiveness that I suspected wasn't directed at Callie, but rather Nathan.

I only hoped it hadn't looked as bad as I feared—Micah and me sitting cross-legged across from each other on the couch, holding hands.

Why hasn't Nathan said anything yet?

I itched to turn around, but his heavy footsteps stopped me. I glanced up from under my eyelashes as he came to a stop beside me. His arms were folded over his chest in that way that always made him look so intimidating, the sleeves of his t-shirt tight on his arms. It and his hair were both slightly damp with sweat, and I couldn't help but be jealous of Callie for getting to spend the last hour with him.

I would have much rather been the one to make him sweat than been stuck sitting on the couch with Micah. Especially after seeing the way Nathan was looking at Micah, with that hint of jealousy he usually reserved for Alec.

"How good are you?" Nathan finally asked Micah.

"At reading specialties? Pretty good." Micah's chin jutted forward in challenge. "I just got done telling Kris what specialties I've been working on, and now we'd like to see what she needs to be focused on."

It was pretty obvious from his tone what Micah was trying to do. Get rid of Nathan.

Nathan had to have sensed it, but pretended not to. "If you can do that, you should be able to read minds, right?"

Micah shrugged noncommittally. "I'm working on it."

During the silence that followed, I glanced at Callie. From the tight-lipped smile on her face, I gathered that she saw what I saw. Boys puffing their chests out at each other. I flashed her a grin, but covered it quickly when Nathan took a step closer.

"Try reading my specialties," he said. "Let's see how good you are before you read Kris's."

He sat on the edge of the coffee table, facing Micah. As Micah grudgingly turned toward him, Nathan's eyes flicked to mine briefly, a hint of amusement gleaming in them, and I couldn't help but wonder what he was up to.

Surely he wasn't simply testing Micah's abilities.

Micah took a hold of Nathan's outstretched hands and repeated what he had told me earlier. Except this time, there was a coldness in his tone. "Close your eyes, relax, free your mind."

Callie and I watched silently as they both dropped their heads, eyes closed. After a few seconds, Micah's lips curled into a tight smile and he lifted his head to look at Nathan. A moment later, Nathan's eyes opened and the two stared at each other as if some silent conversation was taking place between the two of them. From the smug look on Nathan's face, I was now sure this had been his intent all along. Not for Micah to read his specialties, but for Micah to read his mind.

And I desperately wanted to know what Micah saw. Because I was sure it had something to do with me.

Micah gave a barely discernible nod, shifted, moving past whatever had just transpired between the two of them, and lowered his head once again, eyes closed. Nathan grinned to himself before he, too, dropped his head.

When Micah spoke again, his words were clipped. "You're obviously a fighter. I could tell that without reading you, but I can feel a heavy concentration of Ares's bloodline in you. Much more than that of your other bloodlines." Micah hesitated as if to read more before he continued, "Nature, craft..." Micah dropped Nathan's hands as he said the last words confidently, "and intelligence. How's that?"

Nathan stood without an answer and retreated to Callie's side.

Callie looked between Nathan, Micah, and me curiously. "Well? Was he right?"

I resisted the urge to laugh, but couldn't hold back a smile. "Yeah, Callie. He was right." I caught Nathan's eyes briefly before I turned to Micah. "My turn now?"

Before Micah had a chance to take my hands, the sliding glass door opened and shut again, and I heard Alec approach.

"What in the hell are you guys doing?" he called.

Micah rolled his head with a heavy sigh. "You've got to be kidding me."

"Micah's reading specialties," I volunteered cheerily.

"Oh, cool," Alec said and bounded past me to sit on the coffee table where Nathan had sat moments before. "I've always wanted to be read. Can you read my future, too? You do palm readings? Have tarot cards?"

"Just give me your hands," Micah said and instructed Alec on what to do. After a moment, he said, "Medium to the dead, fighter, charmer, and fire manipulation. Strongest to weakest."

Alec made a face like he might have been impressed and started to pull away, but Micah clamped down on his hands, preventing him from standing. Micah's brow furrowed, his lips tight, as he continued to read something from Alec.

What that was, I thought we all wanted to know. Especially Alec.

"Dude, what are you doing?" Alec asked.

Micah shook his head rapidly to silence Alec.

Alec glanced at me, whispered, "He's not gay, is he?"

I choked back a laugh and shook my head. Not that I actually knew for sure, but there was something about Micah that screamed straight. Especially when he looked at me the way he did sometimes.

When Micah finally spoke again, his voice was soft and wary, almost confused, and it came out sounding like a question. "You're surging."

Alec snatched his hands out of Micah's grip. "What's that supposed to mean?"

Micah shook his head like he didn't know how to answer that question. "The evil in you..." he started hesitantly. "It's surging, fighting to break free."

Alec stood quickly. The look in his eyes when he looked down at Micah was that of pure hatred—the perfect face of evil. "That's enough reading for the day."

Alec muttered under his breath as he went to stand on the other side of Callie, and suddenly I was nervous. What if Micah saw the evil surging in me, too?

And what did that mean exactly? For Alec? For me?

I didn't want to know my specialties anymore, but it was too late to back out now, especially when everyone was watching me, waiting. It was out of my control anyway when Micah turned to me, took my hands, and repeated the same process.

"Let me guess," Alec said drily, "Medium, fighter, charmer, and fire."

I opened my eyes just in time to see Micah nod his head. "Yes, but they're much stronger, more pure than yours."

I supposed that made sense. Alex and I had both been created by Hades' four demigods. I should have expected us to share the same specialties. And Alec had told me that they had done something different with me to make me stronger than him. We just didn't know what exactly that was.

"There's something else there," Micah mulled, more to himself than to any of us. "I can't get a good read on it…"

Micah grimaced and my heart jumped into my throat as I waited to hear what he saw. Was it what made me different from Alec? Or was I surging?

He eventually opened his eyes and dropped my hands, having given up. Or so it seemed. He sat across from me and stared, like he was trying to read it through my eyes, by peering right into my soul.

"What is it?" I asked softly.

Micah shook his head. "I'm not sure."

Just like the day before, I got the impression that there was something he wasn't being completely forthcoming about. He had the same look on his face, and even if I didn't know him well enough yet to know what his facial expressions meant, I was starting to think that this particular one meant he was hiding something.

And I had to find out what that was.

CHAPTER 6

Gabby and Richie returned from a recon mission of the warehouse later, and informed us that the Skotadi were going about business as usual despite the absence of several of their guys. Maybe they didn't care that they had lost a few, but I suspected that their lack of reaction was because there were so many of them that they hadn't actually noticed. Either way, since they were still there, and didn't seem to know we were around, we were free to start planning a small attack on them. If there were really that many of them, hopefully we would at least thin their numbers.

The next morning, Nathan went with Richie to the nearest town to obtain more weapons and ammunition. Alec was working with Callie on some self-defense moves in the yard. That left Micah and I alone on the porch, under Gabby's ever-watchful eyes. We were supposed to be working on developing my specialties, but I had so much on my mind that my specialties were the least of my concerns.

"Hey, Micah?"

He looked up from the book in his lap.

"The other day," I started hesitantly. "What did you mean when you said you sensed the evil surging in Alec?"

Last night, I had tried to talk to Alec about what Micah had said and what I thought I'd seen in his eyes, but he'd avoided my questions with perfect, practiced charm. I'd ended up blushing and wondering what had happened to my ability to have a conversation with a boy without fanning myself like a hormone-crazed middle-schooler.

But then, Alec wasn't just any boy. He had talent. And he knew it. I should have been glad it hadn't been worse.

Micah shrugged. "Just what I said. It's rising up in him, getting stronger, threatening to overcome him."

I suppressed a shudder. Was that I what I had to look forward to? And what about poor Alec? I hated to think about what he was going through already. Could he feel it surging? Did he know what was happening to him? He hadn't seemed bothered last night. At least not about that.

"Is that what you saw in me?" I asked Micah timidly, unsure if I really wanted to hear the answer.

"No," he said quickly.

"What do you think it was?"

"I'm not sure. It felt similar to what I feel when I read another prophet, but that doesn't make any sense."

"Why not?" It was interesting that he thought it might be something related to prophesy, especially after I had already suspected that I might have some ability in that specialty. But I didn't understand why he thought it didn't make sense.

"The prophet bloodline isn't associated with Hades," he answered simply. "You really *can't* be a prophet. Seeing as how we can share dreams, you must have something giving you that ability. That must be what I'm seeing, but I just can't pick up on what exactly it is."

The way he was talking made me nervous. Something unknown? Something brewing inside of me that I didn't know about? That no one knew about? Yeah, I didn't like the sounds of that.

"I also know that you didn't want the others to know about the dreams," Micah added with a trace of a smile on his face, "so I didn't say anything,"

My jaw dropped. "You read my mind?"

He chuckled. "I wasn't trying to. I can't help it that you've been practically yelling that to me since you've been here."

There was an awkward silence as Micah stared at me, like he was trying to determine why I didn't want the others to know about the dreams, and I started to wonder if he was trying to read my mind again.

"Stop it," I scolded.

"I'm not doing anything," he said. "I'm just trying to figure it out. Figure you out, *without* reading your mind."

He gave me that look again—the one like he knew me on a level I wasn't aware of—and I jumped up to interrupt the awkwardness that it produced. I paced to the porch railing and took a moment to watch Alec drop Callie to the ground with a leg sweep before I turned to Micah again.

"What else could it have been? What else could enable me to share dreams, if not a prophet bloodline?"

Micah nodded thoughtfully as he digested my question, but didn't answer right away. "There are a few reports of hybrids sharing dreams over the years," he eventually said. "Theories vary from false reports, to Incantation, to soul—"

"Incantation?"

"It's the use of spells," Micah explained. "Kind of like what modern day witchcraft is compared to. The reports on it are scattered, too. No one's really figured out its role in our world. Most don't believe it exists."

I paused before asking, "Do you?"

Micah squinted at me, as if he were looking at me for the answer. "I don't know yet."

I'd hoped to hear something encouraging, something that would make me feel better, but once again I was left with the empty void of ignorance. I didn't know what was going on with me, and the one person who knew more about the inner workings of this hybrid world than anyone else was the master at hidden messages in his words.

The more I talked to Micah, the more uneasy I became. I had set out to get answers from him, and somehow ended up with more questions. And I was left wondering again what he was keeping from me.

I couldn't quiet the annoying voice in my head that suggested I might not want to know. So long as his secrets didn't hurt anyone I cared about, I'd have a hard time *not* killing him if that happened.

Since I didn't want to talk to Micah anymore, and he seemed to realize that without me saying so, he gave me some of his books to read in my spare time. After we went our separate ways, I worked on defensive fighting moves with Alec and Callie for about an hour, showered, then retreated to my room for a little peace and quiet. Feeling guilty, I picked up one of Micah's books, thinking I should at least attempt to get something out of it.

It was boring as hell and my chin dropped to my chest about half way down the second page. I didn't even fight it, and let the book slide off my lap, forgotten, as the peacefulness of sleep pulled me.

I was bolted awake some time later by excited voices in the living room, and hurried down the hall to see what was going on. I used my hands to smooth down the still damp ragweed that had formed on the back of my head while I was asleep, not that I managed to fool anyone.

"Ah, there she is," Alec sang. "Sleeping Beauty."

I flashed him a shy smile and turned to Nathan, who was conferring with Richie and Gabby nearby. "What's going on?"

Gabby fixed me with a steely glare while Richie looked at Nathan to answer me, as if my evil would seep out and infect him if he acknowledged me.

"We've got all the supplies we need," Nathan said, "and we've got a plan for tonight."

I was surprised by my own giddiness. "We're going to get some Skotadi?"

He didn't answer, but then he didn't really need to. He pulled me to the side as the others continued going over strategy.

"Here," Nathan said, placing a knife in my hands. A shiny diamond coated knife. I held it in my palm like I would a bomb, and lifted my eyes to him questioningly. "You're going to need something to protect yourself in close quarters," he explained.

"Can't I just have a regular knife?"

"I'd feel better if you had a coated one."

"But I wouldn't feel better," I returned. "Nathan, you know I'm not good with knives. I'm afraid I'll hurt someone." *Or myself.*

"You're better than you think." His lips curled into a half smile. Then he surprised me by reaching out and putting a hand on my hip. It was unexpected, it was nice, and it caused my pulse to jump. When I realized he was simply securing a knife sheath around my waist, some of my excitement dimmed. "Put it here. I don't care if you never use it, just keep it with you."

"I'd rather have a gun," I muttered.

He flashed me a full smile this time as he produced a pistol from behind his back. "I got you one of those, too."

I sheathed the knife and took the gun gingerly, but not as gingerly as I had the knife.

"It's the same model as you've used before," he told me, and proceeded to show me again where the safety was located. "Remember?"

"I remember."

"It's yours." He waved his hand around the room. "Everyone's loaded. Even Callie."

"Callie?"

He shrugged. "I'm not expecting her to be involved, but like you, she needs protection. Just in case."

"Can she shoot?" I whispered so as not to let Callie hear me.

He nodded, though not very convincingly. "Enough to protect herself. I'm going to keep working with her though."

Again, I had a pang of jealousy. Not that I didn't trust my

best friend spending so much time with Nathan, and not that I didn't want her to work with him—because I did, because I knew that if anyone could teach her to handle the situations we were going to be getting into, it was Nathan. I was jealous only because I wanted to be the one spending the extra time with him, purely for selfish reasons.

As if Callie knew we were talking about her, she glided up beside me with a grin on her face. "Exciting, huh? My first battle."

"Probably won't be that exciting," Nathan said. Callie and I both turned to look at him. I knew she was thinking the same thing as I was—that killing a few Skotadi might not be exciting to *him*, but to us, tonight was a big deal. Then, he explained what he meant. "Tonight's more of a stake out."

"What's that supposed to mean?" I asked, not hiding my disappointment. Haven't we done enough staking out? It hadn't led to anything, so why bother again?

"We're going to follow them," he amended, "see where they go in those vans, what they do, stuff like that. We're after information. We probably won't have much action tonight. There's a good chance they won't even go anywhere tonight."

A few hours later, sitting in the backseat of the Tahoe with Callie—Alec in the driver's seat and Nathan riding shotgun—I realized that Nathan hadn't been kidding about the lack of action. At first, like maybe the first hour, I'd been hopeful.

Micah, Richie, and Gabby were positioned on the ridge above the warehouse, watching. The plan was for them to call us with one of the two prepaid cell phones they had purchased when—if ever—the Skotadi made a move. Parked and hidden along the side of the road as we were in the Tahoe, we would then fall in behind the Skotadi and follow them. After hours of silence, I started to lose hope that anything was going to go down tonight.

In our third hour, a call finally came in. Nathan answered on the first ring, and Micah's voice came through on the speaker phone. "Van headed your way. Four Skotadi, minimally armed."

Alec rubbed his hands together like a kid on Christmas morning and started the engine. "About damn time," he said.

"Let's stick to the plan," Nathan said into the phone. "We'll direct you until you catch up to us."

I heard heavy breathing through the speaker, and imagined Micah, Gabby, and Richie were hauling ass back to their vehicle. "Check back in ten minutes," Micah panted before Nathan disconnected the call.

A few moments later, we saw the van's headlights. Though we were hidden well, parked far off the main road on a bumpy dirt road next to a large green tractor, I still slouched down in my seat as they passed. Only after their taillights disappeared did Alec pull out behind them. We weren't worried about losing them. Out here, there were only so many places they could go, and this road had exactly two turnoffs they could take between here and the nearest town, twenty minutes away. Those side roads didn't really lead anywhere, so we figured they were more than likely headed into town.

Every so often, after rounding a bend or when cresting a hill, we got a glimpse of their taillights ahead of us.

"Don't follow too close," Nathan said to Alec.

"I know how to tail someone," Alec returned. "Being Evil and Doing Evil Things 101. Only class I ever gotten an A in."

"They also teach you how to spot a tail?" Nathan asked.

"Yeah." Alec hesitated, then added, "Point taken. They won't spot us."

And they didn't. We followed them for twenty minutes without incident. Micah called to check in twice, confirming that they weren't far behind us. As we entered town, Nathan called again to relay directions to Micah.

The Skotadi turned into a parking lot, and Alec parked on the street half a block away. From there, we watched as the four Skotadi got out of the van. They walked around the building, coming toward us, before stopping at a side entrance. Leaning forward in my seat to spy the sign above the door, I saw that we were parked in front of *Wild Toad's Nightspot*. With the door open as the Skotadi entered single file, I could hear the thump of base coming from inside and saw the flashing of strobe lights flickering to the beat.

A nightclub. Really?

"Something tells me they're not here for the dancing," Alec muttered.

Nathan and Alec shared a look. "They're taking someone," Nathan concluded.

"Like a kidnapping?" I asked.

Like the poor girl we saw them haul out of the back of the van a few days ago? I met Callie's eyes, and I knew she was thinking the same thing I was. Tonight was going to end up having more action than Nathan had predicted.

Nathan relayed information to Micah, directing them to the location of the nightclub while Alec maneuvered into a parking space behind the building, where we had a clearer view of the van. A moment later, Micah's voice came over the speaker phone, announcing a plan for him and Richie to go inside the club to spy on the Skotadi from there. Again, Nathan and Alec shared a look, but neither objected.

"Just don't let them see you," Nathan warned before he disconnected the call.

After a few long seconds of silence, Alec said, "This doesn't look like a haven for hybrids."

"It's a college town," Nathan added. "Plenty of unsuspecting, drunk humans."

"But what do they want humans for?" Alec mused.

Another wave of heavy silence followed. I didn't have an answer, and if anyone else did, I suspected they didn't want to voice it. We quietly watched the rear of the club and the van, but after twenty minutes of no activity, I started to wonder if maybe they had just come here for a night out. Did the Skotadi take vacations? Have time off?

When the phone rang again, I got my answer.

"Something's about to happen," Micah said urgently. "Looks like two of them are tailing a girl to the restrooms. They're in the back, might be coming out a rear entrance."

Interesting enough, the van was parked next to a red door that could be that rear entrance. They had done this before, I thought, and from this exact nightclub. They knew where to park, how to get out without being seen. My stomach soured at the thought of multiple unsuspecting college students being hauled away in the back of that van to an unknown fate.

The back door didn't open, but the side entrance door did, and two Skotadi rounded the corner of the building, walking toward the van. It was unlikely that they would see us, but we cowered down in our seats as we watched them.

"Let them take her," Nathan told Micah. "We'll follow and intercept on the road before they reach the warehouse. Less witnesses that way."

"Coming out," Micah responded before dropping the call.

The two Skotadi had reached the van and one of them swung the back doors open. A second later, the back door to the club burst open and the other two Skotadi emerged with a young woman, her long, brown hair tossed over her face as she struggled against them, her cries for help muffled by a well-placed hand over her mouth and drowned out by the loud music pouring through the open door. Within seconds, the four Skotadi had her tossed into the back of the van like she had never existed. Two of them jumped in behind her, while the other two climbed into the front.

I had been holding my breath the entire time, and only started breathing again when the van was on the move. They turned right, out of the parking lot. Alec waited a few seconds, then followed. As we passed the front of the club, I saw Micah and Richie clambering into their car.

Alec maintained a safe distance, but considering the size of the small town, the van was never out of our sight. Micah and the others were close behind us. Once we were clear of the town limits and speeding along the dark and winding country road, I leaned forward to grip the back of Nathan's seat eagerly.

We had a good twenty minutes before we reached the warehouse, but I was anxious to stop that van.

Who knew what was being done to that girl right now?

"How are we going to stop them?" I asked the guys.

Nathan glanced at Alec with a hooked eyebrow. Though his eyes remained fixed on the road, Alec grinned. No words had been passed between the two, yet they both seemed to know exactly how we were going to stop them.

Nathan looked over his shoulder. He flinched at our sudden nearness, but didn't back away. His eyes swept from me to Callie, and back to me. "You might want to put on your seatbelts."

He smiled reassuringly at the look of horror likely etched all over my face as I slid back into my seat, but it didn't really help the nervous flutters in my stomach.

"Kris?" I looked up from my shaky fingers as they fumbled over the seatbelt latch. Nathan was watching me. "We'll be fine. It's under control."

"Yeah," Alec chimed in from the driver's seat. "Totally under control."

With that, his foot pressed down on the gas, rocketing the Tahoe forward and closing the distance between us and the van quickly. My nails dug into the door handle as he swerved into the oncoming lane, coming up alongside the van. From my seat, I had a good view as the front end of the Tahoe angled smoothly closer to the back rear tire of the van.

At the moment of impact, my eyes squeezed shut in preparation of a horrific wreck.

Tires squealed, but they weren't ours. As the Tahoe came to a quick, but controlled, near-stop and I realized we hadn't crashed, I opened my eyes.

Ahead of us, the van was spinning off the side of the road. It hit a ditch and flipped over, rolling once before coming to a rest against a tree.

Alec turned the wheel sharply, bouncing the Tahoe off the side of the road, putting us only a few yards from the wrecked van. Nathan jumped out before we came to a complete stop, and ran toward it with his gun drawn.

Gabby pulled their car up beside us, and then she and Richie ran off after Nathan. While Gabby cautiously opened the passenger side door, Richie moved to the driver's side and Nathan disappeared behind the rear of the van.

Callie and I climbed out of the Tahoe, for lack of anything else better to do. We'd already been told to let the other, more experienced ones take care of securing the Skotadi. Alec paused long enough to make sure we were following orders, before he hurried to join the others. Micah walked up beside me a moment later, also banned from joining in by Gabby and Richie.

He was practically bouncing on his toes from the excitement. I felt it too—the adrenaline rush—but I wasn't grinning like a moron like he was. I was about to tell him so, when I was interrupted by a shout, followed closely by three rapid gun shots.

From behind the van. Where Nathan was.

Where Alec was now sprinting.

Where *I* was now sprinting.

Micah lunged for me but I was too fast for him. Nothing, no one, was going to stop me. Even Gabby knew better than to intercept me. I ran past her as she pulled an injured Skotadi through the passenger side door. And then she was right behind me, rounding the back of the van.

Its doors were wide open. One Skotadi lay moaning on the ground, with a single bullet wound to the chest. Another stood with his face pressed against the inside of one of the doors as Alec and Richie restrained his arms behind his back with a plastic tie.

And Nathan…

My shoulders heaved with relief when I saw that he was fine. He was inside the van, toward the front, his back to me as he knelt down in front of the human girl.

A scream pierced the night air, and we all jumped. None of us more so than Nathan, considering he'd been the closest to the source. The girl pulled her knees tight against her chest as she regarded Nathan with wary eyes.

He must have gotten the not so subtle hint that she wanted nothing to do with him. He scooted back, providing her with the space she clearly wanted, and turned to look over his shoulder. When he spotted me, he gave a *'come here'* nod.

He stood to meet me halfway. My gaze fell on a red scratch on his upper arm as I approached, and I grabbed his shirt to turn him toward me. The sleeve was shredded and blood oozed through the fabric.

"Did you get shot?" I asked him, my eyes wide with alarm.

He shrugged. "It's just a flesh wound." But a flesh wound from a diamond-coated bullet wasn't something to shrug at. He must have seen the thought register on my face, because he added, "It wasn't coated."

"You sure?"

He nodded with a hint of amusement. "Pretty sure."

I let go of his shirt, only then realizing that I had still been gripping it, and how close Nathan and I were now standing. I didn't want to step away, but did, knowing that we had an audience.

I looked down at the human girl, huddled in the corner. She had a nasty cut across her nose that was bleeding. Other than that, she appeared unharmed.

Just scared.

I offered her a smile that I hoped she found reassuring. She studied me cautiously before her eyes narrowed on Nathan.

Clearly, she had a head injury. Sound minded girls didn't shoot daggers at Nathan. Ever.

"What did you do to her?" I whispered to Nathan, only partially teasing. From the bland look he shot me, he didn't find it half as amusing as I did.

He leaned close to me, dropped his voice for my ears only. "Talk to her," he said. "See who she is, if she has any connection to the Skotadi or Kala. See if she overheard anything."

I nodded. "What are you going to do?"

He grinned as he retreated to the back of the van. "Forcing a few Skotadi to talk."

The girl watched Nathan as he jumped out the back. She was

still terrified, and it was easy to understand why as she watched all of them—Nathan, Alec, Micah, Richie, Gabby, and even Callie—surrounding the Skotadi with weapons drawn. They, at least, moved the Skotadi out of sight and earshot so we didn't have to hear or see what they were doing to make them talk. Still, considering what the girl had seen so far, I got the impression she might consider us to be the bad guys.

"Hey," I said to her, pulling her gaze to me. "We're the good guys. We're going to help you."

She looked reluctant. "I want to go home."

"Sure. I just want to talk to you first. Is that okay?"

"I want to go home. Now."

"Can you tell me your name first?"

"Jennifer."

"Okay, Jennifer," I said as if I were soothing a baby to sleep. "We'll take you home, but first my friends need to talk to these guys that took you. We want to know why they took you. Do you know?"

She shook her head. "I was at the club and was on my way to the bathroom…and it just went dark," she sobbed. "Next thing I know I'm in here with two of them."

"Did they say anything to you?"

She started to shake her head, then hesitated as if a thought came to her. "Not to me. I heard them bragging to each other."

"About what?"

"It didn't make sense," she muttered. "Something about getting a lot out of me, or something like that."

My confusion mirrored hers. I didn't know what to make of

that. Surely the Skotadi weren't in the human trafficking business. But what else could they have been getting out of her, if not money. Sexual favors? I didn't even want to think about that, and pushed that thought out of my head as quickly as it appeared.

"Did you hear anything else?"

"One of them..." She trailed off as she struggled to remember. "One of them said they were ready to move on to the next step. That they were getting bored playing with *humans*." Her eyes were wide with fear when they lifted to mine. "Why would they say that? Are they not...."

I understood her trepidation. When I'd first learned that Nathan was not entirely human, it had freaked me out a little. And I had been fully prepared for him to admit something unbelievable. This girl was completely blindsided.

I decided she was better off not knowing the answer to the question she couldn't even finish asking.

"They're just a bunch of sick men," I said. "I don't know what they were talking about, why they said what they said, but I do know they're not good. That's why we helped you."

She seemed to accept my explanation eagerly, like she wanted to believe anything other than what she had started to suspect. After a few more minutes of talking to her, it became frustratingly clear that she knew nothing else.

With a promise to have her driven home soon, I left Jennifer sitting in the back of the van, and went in search of the others. Perhaps they had uncovered something more useful.

I found Callie leaning against a tree, distancing herself from the rest of them. I could hear their voices, all loud and angry and menacing. Mostly, I heard Richie, which was surprising.

"You stay with her?" I asked Callie, nodding toward the back of the van.

"Sure thing. I'll do anything but go over there." Callie jutted her chin forward. I followed her gaze and saw exactly where they were, hidden behind some brush.

As I approached, I saw that all but one of the Skotadi were now dead. I knew that they had been injured in the rollover, but I wondered if their injuries had ultimately done them in…or if someone had killed them. Upon closer inspection, I noticed that one of them had definitely been killed by someone's hands. More precisely, a bullet.

Nathan was knelt on the ground, his face only inches away from the last remaining Skotadi. He didn't notice my approach, until the Skotadi looked past him and saw me.

"You," the man rasped.

Nathan stood and swung around in frustration. I hoped it wasn't because of me. From the set scowl on his face as he glared down at the Skotadi, I suspected he had been frustrated long before I came along.

"You need to join us," the Skotadi was saying to me.

"Not going to happen," I returned, earning an evil grin from him.

"Then you will die," he continued, "and so will they." His eyes swept over everyone slowly, finally coming to a rest on Micah. "Especially him."

And with that one statement, I got to witness firsthand the extent of Richie's temper. With something that sounded like a growl coming out of his mouth, he rushed the Skotadi. Before he got within killing range, Nathan intercepted him.

"Not yet," Nathan murmured to him before turning back to the Skotadi. "One last time before I let him have you. What are you doing in the warehouse?"

The Skotadi stared at Nathan without blinking.

Nathan tried another question. This time, his hand shot forward, squeezing the Skotadi around the throat. "What are you doing with humans?"

The Skotadi gasped unsuccessfully for air, and was looking a little pale, even by Skotadi standards, but managed to gasp, "They are our pawns."

"You don't even know, do you?" Nathan spat. "You're a *nobody*. You just run errands like you're told."

The Skotadi rolled his head to the side, to rest his cold gaze on me. "I know enough. I know that she'll be the end of you. All of you."

Nathan's gun was pulled and pressed to the Skotadi's temple before I had time to blink. Nathan was going to kill him. I could see it in his eyes, in the rigidness of his jaw, in the way he fingered the trigger. For a second, the Skotadi knew he was about to die, and he was afraid. It was exactly the reaction Nathan had been looking for.

"You address her, mention her, or so much as look at her one more time, I'll pull the trigger," he said levelly. Once assured he had the Skotadi's complete attention, he asked another question. "Who's in charge?"

With a gun to his temple now, the Skotadi was a little more

willing to talk. "I don't know. I have my superiors, and they have theirs."

Micah spoke up from the back of the group. "How long are you planning to be here?"

"However long it takes."

"What? However long *what* takes?" Nathan shouted.

The Skotadi looked up at him with pure fear in his eyes. "I don't know, I told you. You were right. I just do what I'm told. I don't know anything."

Micah asked, "How many of you are there in the warehouse?"

"Fifty. Maybe sixty."

Sixty? Versus the seven of us. The odds were worse than I had hoped for.

Nathan leaned back so that the gun was no longer pressed to the Skotadi's head. His eyes remained on the man as he addressed the rest of us. "Anyone have any more questions?"

Murmurs of no were passed around me.

"Time's up," Nathan said as he stood. With a nod at Richie, he turned to walk away.

"No, please," the Skotadi pleaded, his voice shaking in desperation before he started to sob.

A Skotadi crying? Never thought I'd ever see that. As much as I despised their race, I knew that they had once been normal people, and I didn't want to see one of them die. Not like this. While I knew it needed to be done, I didn't want to witness it.

I scurried to catch up with Nathan as he approached the back of the van, where Callie stood with Jennifer.

He glanced down at me and some of the harshness in his eyes evaporated. "Did you get anything out of her?"

I gave him a Cliffs Notes version of my conversation with Jennifer.

He raked a hand down his face. "So we got nothing?"

"We know they're doing *something* with humans," I returned.

They are our pawns, the Skotadi had said. It was a start. We just had to figure out what they were doing…and how it was related to Kala to Skotadi conversions. If it was at all.

Maybe they were doing other types of conversions in the warehouse, too. I didn't even want to think about what kind of things they were putting humans through in there. Not now.

As the rest of them took care of the bodies and started clearing up the wreckage, Callie and I volunteered to drive Jennifer home.

"The two of you shouldn't go by yourselves," Nathan argued.

"I'll go with them." Out of nowhere, Micah stepped beside me.

Nathan's jaw tightened, but he said nothing.

Gabby and Richie were reluctant, but Micah gave them a look that signaled his determination to do what he wanted to do, like a boy seeking independence from overbearing parents. It worked.

As Callie slid into the driver's seat of the Tahoe, Micah hopped into the back with Jennifer. I heard him introduce himself to her as I secured my seatbelt, and part of me was glad it was him going with us. Out of all of them, he was probably the least intimidating.

Callie started the engine, but before she pulled away, there was a tap at my window. I rolled it down and Nathan leaned in. While my eyes were on him, his were on Micah in the back seat.

"Still got the phone?" he asked.

"Got it," Micah replied crisply.

Nathan reached past me to hold his hand out to Micah. A second later, he handed the phone to me. "I want you to have it," Nathan said to me quietly. "Call me if there's any trouble."

I took it with a nod, unable to do much else. Not under the heaviness of his gaze as he backed up to let us go. That look he gave me—full of so many possible meanings—was the last thing I saw. In the side mirror, I watched as he joined the others, and wondered what meaning *he* had intended.

CHAPTER 7

We hit them two more times after that. Though we improved on our methods of attack, and prevented them from taking any more human victims, we didn't learn anything new about the Skotadi's plans. Each time we ended up empty handed, I felt the grip of time tightening. Over and over, the Skotadi's words echoed in my head.

She will be the end of you.

I tried not to think about it, to dwell on it, but it was hard not to. Though I'd already known what I was, hearing it come from one of them sort of sealed the deal for me. I wondered if I was only fooling myself in thinking I had some sort of a chance.

She will be the end of you.

I was determined not to let that happen. Even if I couldn't find a way to save myself, I would protect the ones I cared about. I wouldn't let myself hurt them. Even if that meant doing something I couldn't wrap my head around just yet.

Instead of thinking about it, I threw myself wholeheartedly into the missions. It made me feel better to rid the world of a few Skotadi, even if I wasn't the one pulling the trigger. A few more successful missions, and we just might be able to make a run at the warehouse, and get rid of the whole lot of them with a well-planned strike.

For now, we were in the middle of another ambush. This time, Micah, Callie, and I watched from the ridge. Aided by the use of a pair of night-vision goggles, we were able to watch the warehouse for signs of activity. When Micah spotted a van full of Skotadi—five this time—prepared to leave, I phoned Nathan. I could hear his grin through the line when I told him that the Skotadi were upping their numbers.

He wasn't concerned about the extra man, and neither was I. Richie and Gabby had proven to be worthy allies. They both knew how to fight. I knew from experience what Nathan and Alec were capable of. I had all the confidence in the world in those four.

We took our time leaving. By the time we would get to the others, the Skotadi would be dead or restrained, and the living ones would already be undergoing interrogation.

Just as we finished packing up, I heard voices floating up from the valley. From the warehouse. I crawled to the edge with the goggles and peered down. Another van had been pulled up to the door, and I counted seven Skotadi climbing into it, each heavily armed.

They were setting a trap.

Micah's hand came down on my shoulder. "Let's go!"

As we dashed to the car, I called the other phone. This time, Gabby answered. I quickly told her what we had seen and she disconnected the call with a string of curses.

My mind spun with worry. They would be severely outnumbered. Four to twelve. The road we had to take wound down and around the mountain. It would take us about fifteen minutes to reach them, to help them.

I was tempted to call back and tell them to abandon the mission, to run, but I feared it was already too late. The first van was probably already there.

We reached the car and Callie climbed into the driver's seat. She drove while Micah and I prepared our weapons. I did the best I could despite the tremor in my hands.

If anyone got hurt…

This was exactly what I had been afraid of. Someone I cared about getting hurt, because of me. We wouldn't be here—*they* wouldn't be here—if not for me.

I couldn't let anything happen to them.

With Callie driving, the trip took less time than usual. Still, it was the longest ten minutes of my life, and when the ambush location appeared ahead in the headlights, my stomach clenched at the sight.

Both vans were pulled off the side of the road, forming a sort of V, which the Skotadi were using as a shield. Three bodies lay motionless on the ground between the vans and the Tahoe, where I hoped all four of our crew were hovered. At least one of them was still alive, since the Skotadi were shooting at someone.

"What do I do?" Callie shrieked as we sped closer.

"Aim for the first van," Micah answered calmly.

"What?"

"Try to take a few of them out," he continued.

"Oh, man. I don't know about this," Callie squealed as she punched the accelerator.

Two of the Skotadi turned their attention to the car speeding their way. I knew it was a bad idea, but didn't fully grasp how bad until they pointed their weapons at us.

"Get down!" Micah pushed Callie's head between the seats, and threw his body over top of hers. Her foot must have been still on the gas because the car didn't lose any speed as it rocketed toward the vans.

Dropping to my knees behind the passenger seat, I dodged the spray of bullets as I braced for impact.

We hit hard. My head crashed into the dashboard and I lay sprawled across the center console, where Callie and Micah had been a moment ago. Both of them were now curled on the floorboard. Shattered glass littered us. Something warm and wet dripped down my nose, landed on my lip. Blood.

Callie groaned and I reached for her hand. "Callie, you—"

The driver's side door burst open. I was yanked across the seat by a large Skotadi, and dropped to the ground with an unforgiving thud. Gun shots were going off all around me. At least, from what I could see with a quick scan, the car had taken out two of the Skotadi. Seven were left, including the one that had me.

He pulled me up by my hair and I cried out as he tossed me onto the twisted hood of the car. With one hand on me, his other hand moved to his waist. For a weapon. A shiny diamond-coated knife.

My foot connected with his groin before he could grab it. As he bent over in agony, I pulled the knife Nathan had given me from its sheath. I'd prefer my gun, but it was somewhere in the car.

It was life or death now. In a knife fight.

The Skotadi recovered too quickly for me to strike and plowed into me. We rolled off the hood, landing hard on the ground. I ended up on the bottom, the burly Skotadi straddling me, nearly cutting off my air supply.

Though the knife was in my hand, I had a poor angle to work with. But then, with a diamond-coated knife, that didn't matter. I didn't need a kill-shot. All I needed was a scratch.

I bent my wrist and sliced the knife smoothly across his forearm, drawing a steady stream of blood. Nothing that would kill him…yet.

He looked down at me with fireball eyes. Then he saw the knife. I practically saw its sparkle reflected in his eyes.

"You…" he said in a strangled voice. "You—you're supposed to be one of us."

"Not in a million years," I returned haughtily.

I'd never seen diamond injury do its thing, and I wondered if it was immediate, or if it took a while. Minutes? Hours? I hoped it was sooner rather than later, considering he was still sitting on top of me, and technically could still kill me before the diamond claimed him.

And from the look of hatred in his eyes, I figured that was exactly what he planned to do. He raised his hand, and though it wasn't holding a weapon, a few well-placed strikes with a closed fist would get the job done.

Before the first blow landed, Nathan was there, ripping the Skotadi off of me and tossing him to the ground several yards away. As I scampered to my feet, I looked around and saw that most of the Skotadi were dead. Only three remained, two of which were being tied up by Gabby and Richie. The third one, that I had injured, was being tossed around by Nathan.

My knees went out from under me. Alec was there to help ease me down to the ground. As he guided me up against the front of the car, I shot him a wobbly, but grateful, smile.

He frowned as he lifted a hand to my forehead. "Got a pretty bad cut there."

I shrugged. "What else is new?" It was the second time that shattered glass had sliced my forehead. The first time I'd been left with a nasty scar that had healed shortly after I'd started development. I wasn't concerned about it this time. At least not at the moment.

Micah dropped to the ground on my other side, opposite Alec. "You didn't get cut with diamond, did you?" I saw the anxiety on his face, mixed with determination to heal me if I said yes.

"No diamond injury here." I nodded my head toward the Skotadi I had scrapped with. "He wasn't as lucky."

Alec's eyes widened. "You got him with diamond?"

A small sideways grin was my answer.

Alec shook his head in disbelief as he got to his knees in front of me. "We might make a fighter out of you yet." He held a hand out to me. "Want to get up? Come see the effects of your hard work?"

I wasn't so sure I was ready to get up just yet, but I was curious about how diamond injury progressed.

"Just let her sit here," Micah argued. "She hit her head hard."

"I'm fine." I held a hand out to Alec. Anything was better than sitting there with Micah.

Besides, Gabby had finished helping Richie restrain the other Skotadi, and was on her way over. From the looks of the scowl on her face, I didn't want to be anywhere near when she reached Micah. As Alec led me away from the car, one arm around my waist—perhaps unnecessarily, but I wasn't going to complain—I heard Gabby berate Micah for being 'so stupid' for pulling that 'stupid stunt.'

Callie was sitting propped up against the side of the car. She looked up as we angled closer, a timid smile ready. "Not my finest moment."

"You did great," Alec returned. "You guys saved us. We just…" He trailed off as he looked over the mangled and bullet-ridden car. "Well, we'll need another car now."

Though he was hidden from my sight behind a large tree several yards away, I could hear Nathan talking to the Skotadi in a low voice. I couldn't make out what was being said, and I desperately wanted to.

"You okay, Callie?" I asked her.

She waved her hand. "Yeah, yeah. Go. I just want to sit here for a little bit."

I turned out of Alec's grasp and made my own way to Nathan. The Skotadi was slumped against the tree; Nathan knelt on one knee in front of him. The Skotadi looked up as I approached, with Alec right behind me.

"Getting anything out of him?" Alec asked Nathan.

"Nothing that makes sense." Nathan glanced at me. "You alright?"

His voice was clipped, reminiscent of the days he hadn't been so nice to me. When I'd been a pain in his ass, as he'd once told me. And I'd thought things had changed.

"I'm fine." I sounded like a broken record, but it was all I could manage under Nathan's hard glare.

What was his problem?

The Skotadi laughed, a sadistic, blood-curdling laugh. "Fine? Far from it. Dead. That's what you'll all be. Soon."

"I think you're the one that's dead," Alec retorted. To me, he whispered, "Diamond deliria."

So diamond turned its victims into lunatics before it kills. Good to know.

"I sacrifice for the good of better," the Skotadi mumbled, earning a snort out of Alec.

"What are you planning?" Nathan asked.

The Skotadi started to laugh before choking and coughing. "You no stop it. The gods no stop it. You think you do?"

Nathan stood quickly and turned away in frustration. His hand shook as it raked through his hair, the muscles in his back visibly taught and stiff with each movement.

"Stop what?" Alec tried.

"War going to the gods soon…"

My brow furrowed as I glanced at Alec. *What in the hell was that supposed to mean?*

"He's been talking nonsense," Nathan muttered, turning

back to us now. "Keeps circling around the gods getting away with something for too long, and that they are going after the gods, and nothing can stop them. Over and over…"

Alec stepped in front of the Skotadi. "What about turning Kala into Skotadi? Is that a part of your plan?"

The Skotadi might have tried to grin, but it looked more like a grimace. He was hurting, that much was clear no matter how hard he tried to pretend he wasn't. "Only the beginning."

A cold chill snapped down my spine, and I rubbed my arms to fend off the resulting goose-bumps.

"Get rid of him," Nathan muttered to Alec. With a dark look at me, he stormed away.

Even though Nathan was gone, Alec shook his head in response. "I think I'll let him suffer."

I spun around to the sound of two rapid gunshots behind me. Several yards away, Gabby and Richie stood over the motionless bodies of the other two Skotadi. From their grim faces as they conversed with Nathan, it was apparent they hadn't fared any better at gathering intel.

Aside from crazy rants, we'd gotten zilch. Though nothing the Skotadi had said made sense, his words still filled me with dread.

Only the beginning…

Nothing can stop them…

We didn't have a clue what they were planning. Of course we couldn't stop them. And we were no closer to finding a way to stop Alec and me from becoming Skotadi.

The grip of time squeezed tighter.

* * *

Finding a new vehicle was the next day's mission. Fortunately, with Micah's access to Kala funds and what was left of the money Alec had withdrawn from his Skotadi-funded bank account, we had more than enough to get something decent. Richie and Nathan came back with an Expedition, a big hefty thing that rivaled the Tahoe.

Two whole days went by without Nathan so much as glancing in my direction. I wasn't sure why exactly. Either he was mad about my role in the attack, though I didn't understand why—it wasn't like I'd had much control over what happened—or he was just being moody Nathan. Something known to happen from time to time.

Evening of the third day, he finally acknowledged me when we crossed paths in the hallway outside the bathroom.

He hesitated before placing a hand on my shoulder. "Hey."

I looked up at him and waited. My breath hitched as I remembered how to inhale and exhale. Words weren't exactly forthcoming.

"I was wondering…" He shrugged to emphasize the casualness of his invitation. "You want to work out tomorrow?"

I nodded, and hoped it wasn't obvious how hard I was trying to mirror his easy-going demeanor. On the inside, I was jumping with excitement. "Sure."

"Dawn," he had said. That was why I was now gladly and willingly up before the sun, lacing my shoes and bracing for the

cold mountain air. Nathan was waiting for me on the back porch, but didn't turn as I walked up beside him, choosing instead to fixate on the sunrise peeking above the mountain tops.

"Want to warm up with a run first?" he asked.

We had gone running a few times before, to build stamina, as he had claimed. I hadn't been a fan of it then, but if it offered me an hour of alone time with him now, I was definitely up for it.

"Sure thing, Sensei," I said, referring to him with the old nickname I had loved. He'd hated it. Which was probably why I'd loved it so much.

His eyes slanted sideways and his lips curled into a subtle grin, but he said nothing. He handed me a knit cap similar to the one on top of his head, and I pulled it down over my ears.

"Ready?"

He didn't wait for me to reply before taking off, forcing me to run after him. He led me across the yard before we ducked into the woods, onto a well-beaten trail that he had apparently known about. It was obvious from the gracefulness with which he maneuvered the bends and dips in the path that this was not his first time running on it. Knowing that he had been out here, probably every morning before everyone, including myself, woke up filled me with a strange longing. I wanted to join him, to be let into every aspect of his life—even if it was running.

The air was brisk and stung my lungs as my breathing accelerated, but in a good way. The visible puffs of air in front of me induced a sense of accomplishment and renewed determination. I was doing this…and doing it well. Nathan glanced over his shoulder a few times. The brief twinkle in his eye when he saw that I was keeping up with him only pushed me harder and faster.

Surprisingly, I was loving every moment of the run. The view was extraordinary—the mountains, the trees, the slightly foggy air were all refreshing sights. But the view just feet in front of me was the best one of all. A broad-shouldered, sturdy Nathan, in black track pants, a grey hoodie, and a beanie. Now *that* view was truly impressive.

I was again relieved to know that Nathan had an aptitude for nature. After several forks in the trail, I was lost, but I knew he wasn't. We jogged, winding our way up the mountain for half an hour before he finally stopped, and only then did I realize where we were.

Well, I didn't technically know where we were, but the scenery was spectacular, and it was obvious that he had meant for us to emerge from the woods in this exact spot. Perched atop the mountain, on a rocky overlook, the West Virginia wilderness was spread out in front of us, and I could see for miles. Beneath us, a narrow river snaked through the trees. In the distance, an eagle soared, and as I fought to catch my breath, I thought I heard him squawk.

"Being out here reminds me of our time spent trudging through the Blue Ridge Mountains," Nathan said wistfully.

Back when things were simpler. Before I'd learned the truth about who and what I was, when it was only a pack of Skotadi hunting me down. Easier, true. But not hardly enjoyable.

"You say it like it was a fun time." I hated that I sounded so out of breath, especially when he'd barely broken a sweat, and leaned forward, placing my hands on my knees as if that would help.

"It wasn't that bad," he said, and there was something in his tone that told me he was implying more. Much more.

In retrospect, I supposed I agreed with him. In those days, we had been falling for each other, though we hadn't known it yet. I'd give anything to go back to the days following Nathan through the woods, sleeping in a tent with him, peeing behind a tree. A comfortable silence settled between us as we took in the view, and I wondered if he was thinking the same things, remembering the days we had spent together, and missing them as I was.

After a moment, he knelt to pick up a stick and used it to carve circles in the dirt. "Hey, Kris," he started hesitantly. I'd finally managed to start breathing normally again, but my next breath came in a rush when he looked over his shoulder at me. "I want to apologize for the other night. I shouldn't have acted the way I did toward you."

So, he had been mad at me. The puff of air I'd been holding finally slipped past my lips. I didn't—or couldn't—say anything. Nathan looked back down at the ground and continued to play with his stick.

"I appreciated your help," he continued. "I always appreciate your help. I just…" He dug in the dirt as if the right words were buried there. "I'm frustrated that we keep hitting this wall, we're not getting anywhere and…I don't want you to get hurt. It's hard enough fighting these guys, and I can't always keep an eye on you, too. When I saw you and that Skotadi fighting, and I couldn't get to you…"

Nathan looked at me then, and I saw that the root of his anger the other night had come from his inability to help me sooner. His eyes were lined with guilt.

Unnecessary guilt as far as I was concerned. But I knew Nathan, and he took things like that personally. I figured there was only one way I could get him to move on from this with his ego intact.

And, hey, I would get something out of it, too.

"Maybe you could teach me more, get me all fit and trained so that I can fend for myself, and you won't worry about me."

"I'll always worry about you," he murmured softly. I didn't miss the undertone in his voice, or the way his eyes dodged mine.

"But it might help." I was so bored studying with Micah all the time. I needed some more excitement in my life, and a way to burn off some of the excess steam built up from being around Nathan without really *being with* Nathan.

He nodded and stood. "You're right."

I beamed. "Really?" I hadn't expected him to agree so quickly, not without at least some begging on my part.

"Really. I've spent a lot of time preparing Callie, but not enough time helping you master what I know you can do." He paused and a mischievous glint lit his eyes. "Consider the skills I have to offer an early birthday present."

My mouth dropped open.

"A few weeks, right?" he asked. "On the twentieth?"

How did he know?

As an afterthought, I figured I should probably be asking

what he *didn't* know about me. He seemed to know so much—more about my past than I knew, my favorite foods, my habits. And now my birthday? Funny, considering I had barely remembered.

"I'm not really all that excited about it," I muttered.

"Why not?"

"It's not like it's going to be a good year," I scoffed. "It's not going to be any better than seventeen was, and that was a bad year."

"You don't know that."

I gave him a bland look. "It's not looking all that promising."

His eyes drifted from mine, and I suddenly felt bad that I was only reminding him of all that was screwed up in my life. Here he was trying to be nice, to talk about something other than all the depressing stuff we were faced with every day, and I was squashing it like a bug.

Before I could offer an apology, he said, "I know what will cheer you up."

"What's that?" A kiss maybe? That would definitely work, but I wasn't optimistic.

He smiled. "Let's put in a little one-on-one rink time," he suggested, then added, "Now. Without Callie."

Yep, he definitely knew me, and knew how to cheer me up. His offer to restart training right away, *today*, was probably the only thing that could have managed to do so. Aside from planting a big kiss on me of course.

But I would take what I could get, and it was good enough. For now.

CHAPTER 8

He sure knew how to make me happy, except when he was pissing me off. And now, he was pissing me off. At first, I'd been excited to scrap with him. I'd always enjoyed it, and today was no exception. Until he started egging me on, telling me that I could do better—and not in a friendly way.

He was harder on me than he used to be, and much harder than he was on Callie. I realized it was only because he believed I could do it, that I could be good, and he was trying to help me capitalize on my ability. So I let it go at first.

Then it became obvious how much he had been holding back on me before, when I'd thought I had actually been getting good. I was in the midst of a reality check, and I wasn't happy about it.

It wasn't that I was doing that badly now, but he managed to block, sidestep, and avoid everything I threw at him. I was giving him my best, and he was practically laughing at me.

"You can do better than that!" He swatted my fist away, dodging a kidney strike. I quickly followed with another, which he blocked effortlessly. "What was that? I thought you wanted to hit me."

I snarled at him and he grinned. As I regrouped, I saw that

we had drawn an audience. Callie had been watching all along, taking pointers, and looked appropriately uncomfortable and scared. Now, when I glanced around, I saw that the others had joined her. Even Gabby and Richie.

Knowing that they were watching only angered me more. My vision blurred momentarily as I zeroed in on Nathan, and I wondered if that was where the expression *'seeing red'* came from. If so, I was definitely seeing it.

I threw a right jab. He dodged it, and taunted, "Is that all you got?"

I swung an uppercut and missed. Even as Nathan was leaning out of the way, I quickly followed with another jab…that connected with his nose, hard.

I heard the crack, felt the pain in my hand, and heard everyone go *"Ooh!"* in unison behind me. I had finally done it. I'd gotten Nathan, and I'd gotten him good. I stared triumphantly at the top of his head as he hunched over, face in his hands.

I was still glaring at him when Callie stepped into my line of sight, holding a towel out to him. At her appearance, I snapped out of the enraged spell I had fallen under, and the only thing I could think about for a few moments was…*where had I just been?*

How much time had passed, with me staring down at Nathan, for Callie to run into the house and return with a towel? And why didn't I remember that time passing?

Then, I saw why she'd gotten the towel, and I totally forgot that I had just missed a few seconds of my life. As Nathan straightened with the towel covering his face, I caught sight of the blood on his shirt, and I pushed everything else to the side.

"Oh, my God," I gushed, rushing forward to assist him, though I had no idea what to do. He was bleeding—bad. Because of me. "Nathan, I'm so sorry."

His eyes lowered to mine. With the towel in the way, I couldn't be sure, but I thought he was smiling. "What got into you?"

I sighed in relief. He wasn't mad. But his question only piqued my curiosity more.

What had gotten into me?

Something obviously had—and I hardly remembered. The last few minutes were so hazy, so clouded. I barely remembered the moment I'd connected my fist to his face. But from the looks of the damage I'd done, I'd apparently done a good job.

It was as if it hadn't been me…or my fist.

As much as my out of body experience freaked me out, it was nothing compared to what I felt when I looked up and met Alec's eyes. He had seen the whole thing. Something about the expression on his face told me that he knew exactly what had happened. And it was something neither of us were prepared for.

* * *

"You alright?" Micah's voice snapped me out of my daydream, and I could tell from the look on his face that he'd asked me this simple question repeatedly before I'd registered it.

"Huh?" I said as I blinked the fog away.

"Where did you go?"

"Nowhere," I said hastily in an attempt to blow it off.

Truth was I have been obsessing all morning. It has been two days since the nose break heard around the world. Nathan and I have not scrapped since so that his nose could heal. Instead, he and Callie have been working on target practice with the guns. Except today. This morning, he had gone with Gabby and Richie to do some surveillance on the warehouse.

We had run together the last two mornings, and that had been nice, though I didn't enjoy it as much as I did the hand-to-hand, sweat-producing, body-wracking fighting. We also hadn't talked much. Just ran. I supposed I understood the need for a break from the fun stuff. I wasn't so sure I was ready to do it again anyway. Not yet. Not until I knew what had happened to me.

So much for our plan to whip me into shape.

The hiatus with Nathan left me to practice exclusively with Micah. Again. I wasn't completely into it. I kept thinking about those lost moments—from the second I'd popped Nathan in the nose to when Callie stepped in with the towel. It wasn't normal to check out like that. It wasn't right, and it was downright scary not knowing what had come over me. Where had I gone? And even more pressing—what was happening to me?

Even as I asked those questions, I wasn't sure I wanted to know the answers. So, instead of talking to anyone about it, I silently obsessed over it.

Besides, Micah was definitely not the one I would to talk to about this. Alec was a better choice, but he had been elusive and was currently off doing whatever it was that Alec did.

"Okay, well, if you're not going to talk about it, then let's get back to practicing," Micah said sternly.

I squinted my eyes at him. "Stop reading my mind."

"Stop yelling your thoughts at me."

"I'm not—" I came up short, my defense falling flat when I realized I probably had been screaming them out. I supposed it wasn't his fault I couldn't keep my thoughts to myself. Considering I had a hard enough time not speaking before thinking, I could only blame myself.

I really had to learn better impulse control.

"Forget it," I said. "Where were we?"

"Element manipulation," Micah said with an authoritative tone that only reminded me that I hated how smug he could be at times.

Sometimes I wished I could smack that permanent smirk off his face—without the threat of Gabby's and Richie's wrath. Seeing as how I sort of wanted to live, I was forced to overlook the things I was starting to hate about Micah.

"Right. Element manipulation," I said like nothing was wrong. "And how do I do that?"

Micah cocked his head to the side, looking at me like he was a teacher scolding a student for not completing an assignment. "Haven't you been reading?"

"Yeah," I chuckled, "when I'm having a hard time falling asleep."

He frowned. "Not funny, Kris. How do expect to learn? You have to put in some effort, you know?"

I shrugged. "Alright. Let's put in some effort then. Tell me what I need to know." I paused, then added, "I'm just not reading that dumb book."

I was more hands-on anyway. Last thing I wanted was to feel like I was back in school. Despite the circumstances, I was rather enjoying my little hiatus from standardized education.

Micah shook his head, but said, "You specialize in fire manipulation. Personally, I don't have any experience with fire. But I know how to manipulate elements in general. It's all about meditation and concentration."

"What elements can you manipulate?"

"Water, earth, and air," he answered. "I'm best at manipulating air."

Now, I was intrigued, and the grin growing on my face was genuine. "What can you do with air?"

Micah pursed his lips without answering. I expected him to lecture me about reading the book to learn what air manipulators could do. But he said nothing. Just stared…and stared.

A soft breeze tickled my neck, stirring my hair as if someone were standing behind me, blowing on me. I nearly turned around, convinced Alec was pulling a prank on me, but then the breeze strengthened. A strong gust blew my hair into my face like someone was holding a blow-dryer to it. As I struggled to contain the unruly strands, I caught the look on Micah's face.

He was *showing* me what he could do with air. The satisfied grin on his face was infectious and, before I knew it, I was laughing.

Laughing. I hadn't laughed, really laughed, in…

Well, it's been a long time.

"Pretty cool, huh?" He bordered on bragging, but I didn't

care. I'd probably brag too if I could do what he'd just done.

"That was awesome," I admitted as I combed my hands through my hair to fix what the unnatural breeze had done. "How do you do it?"

"Like I said, it's mostly about meditation. You've got to concentrate on what you want to achieve," he explained, then pointed to a stone by our feet. "If I wanted to move that rock, I'd focus on it, repeat what I wanted it to do over and over in my head…"

The rock shifted and I jumped back in surprise.

He'd just moved a rock with his mind. I'd officially entered the Twilight Zone.

"How…"

"Focus," he said slowly. "You're specialty is fire. You don't have anything to look at, to focus on. That makes it harder. Maybe just think about fire in your head. See what happens."

I wasn't in any type of condition to be meditating with all that was running through my head, between my anxiety and seeing what Micah had just done, but I followed his instructions. I doubted it would work anyway. As Micah's soft voice floated around me, I closed my eyes and cleared my mind of everything but thoughts of fire. At Micah's suggestion, I envisioned a tiny flame on the end of a match, growing, spreading, engulfing everything in my mind's eye.

Fire…fire…fire…

Micah called my name sharply and I opened one eye to look at him. That was when I saw it.

The glowing orange-red ball in my right hand. Both eyes

opened now, I took in the clear view of a golf ball sized fire ball swirling in my palm. Though it wasn't burning me, the sight of fire against my skin kicked my survival instincts into gear. And I freaked out.

I'm not ashamed to admit that I screamed like a girl while waving my arm frantically in all directions. In the process, I inadvertently propelled the fireball like a flaming baseball into a nearby tree. Though the fire had been small, the fully grown tree was engulfed within seconds. As my heart hammered in my chest, the tree was reduced to a smoking skeleton of scorched limbs.

After checking that my hand had not fallen to the same fate as the tree—not one burn, thank God—I turned to Micah. "What the hell was that? You trying to kill me?"

He stood motionless, looking at me with awe. "I've never..."

"What?" I screamed at him.

"I've never seen anyone do that. Ever."

Great. What was that supposed to mean?

"Only the earliest hybrids have been known to throw fire," Micah continued. "Most hybrids can't even yield it anymore."

"I'm supposed to be as strong as the early hybrids," I reminded Micah, but he didn't seem as relieved as I would have liked.

He was still in shock over what he'd seen me do. I didn't consider that a good thing.

He finally looked me in the eyes. "That was the first time you tried it," he said matter-of-factly. "I'm as strong as you. Stronger even, since I've been developing longer, and I can't manipulate my elements like that. It took me months to get anything to happen."

"So?" I tried to keep the nervousness out of my voice, but couldn't. Not with the way Micah was staring at me like I was some freak.

He didn't get a chance to answer before Alec and Callie appeared, walking toward us.

Alec motioned to the smoldering tree with a grin. "Hey, Kris," he called, "I can't find my lighter. Light my cigarette?" His grin dropped when he got close enough to see my face—and lack of amusement—clearly. "You okay?" he asked with genuine concern.

"Did you do that?" Callie squeaked.

I nodded numbly.

Alec turned his attention, and developing rage, on Micah. "What happened?"

Micah dodged that question by asking Alec one of his own. "Can you do that?"

Alec hesitated and glanced at me before looking away quickly. "No."

Awesome. Just what I wanted to be—the weirdo in a herd of black sheep, with supernatural powers unparalleled by others with supernatural powers, and surrounded by people who have seen some weird shit, but looked at me like they have never seen anything quite like me before. It didn't fill me with the sense of security I hoped for these days.

"So what," I asked, looking back and forth between Alec and Micah, "I'm developing faster than Alec now? Is that what this means?"

Micah shrugged one shoulder, not appearing certain about that theory. But what else could it be then? Why was I doing things I shouldn't be able to do yet—when hardly trying?

The ringing in Alec's pants' pocket interrupted me from completely freaking out. Suddenly, I had more to be concerned about than rapidly developing specialties.

They never called.

Alec answered quickly and put it on speaker phone for all of us to hear as Nathan's voice came through. The fact that it was him calling settled some of the galloping in my chest. He was fine, obviously. I didn't need to worry about him. But what about Gabby and Richie?

I could hear the apprehension in Nathan's voice as he asked for all of us to drive down to the cliff overlooking the warehouse. With one urgently spoken word, everything and everyone around me disappeared.

Now.

Something had happened. Something was wrong.

I didn't have a guess as to what it could be, but I knew it couldn't be good if it had Nathan on edge.

CHAPTER 9

I was relieved to see Nathan waiting for us when we pulled up. I got the confirmation that he was okay, but I could tell from the look on his face that something big was going on. Though I didn't know them very well, and what I did know is that they didn't like me very much, I felt a pang of concern for Gabby and Richie. I hoped nothing had happened to either of them, and Nathan didn't call Micah down here to do some diamond injury curing.

Nathan didn't say a word as he led the way from the road to the overlook. It was a slightly uphill hike that was just long enough and steep enough to cause a little bead of sweat to pop out on my forehead. Gabby and Richie met us at the top, and neither of them were writhing in pain or muttering gibberish.

So what was the problem, and why the glum faces?

I opened my mouth to ask, but was interrupted by Micah.

"They're gone," he said in a hauntingly soft voice.

Who? The Skotadi? Gone? How did he know that, I wondered, and then I remembered who I was questioning.

Of course. I had read in that stupid book of his that some prophets could sense Skotadi from a distance. Micah, as arguably the strongest prophet alive, surely had that ability.

"Are you sure?" Nathan asked him.

Micah nodded. "Positive. I can usually sense them in the car on the way here, and it gets stronger the closer I get. Now, I'm getting nothing. I can't feel them at all. They're gone." He hesitated, then added, "And I think they left in a hurry. Maybe middle of the night."

Alec scoffed. "You can get all that from just standing here?"

Micah glared. "Yeah. I can."

Alec narrowed his eyes at Micah, and looked close to firing a smartass comment in return. It was obvious that Nathan wasn't the only one that didn't like Micah. The animosity between Alec and Micah didn't go anywhere though, since Richie interrupted their testosterone-charged staring contest by suggesting that we all go check out the warehouse. Then, there was something more important to worry about than who would get first dibs on kicking Micah's ass.

"Go check it out?" I spun on Richie. "Are you crazy?"

"I'd think you would be eager to see what they've been hiding in there," Gabby said coolly. She was intimidating for being such a small framed girl, but I refused to let her know she scared the hell out of me.

"Let's go see what they might have left behind."

That last statement came from Nathan, and was what started us all down the embankment to the warehouse.

I wrung my hands nervously as we approached the building. Sure, I trusted Micah's weird ability to sense a group of Skotadi. I trusted that he believed they were gone, but it still freaked me out to go inside their warehouse. Part of it was fear that a few, not enough for Micah to sense, had stayed behind to ambush us. Most of it was fear of what we might find.

What if it was something I didn't want to see, to find out? What if we found that there wasn't a way to alter the path I was destined for? The words that Skotadi muttered in the woods just before Richie put a bullet in his head still haunted me. What if we were about to stumble upon something bigger than what we were prepared for?

My skin prickled as we entered the building. Inside, it was cold and dark. The windows were haphazardly covered with black garbage bags, with weak bands of sunlight spilling through the occasional gap. It was a big, and old, and creepy building, but I was glad to see that it was open and spacious, which left few places to hide.

Our footsteps echoed ominously off the concrete as we fanned out. I jumped when Alec suddenly called out from beside me.

"Come out, come out, wherever you are!" he shouted. Gabby shot him a scathing look, and he shrugged his shoulders. "Wouldn't you rather know if there's anyone left now, than to keep looking over your shoulder?"

Before she could answer, Micah chimed in with a confident, "There's no one left."

"We should split up," Richie suggested. "We can cover more ground before the sun sets and we can't see at all."

Richie, Gabby, and Micah—because they wouldn't let Micah out of there sight of course—took one phone and said they would canvas the lower level. The rest of us climbed up a shaky set of metal stairs to a cluster of rooms that looked as if they might have served as offices.

The first room we came across was mostly empty, aside from some boxes that, from the amount of dust layered on them, had obviously not been touched in some time. Same went for the second room. The third room we entered had more boxes, but with less dust, and appeared to have been some sort of storage room. Likely for the Skotadi, since this room had been used more recently. It also appeared to have been emptied quickly.

Chances were that whatever they had kept in this room had been taken with them, and the boxes that remained held nothing of importance. We paused to sort through them anyway, just in case something worthwhile had been left behind.

After a few moments it became clear that nothing would be found there. Turning away from another empty box in frustration, I caught a glimpse of Nathan as he wandered through a door into another room. With a quick glance at Alec and Callie, who were busy sifting through a cluster of boxes in the corner, I followed him.

He looked up when I entered, and I saw the bluish hint still left in the corner of both of his eyes, all that remained of the broken nose I had given him. Seeing the bruises now only made me feel all the more guilty.

"Hey, Nathan…" I started hesitantly. I didn't know how to apologize for what I had done. Mostly because I knew that he wouldn't expect, or want, an apology. As far as he was probably concerned, one wasn't necessary. I had only done what he'd encouraged me to do.

It was the rest of it that I felt I needed to apologize for. The out of body experience I had encountered the moment I'd connected my fist with his face, the fact that I didn't really remember doing it, and that I still couldn't explain what had happened. But how could I apologize for all of that when I didn't really want him, or anyone, to know what had happened? Not before I could explain it.

"Don't," he said like he knew exactly what I was trying to do. And of course he did. It was Nathan. He always knew what I was up to, sometimes even before I knew.

Sometimes I really hated that. "Yeah, but…"

"But nothing, Kris. You did what I wanted you to do. You hit me." He rolled his head with a smile. "Just a little harder than I anticipated."

I sighed, and then said the rest in a gush, "I'm sorry I broke your nose."

His smile widened. "No, you're not."

My mouth gaped open. Did he really think I'd wanted to break his nose? Surely not. But then, well, I had been pretty pissed at him at the time.

He used my hesitation as an opportunity to close the door on the whole incident. That was fine. I'd apologized. Maybe not for *all* of it, but he'd gotten the message.

He turned toward the desk in the corner of the room. It, too, had been cleared, except for one piece of paper placed neatly in the center. He picked it up and examined it.

Since I couldn't read it without stepping close to him—and being close to Nathan wouldn't help me with that impulse control I'd been working on—I watched Nathan's reaction as he read what was written on the paper. A muscle in his cheek twitched and his eyes hardened.

"What is it?" I asked.

Wordlessly, Nathan handed the paper to me. It was a letter addressed to him. From Lillian. My chest tightened as I read the words.

Dear Nathan,

I don't know how you did it, but apparently you found us. I'm not sure what it is that you and your pet are looking for, but I can assure you that you are wasting your time. You won't find us again. You can't win. Give up and let us have the girl. You're only postponing the inevitable. Until next time, when I find you...

Love,

Lillian

I had hoped she'd been killed when Nathan and Alec blew up her underground Skotadi compound in Kentucky. We hadn't heard or seen anything from her since. Until now. She was alive and still looking for me. And still referring to me as Nathan's *pet*.

He was across the room, rummaging through a filing cabinet, when I turned to him.

"This is the second time she's called me your pet," I said to him. "What does she mean by that?"

Nathan shrugged without turning to look at me. "We were dating when I found you. She knew what I was doing, checking up on you, protecting you. We got into a few fights about it."

They used to fight about me? About Nathan protecting me when I was a kid? That was…weird.

"Why did she care so much?"

Nathan slammed one drawer shut and opened another. As he flipped through the files, he answered, "She didn't want me to get caught, I think. I don't really remember now. It was so long ago." He stopped what he was doing to look up at me. "I was breaking just about every Kala rule there was."

I half smiled. I doubted I would ever grow tired of hearing how Nathan had risked everything by helping me. In learning about the actions he had taken over the years to protect me, I'd uncovered the deeply rooted, though heavily guarded, feelings he had for me. I'd learned that he genuinely cared for me. Even if it had only started because he'd felt sorry for me, the pathetic little girl who had no one else.

Except for him. He had always been there.

His girlfriend had known…and hadn't liked it. It wasn't like it could have been a jealousy thing. I had only been three when he'd first started protecting me. And I had only been eleven when Lillian was changed to a Skotadi.

The same year Nathan had removed me from foster care.

When the Skotadi had lost track of me.

"Hey, Nathan?"

"Hmm?" He was flipping through a file he had withdrawn from the cabinet, and not paying much attention to me.

"Was Lillian changed before or after you took me out of that foster home?"

He tossed the file, apparently having come up empty on

finding anything useful in it. He glanced at me distractedly. "Huh? Why?"

"I have a theory," I said slowly as I sorted through my jumbled thoughts, hoping I was wrong. But afraid I was right. My pulse thundered in my ears. "Just go with me. Was it before or after?"

He tossed his head back as if to think. He pondered for only a second before his eyes flicked to mine, hard and serious. "Kris, don't…"

"Just think about," I insisted. "What if it wasn't a coincidence?"

He shook his head as if to prevent my suggestion from planting, as if the idea was too painful to consider.

"She knew you, your strengths and your weaknesses," I added. "They knew you were messing around in my life, and she knew you better than anyone."

I saw from the look in his eyes that Nathan had never considered the possibility before. Honestly, I didn't know how he hadn't thought of it sooner. But I could also see that he didn't want to believe it.

"You don't think it's possible that they targeted her and changed her to use her to find me?"

He shook his head, but it wasn't very convincing. Neither was his voice. "No, I don't."

I did. The more I thought about it, the more convinced I became. And it made me sick.

Because of me, Nathan's life, and Lillian's, had been turned upside down. I didn't like her, but I still felt guilty that she was the way she was now because of me. And I hated what it had done to Nathan. It was all my fault. All the pain that Nathan has been through was all because of me.

He must have seen the devastation on my face, because he crossed the room to where I swayed unsteadily as a chip was chiseled out of my heart. He cupped a hand to the back of my neck, forcing me to look up at him.

"I don't want you to be thinking what I know you're thinking," he said softly.

I couldn't help it. Gradually, I was only being reminded of how much easier things would be if I weren't here. No more questioning the fate of humanity, no more fighting for my soul, no more heartbreak.

No more ruining the lives of everyone around me.

"Everybody would be better off if I had died in that accident." The car accident that, by all means, I should have died in. I'd only survived because Nathan had saved me.

Nathan gripped my chin forcefully, making me hold his gaze. "Not me."

"Maybe fate was trying to correct what you had interfered with all along?" I was in a downward spiral of self-loathing now, all my most negative thoughts rising to the surface, all the little things I had buried coming forth, all at once. The end result was shattering. "My foster dad, who would have raped and killed me, the car accident I should have died in? Maybe I was supposed to die when I was three, and fate has been trying to correct it ever since?"

Wallowing in self-pity had never been a trait I admired in

anyone, least of all myself, but there I was, immersed in it. But what I said, I truly believed. What if Nathan had been throwing a kink into fate's plan all this time?

"It's best for everyone I know, not to mention all of mankind. I shouldn't be here," I concluded numbly.

"Listen to me, Kris," Nathan said, his hard grip on my chin softening into a gentle caress of my cheek. "I want you here. I *need* you here. Don't you give up on fighting this just because you think it's fate's plan. I'm sure as hell not going to stop fighting for you."

"Nathan—" I didn't really know what to say to that, and I didn't get a chance to make something up, because he interrupted me.

"No," he said forcefully. "I don't want to hear anything like that come out of your mouth again. You're here for a reason. As much as I hate to admit it, I think Micah might be onto something. With you, him, and Alec all fighting on the same side? This war could finally end. Maybe *that* is fate's plan for you."

My mouth opened, but any attempt at a reply was shut down by his finger to my lips, and I knew he had more to say, so I bit back my weak argument. Something told me I wouldn't get anywhere with negativity anyway. Not with him—Mr. Optimistic.

"Am I glad that Lillian was turned? No," he continued, "but I'm also not standing here, wishing for the ability to go back and change things, wishing that the last seven years had been different. It sucked when I thought she died. A lot. But I also moved on, Kris. I'm not trying to rewrite the past, and I'm sure as hell not going to dwell on it. What's happened as a result of all of this, all that we've gone through, all that Lillian has gone through, has led us to where we are right now. And honestly, I'm happy where I'm at."

He hesitated, sucked in a deep breath, and held my gaze firmly as he concluded the best damn pep talk in the history of pep talks. "I'm glad I'm here with you now. I wouldn't want to be anywhere else. I'm glad everything that's happened between us happened, and because of that, I wouldn't change anything. And I need you to fight, with me, with all of us. We've come so far, you can't give up now."

Any response to his words was lost to me. They were just too amazing to respond to. They filled me with a sense of hope I hadn't felt in months. For that, and for so many other reasons, I was hit with an overwhelming desire to kiss him.

And I was pretty sure he wanted to kiss me too. His head dropped ever so slightly toward mine, and I knew it was going to happen when his gaze lowered to my lips and he licked his own in preparation.

I wasn't left disappointed.

It was a perfect kiss to follow his perfect words. It was everything I needed—soft and delicate—like he knew I was in a sensitive place and needed a sensitive kiss, full of reassurance and promise. The gentle brush of his lips across mine was mirrored by the soft caresses of my face in his hands. Pent up desire brewed just under the surface, waiting and wanting release, but he held it in check, like he knew that wasn't the type of kiss I needed right now. He knew what he was doing and, good God, did he do it well. So well, that my response went from grateful to full on hot and bothered in a matter of seconds.

Nathan pulled back, my face still in his hands, and pressed his forehead to mine as if to cool down. I wasn't sure if he intended to cool himself down, or me—maybe both—but when his eyes met mine, I saw the war raging behind them, and the decision in them when he made it.

His mouth crashed into mine with a definite urgency. What he had been holding back just a moment ago burst free, and I knew that this kiss was going to be even better than the last.

Too bad Callie had the uncanny ability to ruin just about every moment Nathan and I had alone anymore. As the sound of her footsteps stopped in the doorway, Nathan practically hurled himself halfway across the room from me. Not that it mattered. From the look on Callie's face, it was obvious she had already seen us. And felt bad about the interruption.

She hovered uneasily just inside the door, looking back and forth between the two of us. "I'm sorry. Again," she added with a small chuckle. She pointed over her shoulder. "Micah called. They found something downstairs."

I glanced at Nathan. His eyes met mine briefly before darting away. As much as that kiss was still on both of our minds, I could tell he was curious about this *something downstairs*. As was I.

"There's nothing up here," he concluded. With a nod of his head, he motioned for me to follow Callie out of the room. He caught me at the door. Callie was ahead of us, and out of earshot. "I meant what I said," he murmured. "It doesn't matter why Lillian was changed. Not anymore."

My nod of acceptance came up short when he leaned in and

touched his lips to my forehead. He lingered for only a second before ushering me the rest of the way through the door, after Callie, which was hard to do now that my legs felt like lead.

Callie had turned to wait for us, and her eyes danced with a silent question when they met mine. I returned a smile meant just for her, my own silent promise to give her details later. That smile fell quickly when my eyes found Alec's from across the room, and despite all the joy I felt, another little piece of my heart broke.

CHAPTER 10

We found the others on the opposite side of the warehouse, in a small room tucked away from everything else like it was on purpose. From the looks of the room, I understood why. Whatever this room had been used for, it was something different, something secretive. Something disturbing.

It gave off a bad vibe, and I rubbed my hands over my arms as if to protect myself from whatever evil lingered inside. The addition of red streaks on the walls, which I really hoped was paint, the mounds of various shapes and sizes of candles, and the perfectly drawn symbols on the floor added to the mystery. I'd only seen symbols like that in movies…usually of the really disturbing, devil-worshipping type.

A few of the larger candles were still lit, providing us with just enough light to see that something ritualistic-like had been going on in this room. If not devil-worship, then something equally alarming.

"This is where they did it, isn't it?" I asked no one in particular. Micah looked up from where he was crouched in a corner of the room, looking at additional floor markings, and I focused on his gaze. "This is where they did the Kala-to-Skotadi conversions?"

Micah nodded, but no one said anything, as they all had seemingly reached the same conclusion, and were silently mulling over the discovery. It was a good discovery, one that we have been looking and waiting for.

If only we could figure out what the things in the room had to do with the conversions. I'd always suspected they involved a drink of tainted Kook-Aid. But this? This suggested a level I had not considered. Something I'd been severely unprepared for.

What in the hell were we dealing with?

Alec ran a hand hesitantly over the streaks on the wall, apparently wondering as I had about the origination. "It's blood," he announced softly, sending every bone in my spine into its very own dance.

"To summon the gods," Micah added, his voice eerily calm. From his little corner of the room, a candle flickered and he turned to us with it to light up the rest of the room. "For Incantation. They're using Incantation to do it."

Nathan and Alec both scoffed in response to Micah's idea, but I was curious. I'd heard that word before, hadn't I? Micah had told me about it, when I'd asked him how I was able to share dreams with him if I weren't a prophet.

"Witchcraft?" I asked timidly. "They're using *witchcraft?*"

No one was quick to answer. Finally, Micah amended, "Spells. They're using the elements to summon the gods with spells. If the gods are invoked in the right way, they will aid you in whatever you ask of them. There are different spells to achieve certain…things, but I've never heard of a spell for this."

Yeah, sounded like witchcraft to me. So the Skotadi were

using some form of witchcraft and magic—Incantation, as it was known in the hybrid's world—to do their conversions, and were using the help of the gods? That didn't sound good. Not to me. Nor did it sound as farfetched as Alec and Nathan were acting.

"So, this is all witchcraft?" I asked, spreading my arms out to indicate the room.

"No way," Alec interjected before Micah could answer. "Only kooks think Incantation exists."

"There's no solid proof that it exists," Nathan added, surprisingly in agreement with Alec. I doubted I would ever get used to seeing the two of them being on the same side of any disagreement, but if anything could bring them closer, it would be their mutual dislike of Micah.

"It's nothing but a myth," Alec concluded.

"Our entire world, our existence, is all based on myths," Micah returned. He gestured to the candles and the glass jars filled with various objects and materials. I expected to see a jar filled with eyeballs somewhere, but didn't. Granted, I was afraid to look too closely, just in case there was one hidden there somewhere.

"This stuff is all used in Incantation," Micah continued, "to call upon the gods. Whatever they were calling them for was done in this room, and it was something big, something we need to pay attention to. Only a very powerful Incantator could be capable of this, and we can't blow that off."

"The Skotadi don't do Incantation," Alec insisted. "I would know if they were."

"Just because you haven't seen it, doesn't mean it doesn't

exist," Micah said.

"If Incantators are out there, don't you think we would have heard about them by now?" Nathan argued.

"What about the legends?" Micah countered. "There are centuries' worth of stories. What if there are so few Incantators that they're easy to hide? And maybe they don't even know what they're capable of until they try it, and then they can't talk about it, for fear of being ostracized."

As he stated his defense, Micah glanced in my direction. As usual, the heaviness of his gaze unsettled me, but the look he gave me now was different from the others. It wasn't deep and penetrating, but rather scared and uneasy, like we shared a shocking secret that I wasn't technically in on.

I cleared my throat to break the hold Micah had on me. "Why is it so hard to believe the Skotadi capable of Incantation?" I asked of Alec and Nathan, since they were the two dead-set against the idea.

From what I've seen and heard so far, Micah had a good argument. The room looked like a voodoo shop.

Nathan answered me. "There are a few gods and goddesses capable of working magic, but none of them procreated with humans. None of our bloodlines are linked to them, so it's not possible for hybrids to have that specialty." He looked at Micah as he emphasized the last few words.

Okay. I understood their reasoning. But why were they so against the idea of their history being wrong? It wasn't that ridiculous to consider the existence of a previously unknown Incantation bloodline out there somewhere, being kept secret, as

Micah suggested.

"There's more to it than that," I said, surprised at how confident my voice sounded. "What is it you're not telling me?"

Alec and Nathan exchanged a look, which only confirmed my suspicion.

"It's the legend," Micah chimed in. "They don't want to accept that it might be right."

"What legend?" As I looked around at everyone, it became apparent that Callie and I were the only ones in the dark. Even the almighty Gabby shifted uncomfortably in response to my question, her eyes flicking to mine before darting away.

"More like a folktale," Alec grumbled.

Micah ignored him to answer me, since no one else was forthcoming. "Centuries ago, a prophet, actually the most powerful prophet at that time—"

"She was an old crazy bat," Alec interrupted, but Micah continued unfazed.

"She had a vision," he said, "of an Incantator bringing about the end of everything—of us, of our world. *Everything*, Skotadi and Kala alike. Her vision led to a bad time in our history, where anyone even suspected of Incantation was executed, without question. Hybrids, demigods, everyone was terrified. It got twisted into human history over time, and is now what the basis of the persecution of witches in the 1600s came from."

"None of them were ever found to be Incantators," Nathan added in opposition of Micah's story. "Let alone *the* Incantator."

"Maybe because she wasn't born yet," Micah returned coolly.

"She?" I asked.

Micah nodded. "The prophet saw a girl, capable of bringing an end to all of us."

Micah had a way of making my skin prick, but never had his words caused the hairs on my neck to stand on end quite like this before. I'd thought learning that I was destined to be the greatest evil to walk the earth would be the most bone jarring moment of my life. I had been wrong. Because even if no one said it out loud, and I didn't know if anyone else was even on the same brain wave as I was, but I had a deeply rooted suspicion that this prophecy, this Incantator, was linked to me.

I was destined to lift the Skotadi, and bring an end to the Kala. It was likely that my path would intersect with this great Incantator they all feared. If the prophet's prediction that an Incantator with this kind of power was coming, I knew she was here now and our paths would be crossing soon. Not only did I fear myself, but now I feared this unknown enemy.

Even if the others doubted it, I believed. How could I not, after all I have seen and heard and learned about this new world, and myself? For all we knew, she was the one behind these conversions, and this was her room we were standing in. Micah had said only a very powerful Incantator could pull of something like this. Surely *the* Incantator would have the strength to force someone's soul to…switch sides.

What were our chances, if we were up against someone like this? Did I have a chance?

I felt the heaviness of several sets of eyes on me, and I kept my eyes downturned to avoid meeting any of them. Too much was swirling around in my head and I didn't want any of them to know just how freaked out I was. If I was going to do this, I had to be strong. For now, faking strength would have to do.

Because I had to do something—anything—to cover up the chills that had gripped me, I stepped closer to the markings on the floor in the center of the room, studying them though I had no idea what they meant. I had no plan, no reason to do so, but I stooped there, in the middle of the room, and brushed a finger over the crescent shaped drawing at my feet.

It was drawn in a powdery material, almost, but not quite, like chalk. Lifting my hand, I studied the powder on my finger. It was…shiny. As I moved my finger around, light from the candles glistened off of tiny specks. They weren't…

My breath caught.

They weren't specks of diamond, were they?

I tried to open my mouth, but found that I couldn't. The only thing that worked were my eyes. I saw my hand frozen in the air, my finger sticking straight up, held there against my will. I felt as if I were suspended in a pool of thick jelly, unable to move.

I heard the others' muffled voices, full of panic, as stars swarmed my vision. A bolt of electricity shot up my arm, producing a scream from me that sounded more like a whimper to my ears. I saw a flash of color, perhaps the same color as Nathan's shirt, rushing toward me. I tried to reach for it, but couldn't.

And then I saw nothing.

I was thrust into the land of nowhere, surrounded by nothing, for a long time. At some point, I felt a presence join me, but still saw nothing. After a while, I started to wonder if I had imagined the feeling of something, or someone, else being there. On some level, I knew it was still there…only not. It was more like…

Like it was a part of me.

Relentless darkness, made worse by thick fog, limits my vision. Only the lantern in my hand permits me hope of finding it. Of finding him.

My thin white gown sweeps across the fog covered ground. I watch my sandal-clad feet, faintly illuminated by the lantern's light, as they push forward, one in front of the other. I take tentative steps that will lead me to freedom…a freedom I have not known for centuries.

To a love I have not seen for far too long.

Aside from in my dreams. But they are not the same. They do not give me the strength that his true presence does. I am on my own, and can only rely on my own faltering powers.

Oh, how I miss him. How I need him.

A vision of him fills me. Tall and lean, with wavy dark hair, softly curved shoulders. Beautiful in every way. My love. My curse. In my mind's eye, he turns and I see him.

His eyes—the color that emeralds were named after—meet mine. With a smile, his hand lifts to welcome me. I reach for it—of course I reach for him—but my hand slips through his, his arm wafting away like a cloud. To my horror, he fades. Disappears.

It's then that I remember he was only a vision. He wasn't real.

But he is out there.

And I will find him.

And then everything will change.

Micah.

I woke with a start. The seconds ticked by as I stared at the ceiling of my room, orienting myself. I listened to Callie's slow and steady breathing as she slept soundly beside me. Other than that, the house was quiet and dark.

As I lay there, I wondered how much time had passed, and how I had ended up in my bed when the last thing I remembered was being on the floor of the warehouse. Then, the details of the dream—or whatever it had been—rushed me.

It hadn't been anything like my usual dreams with Micah.

I wasn't convinced it had been Micah in my dream anyway. I hadn't been me. And the man had looked slightly different. Older, with shaggier hair than Micah, a little more height than Micah, but a close resemblance none the less.

A brother, perhaps? Father?

Why in the hell was I dreaming about Micah's father?

And whose shoes had I literally been walking in, whose eyes had I been seeing through?

I grunted as I threw back the covers and got to my feet.

Another dream, another mystery. My life was full of them.

I wondered if Micah had any knowledge of the dream, and resigned to ask him the next chance I got.

For now, Mother Nature had me scurrying to the bathroom.

After I finished, I stopped at the sink to inspect my finger. The powdery substance had been wiped clean. As I ran my hands under the water, I wondered what it had been.

Whatever it was had led to one crazy trip out. One that I

never wanted to repeat.

On my way back to the bedroom, I saw a bluish glow coming from the end of the hallway. I continued past my room, and the others, to find the source of the light.

I found Nathan sitting at the kitchen table, a laptop in front of him. He hadn't heard me approach and I stopped in the entryway to watch him for a moment. Whatever he was doing, he was hard at it, with a slight scowl on his face. He didn't remove his eyes from the screen as he lifted a cup of coffee to his mouth.

I glanced at the soft green numbers on the microwave. 2:27, drinking coffee. Must be serious.

"What are you doing?" I asked softly to announce my presence.

He looked up as I rested my forearms on the back of the chair across from him. "Research," he said, stretching his arms above his head as he reclined in his seat.

"Went out and bought a computer to do research?"

He nodded and, as if predicting my next question, added, "Richie hacked into the neighbor's WiFi."

I didn't know the guy very well, and hadn't particularly liked him since the moment he'd pulled a gun on me, and looked ready to do it again if I so much as looked crooked at Micah, but I had to admit he was handy to have around.

"Looks like you've been at it for a while."

"Since we got back. Since…whatever it was that happened to you." He hesitated, looked across the screen at me. "What did happen, Kris?"

I shrugged and rounded the table, edging closer to him.

"Exhaustion? Mental fatigue? Stress?"

He wasn't amused. "You passed out when you touched those markings." He said it like he knew damn well that I already knew that, and wasn't going to let me get away with blowing it off as nothing. No matter how much I wanted to.

I sighed. "I don't know, Nathan. All I remember…I felt paralyzed and then, there was this surge of energy. I saw stars and blacked out."

From the angle I now had, I could see what he had pulled up on his screen. He made no effort to conceal it from me, so I took the opportunity to study it.

"Really?" I raised my eyebrows curiously. "The Historical Society of the Salem Witch Trials? Couldn't find a good porn site?"

Not even Nathan could hold back a short laugh. His eyes were twinkling when they lifted to mine, and suddenly I was thinking of Nathan…and bad, bad things. I thanked God that the faint light the computer put off wasn't enough to illuminate my flushed cheeks.

Feigning indifference, I sat in the chair next to his and leaned forward, eyeing the website curiously. "Is this your way of accepting that Micah might be on to something?"

He shrugged. "After seeing what happened to you in there…I guess it is.

I swallowed hard, the dirty thoughts in my head a moment ago completely forgotten. "What? Now you think I'm a witch?"

"No," he said automatically. "But I believe that witchcraft, Incantation, or whatever you want to call it had a part in what happened back there. When you touched those markings…"

"I don't think it was the markings," I admitted quietly. "I think it was whatever substance they used to make the markings. When it touched my skin, it was like an electric current shot up my arm. And…" Nathan waited patiently as I swallowed, gathering the nerve to come clean about what I'd experienced.

"I had a dream. Or a vision. I don't know what it was," I finally said. "I was someone else, I think, but I don't know who. She was holding a torch, walking through a thick fog, looking for someone."

"Do you know who?"

"A man. She thought of him as her love, but also her curse. What could that mean?"

Nathan genuinely looked as puzzled as I felt. "I don't know." He dragged a hand down his face with a groan, and I could feel the frustration seeping off of him.

"Nathan, get some sleep," I suggested softly. "We're not going to solve everything tonight."

He nodded solemnly, like he had really hoped to come to some sort of revelation when he'd sat down in front of the computer tonight, and was reluctantly accepting defeat.

"We've got more angles to work with now," I added with forced cheer. "We know how they're doing the conversions, we've got the rest of the warehouse to search yet. We'll find something."

I had to admit, I was impressed with the sense of confidence I had gained from trying to lift someone else's morality. Hadn't our roles been reversed just a few hours ago? Right before witchcraft and magic and the world of Incantation entered our lives.

With a sigh, Nathan shut the lid on the computer, casting us into darkness. Only the soft glow of the numbers on the microwave permitted us to see each other. His eyes, when they turned to me, sparkled a subtle silver. I felt a pull toward them, and might have even moved forward just a little. Before I got too close, he bolted to his feet, putting an end to the spell he had unknowingly put on me.

The almost-moment reminded me of our kiss in the warehouse earlier. I wanted to bring it up, to talk to him about it, but I couldn't find the nerve. And it was clear from his abrupt actions that he was still running away, trying to keep his distance. Unspoken words hung between us as we walked side by side down the hallway, toward the bedrooms.

Nathan surprised me when he passed his room to walk with me to mine. I stopped there, with my hand on the doorknob, and turned to wish him a good night. The words dried up in my throat when his hand lifted to brush a stray hair behind my ear, and then he leaned down to plant a gentle kiss to my forehead.

He hovered there, his lips barely grazing my skin, as he took deep and steady breaths, as if he were fighting a war with himself. Making a noise that sounded like a growl, he leaned into me, momentarily pressing his hip to mine, and all my senses were triggered, my body on high alert. My chin lifted in anticipation of more. For a moment, when his hooded eyes lowered to mine, I thought something phenomenal was about to happen, with me sandwiched between him and the door at my back. Then his eyes widened in sudden clarity, and with one more fleeting kiss to my forehead, he backed away.

"No more dreams, okay?" he said gruffly as I swayed unsteadily on my feet.

I had to gulp for air a few times before I managed to whisper, "Only ones I want to have."

Not that he heard me. He was gone.

CHAPTER 11

I was rewarded with a dreamless sleep. When I woke up, Callie was gone. A quick glance out the window confirmed that it was late morning, and I had slept in. The house was quiet as I padded out to the living room. Spying outside, I saw a steady downpour of rain. No one was training or working on target practice. Both vehicles were gone from the driveway.

What the hell? They left me?

A clatter from the kitchen spun me around as my heart lurched into my throat. I froze and listened for muffled voices, soft advancing footsteps—or for a Skotadi to charge, or a witch-girl to fly at me.

The sloshing of water in the sink followed by the groans of complaint by a familiar voice calmed my jitters, and I headed into the kitchen to witness what I needed to see to believe. Even then, I was sure I must be hallucinating as I stopped to watch Alec washing the dishes.

"Well, well," I announced from the doorway. "Alec doing housework."

He glanced over his shoulder with a grin. "Shut up and help me."

I folded my arms and leaned against the doorframe. "Looks

like you're doing a good enough job by yourself."

He barely moved a muscle, but somehow managed to fling a soap and water missile over his head in my direction. It missed.

"Alright," I sighed. "If you're going to get violent about it."

I joined Alec at the sink and began drying the dishes he had already washed. A few moments of comfortable silence settled between us as we worked side by side. As I replaced a few glasses in the appropriate cabinet, I broke the silence.

"Where is everyone?"

"Micah threw a tantrum, made Gabby take him into town to get something that he wanted. Probably a new dolly," Alec answered. "Since there was a chance for a mall trip, Callie went with them. Richie and Nathan went to the warehouse to sort through the rest of the stuff there. They should be back soon."

"And you volunteered for kitchen duty?"

"Hardly. I drew the short straw. I wanted to go to the mall, too, but they wouldn't let me." His eyes slanted toward me. "But now, being stuck here isn't so bad."

I managed to avoid the undertone in his statement by moving to another part of the kitchen to put away the stack of plates I had dried. Alec's back was to me as I slowly made my way back to the sink and I took a moment to take him in.

We hadn't had the opportunity to spend much time together lately, and I was grateful for the chance to reconnect with him a little bit, even if it was over a sink full of dishes. It would still allow me the opportunity to figure out what it was about him that I had been drawn to in the first place.

What wasn't there to be drawn to? Alec was great, he really

was. Just about everything that came out of his mouth made me laugh. He was cute, ornery, and any girl would be lucky to have his attention. I did care about him. A lot.

I wondered about Nathan's insistence that I had unsorted lingering feelings for Alec. Sure, I could acknowledge that I had some feelings for Alec, but they weren't as strong as they had once been. Since my time with Nathan, my feelings for Alec had changed, had lessened. But...

Was something still there? More than I realized?

"Why are you looking at me like that?" Alec's voice broke through my concentration, interrupting my thoughts.

"Huh?"

"Trying to undress me with your eyes?" He grinned. "I wouldn't mind if you were."

"Shut up, Alec," I said, though it didn't pack much of a punch with the smile on my face.

His grin grew and his eyes remained on me as I reclaimed my spot at the sink beside him, but he didn't say anything. It was a little unnerving, Alec being quiet. I wasn't used to it.

"What?" I asked.

He shook his head. "Just trying to figure you out."

I dropped my head to avoid his gaze. "Am I that difficult?"

He finally shifted, releasing me from the hold he had on me. "Girls are complex by nature, but you, Kris, are probably the most confusing one I've ever encountered."

I gaped at him. "Me? How so?"

He resumed washing the dishes, his eyes mercifully turned away from me as he spoke. "You've made it pretty clear how you feel about Nathan. I know you want him, but…" He turned to me—no grin, no smile, no joking—in all seriousness. "There's this way that you look at me sometimes."

Shit. That was the same thing Nathan had said.

Did everyone see something I was blind to?

Alec turned back to the sink, pulled the plug to let the water out. "Makes me wonder, that's all."

Holy hell, what was I supposed to say to that? "I don't…I didn't…" I stammered meekly.

Alec turned to me and leaned against the counter, his patented grin back where it belonged, on his face. "You don't even realize how bad you want me," he teased. I narrowed my eyes at him, and he continued, "You must really have it bad."

"Maybe somebody's over confident," I returned quickly.

"No," he said, shaking his head. He moved as if to walk by me, but stopped and lowered his mouth to my ear. "But just so you know, I've got it pretty bad, too."

He bumped his shoulder against mine as he continued by, leaving me weak-kneed by the sink and forced to set the dish in my hand down. Good thing, because I surely would have dropped it when I heard Alec address someone on his way out of the kitchen.

"'Sup, Nathan," he called cheerily.

Oh, my God.

I stiffened, my back to the door, as I waited to hear a response from Nathan. Nothing followed, and I knew that he wasn't going to give one.

How much had he seen? How bad had it looked?

It had to have looked bad. Really bad, judging by his silence.

I didn't want to do it, but as the silence dragged on, the suspense got to be too much. I glanced over my shoulder to see Nathan standing in the doorway, soaking wet from being out in the rain, and looking after Alec as he walked away.

Anger was the usual emotion that Alec induced in Nathan, and was what I expected to see now. But when his eyes turned to me, for the first time ever, I saw a disappointment on his face that I knew I never wanted to see again.

Before I could say anything—or think of something worthy to say—Nathan turned and walked away without a word. He went in the opposite direction of Alec, and that was probably a good thing. I had bigger things to worry about than breaking up another fight between them two.

One thing was for sure. I had to figure out what I was doing, before I lost Nathan for good. That would be so much easier to do if I weren't so obviously attracted to Alec.

* * *

As if the day wasn't already off to a bad start, Micah returned with Gabby and Callie soon after. He had books—lots of books—and called us all into a sort of meeting in the living room. Nobody was less thrilled than me.

I quickly learned that my trepidation was rightfully earned.

"Look at these," he said to no one in particular, tossing the books down on the coffee table. No one moved, so he added pointedly, "You'll find the proof that Incantation exists. It's been here all along, and they're using it."

If there had been a cricket in the room, we would have heard it. Only Richie obliged Micah by taking a book off the table and flipping through it.

"Let's just pretend that you've actually found proof," Alec said conversationally. "What point are you trying to make, other than showing us you're right?"

Micah spun around to Alec, excitement lighting up his eyes. "Alec, you saw what Kris did with that fireball."

What? What did that have to do with anything?

The horror on my face was caught by Nathan, before he turned his attention to Micah. "What fireball?"

Uh-oh.

Micah seemed to sense the dangerous territory he was about to navigate, and some of his excitement dimmed. His voice, when he addressed Nathan, was subdued, cautious. "I've never seen anyone manipulate an element like her before. She conjured fire better and faster than those that have been doing it for years—on her first attempt."

Nathan glanced in my direction before narrowing his eyes at Micah. "So?"

Micah swallowed hard, looked from me to Nathan. "I think Kris might be descendent of Hecate."

My first thought: what an odd name; second thought: who in the hell was Hecate? Better yet, why would Micah think I might be descendent of this person, and why did his suggestion provoke everyone else in the room—with the exception of Callie, who was just as confused as I was—to start arguing amongst each other as to why there was absolutely no way in hell for me to be descendent of this mystery person with the weird name?

"Why would you think that?" Nathan asked Micah once everyone had settled down enough that he could talk over them.

"Legend has it that Hecate was imprisoned by Hades shortly after the start of the war," Micah started.

"We all know that," Alec sneered at Micah. "What does that have to do with Kris?"

"What if Hades used Hecate to create another demigod? Maybe he used five demigods to create Kris, and that's what makes her different from you?" Micah asked Alec. "It would explain a lot of things."

"First of all," I finally spoke up, turning to look into the eyes of everyone in the room one at a time, ending with Micah. "Who is Hecate, and *what* could it explain?"

"Hecate is the goddess of magic," Micah said softly. "If you carry her bloodline, you would be capable of Incantation. It would explain why you're developing faster than you should, why you can do things you otherwise wouldn't be able to do yet. It could be that fifth specialty that I'm reading in you, but can't pinpoint."

A descendent of a goddess of magic, of witchcraft. "What? You think I'm the Incantator?" I squealed.

"No, no, not that," Micah gushed. "Just, that you're capable of it. It's fueling your other specialties, making you even stronger."

"You came up with this just because she's developing quickly?" Nathan asked with more than just a hint of disapproval.

"No," Micah admitted reluctantly, "there's more."

More? Seriously? How much more could there possibly be?

I wasn't so sure I wanted to stick around to hear what else he had to drop on us, but again, my curiosity won out. Besides, this whole conversation was about me. I supposed I couldn't just up and leave like I really wanted to do.

"We've all heard of the legend of Hecate," Micah said to the others.

Obviously, Callie and I hadn't heard of the legend. The rest of them grumbled their acknowledgement.

Micah spoke to me directly, since the others didn't need the history lesson. "Hecate sided with Zeus and Poseidon, but she held so much power because of her magic that Hades captured and imprisoned her, rendering her powers useless, except for his own vices. Before she was captured, she had a secret love affair with another god, Asclepius. Legend has it that they fed off each other, made each other stronger, as their souls were like one. They were what modern day soul mates are based on.

"When Hecate was imprisoned by Hades, being away from Asclepius weakened her. She was further weakened by her desire for him, a desire that would forever remain unfulfilled. You see, Hades placed a curse on her that if she were ever to reunite with Asclepius, she would kill him, assuring that Hecate would never try to escape, and would remain weak and for Hades' manipulation."

A quick glance around the room confirmed that the others had heard of this legend before. Micah wasn't spinning some wild tale for me. Even if it was an interesting story, there was much I still didn't get.

"Micah, what does all of this have to do with me?"

He looked me squarely in the eyes. "I'm descendent of Asclepius."

From somewhere, from someone in the room, came a gasp. Micah was staring at me as if he expected his revelation to have some sort of effect on me. It didn't. I had no clue what it meant. So what if, for argument's sake, I came from this Hecate character's bloodline, and she had a secret love affair with the guy that supplied one of Micah's bloodlines. So what if they had been soul mates?

So why was everyone looking at me like they were? Especially Micah. He hadn't taken his eyes off of me once.

"There are stories of others like us, Kris," he continued, gesturing toward the books on the table. "Others who were thought to be descendent of Hecate and Asclepius, who crossed paths because they found each other, because they too were soul mates." He paused with an apologetic expression on his face, and too late, I realized why. "The bond we have, the dreams, it's all because their connection was passed on to us."

My face fell as I felt all eyes turn to me. One set in particular.

His voice was like thunder in my ears. "Dreams?"

I glared at Micah, making sure he understood the gravity of what he'd just done. It was out in the open now. They all knew about the dreams. Nathan knew.

When I turned to face him, his eyes were already on me, waiting, questioning. He must have seen the answer written on my face. "You're sharing dreams with him." It was a statement, not a question, but I nodded my answer regardless. That muscle in Nathan's cheek twitched. "How long?"

Afraid to answer, I hesitated. Long enough that Micah found it necessary to answer on my behalf. "Since she started development," he said, "and we formed the connection."

Though I knew Nathan heard Micah, he gave no indication that he had. His complete focus remained on me as he waited for my answer.

"Months," I said softly.

I didn't know what I expected Nathan to say or do, if anything, but his first action would have been the last on a long list of possibilities.

He turned to Alec. "Did you know about this?"

Standing in the corner with a fist to his face as he attempted to conceal a smile, Alec said, "If I did, this wouldn't be the first you were hearing about it, as much fun as this train wreck is to watch."

At another time, in another situation, I might have cracked a smile at Alec's quip. Hell, Nathan might have even found it a little funny. But nothing about this moment—this train wreck—was funny to either of us. Nathan's steady gaze remained fixed on me for a long time. The silence of the others moved in around us like a heavy fog, giving me the sensation that it was just the two of us alone in the room.

But it wasn't, and Micah made sure to remind us of that. "We were born with this connection, Kris," he said as if nothing else more important than his stupid revelations was going on right now. "We could use this, take advantage of it now that we know. Use it to beat the Skotadi at their own game."

I watched as Nathan's gaze finally moved and settled on Micah. I expected some sort of reaction from Nathan—most likely a strategically placed fist to Micah's face—but his lack of reaction was even more unsettling than the alternative. He turned and walked away without another word.

Gabby and Richie watched him carefully, and only relaxed when the front door slammed shut behind him. Looking out the window, I saw him pause briefly before bounding down the steps. He cut across the yard, heading toward the trail in the woods.

I wanted to follow, to try to explain to him that the dreams meant nothing to me, not like they obviously did to Micah. I decided against it; opted to leave him alone—to let him clear his head. God knew he needed it.

As did I. I didn't yell at Micah, didn't tell him all the hateful things I otherwise would have. I didn't even look at him before I retreated down the hallway to my bedroom.

It was just too much. There was so much to absorb, to consider, that I didn't know where to begin. But all of that was trumped by the memory of the look on Nathan's face.

First, his witness of my encounter with Alec in the kitchen. Then, this bombshell of Micah's. I started to worry that the stars weren't aligned for Nathan and I after all. Maybe this would finally seal the deal—we weren't meant to be together, no matter what I thought, no matter what I wanted, and what I knew in my heart he wanted too.

And despite the possibility that I might be descendent of a

goddess of magic, making me an Incantator, and destined to be soul mates with someone I could barely stand, the thought that Nathan and I would never be together was the one that crumbled me onto the bed in a fit of tears.

CHAPTER 12

If Micah thought we were going to start picking out china patterns together, he was seriously mistaken. If anything, I wanted to pound the hell out of him, and probably would have if not for Gabby and Richie hovering around like they knew exactly what I was thinking.

I was sure Micah was getting an earful of my thoughts, because, aside from working with me on my specialties once a day for a few hours, he kept his distance.

As did Nathan. While I desperately wanted to talk to him, to fix everything—if I could—I gave him the space he obviously wanted. It was like a slow, miserable death for me inside, but I figured a little time for him to see how ridiculous Micah's claims were would be worth every minute in the long run.

And Alec? Well, Alec was just pissed. At Micah, simply for existing. I was pretty sure he wanted to beat up on Micah as much as I did. Maybe more. Unlike Nathan, he wasn't avoiding me, or Micah.

Surprisingly, Alec took to hanging out with me and Micah more as we worked on reigning in my specialties. Perhaps to be an ally for me. I knew it wasn't to protect Micah. I doubted he would stop me—and would most likely join in—if I raised a hand to Micah.

Alec was with us now on the back porch, where we had met about an hour ago. So far, I have yielded fire twice…and extinguished it without catching anything or anyone on fire. It seemed I was a natural at manipulating fire. My other specialties were a different story.

For one, they were much harder to practice.

My fighting skills I would typically work on with Nathan, and that wasn't happening anytime soon. I'd yet to fully understand what my 'charmer' specialty was all about. To me, it sounded like a joke—the ability to woo people into liking and trusting you, and then convincing them to do what you wanted. Yeah, right. Micah had to be wrong about me specializing in that one. That left conferring with the dead, and I so didn't want to try that now. Not with witnesses.

I'd tried once, alone in my bedroom, to reach Gran. The attempt had resulted in me staring at the wall for thirty minutes, and feeling like a complete idiot when nothing happened. I wasn't ready to do it again. The thought that I might actually reach her freaked me out way too much. I wasn't ready to try it again.

Perhaps that was why I had failed? Because I wasn't really ready? Either way, I wasn't doing it again. Not now. Maybe never.

"If you don't want to try channeling the dead," Micah was saying, "then try charming me. Or Alec."

"She don't need to charm me. Not like that," Alec said drily from the porch swing.

He was leaning forward, elbows on knees, and head in his

hands as if hanging out with Micah and me caused him excruciating pain. He glanced up at me and I flashed him a smile to portray my gratefulness, for both his presence and his backhanded compliment, before I turned to address Micah.

"I don't even know where to start. How do you charm people?"

Micah lifted an eyebrow and looked at Alec. "Care to elaborate?"

Alec blinked slowly and gave Micah a look I'd come to realize meant that his tolerance level was quickly fading. "I guess it comes naturally to me."

I threw my hands up and glared at Micah. "See? I can't do it. I don't want to try to do it."

Micah was relentless. "Look. You're good with fire and fighting. We just need to work on your meditation so th—"

Alec crossed the length of the porch in a few strides, coming to my side. His eyes were filled with rage, and a tiny spark lit the black of his pupils, as he leveled his gaze on Micah. "Stop pushing her," Alec growled.

"I'm only tr—"

Alec lunged, grabbing a hold of the front of Micah's shirt, and propelled him into the side of the house in one swift motion. He hit so hard I suspected there to be a hole the size of Micah's head punched through the siding.

With his nose nearly touching Micah's, Alec snarled, "If Kris doesn't want to do it, she doesn't have to do it. Now, she might not do what I know she wants to do, because she's a good girl, but I can promise you that I am not a good guy and I would have no problem knocking you out. In fact, I know I'll enjoy it."

With Alec and Micah staring each other down, only I saw the faint orange glow emitting from Alec's clenched fist. He was conjuring fire—though a small one compared to what I'd created—and he didn't even know it. Realizing he was close to not only beating, but combusting, Micah's head, I stepped into the danger zone.

"Alec?" I said gently so as not to startle him.

His teeth gritted together with forced control. "What?"

I placed a hand on his shoulder. "Look at me, Alec."

Standing beside and slightly between the two of them now, I could see what Micah saw, and it scared the hell out of me.

That spark in Alec's eyes was now completely engulfed.

"Alec?" I tried again, and this time, his gaze drifted to meet mine.

The second his focus turned to me, the flames—both in his eyes and in his hand—extinguished, and I breathed a sigh of relief. "I need to take a walk," I said to him. "Do you want to come with me?"

Alec's eyes flicked back to Micah, who he still had pressed against the wall.

"We can argue over who wants to beat up Micah more," I added with a grin that was only partly teasing when I tossed it in Micah's direction.

With one final abrupt shove into the wall, Alec let go of Micah's shirt. As he backed away, his eyes held mine, and he nodded slightly. "I need to get out of here," he said gruffly.

I hesitated, watching as Alec bolted down the porch steps

ahead of me, and wondered if he simply wanted to be left alone.

"Alec?" I called after him. He turned, hands stuffed in his pockets, and a small sad smile curling his lips. "Can I come with you?"

I was rewarded with a full-on grin. "Do you really have to ask?"

I joined him and we walked around the side of the house, to a quiet corner on the front porch. Just enough to separate us from Micah.

In the yard, Nathan and Callie were working on target practice, and the rumble of her shots reverberated through the crisp mountain air. Alec rested his elbows on the railing, appearing to watch them, but I saw the distant look in his eyes that meant he wasn't really seeing what was in front of him.

"Alec, what's going on?" I asked softly. "Aside from hating Micah?"

He scoffed. "I can't stand him."

"I've gathered that much, but what's happening to you?" I hesitated, not sure if I should mention what I saw. Was Alec even aware of it?

"I don't know, Kris," he mumbled miserably. "I've been getting these impulses, this need to hurt someone, for a while now. I've been able to keep them under control, and fighting the Skotadi had helped alleviate some of it, but sometimes it hits me hard…"

"How long has this been going on?"

"Months. Worse the past few weeks. It might be Micah making it worse, I don't know."

I could understand that. Micah was supposed to be our enemy. There was a deeply rooted seed in both of us to dislike him. But while Micah claimed I had a connection to him that might prevent me from hurting him, Alec didn't. It must be torture for him to be around someone he was created to hate.

"Does anything make it better?" I asked with a hopeful ring in my voice. I wanted there to be something, not just for Alec, but myself as well. If this was what I had to look forward to, I had to learn how to deal with it.

"This is helping," Alec said. "Talking to you, being with you, helps."

He turned to look at me then, and I smiled at the warmth in his eyes. Not because they were enflamed, but because I believed he truly viewed me as a bright spot on the dark horizon.

"I'll be here," I told him. "Next time you feel it, come find me, okay?"

He looked away with an indifferent nod. I grabbed his arm, forced him to meet my eyes. "I mean it, Alec. I want to help. Come find me."

He gave me a smile that was painfully sad, and very uncharacteristic. "Yeah, Kris. I'll find you."

I suspected a double meaning to his words, but I couldn't determine what it might be. Instead of pressing, I opted to just be there for Alec—without question, without trepidation—because I knew that was what he needed.

As we stood side by side, listening to Callie's thundering gunshots echoing through the valley, I knew I was more determined now than ever to find a way to stop this. Not only for myself, but for Alec.

Especially for Alec.

* * *

I was so determined, I spent the rest of the afternoon reading Micah's books, orienting myself to the world of Incantation. I'd secretly hoped to stumble upon some clue as to how the Skotadi were using it to manipulate Kala into turning Skotadi, but really, I just learned general information about where it originated and how it was used. After a few hours, I came to the conclusion that these books didn't have what I needed.

Micah had said that different spells were used to achieve different results. I needed a book that focused on the spells, not superficial information and history. Maybe there was a spell out there that I could find and reproduce.

It was a long shot, but what alternatives did we have at this point? This was how they did it, so this must be how we can undo it. If I was really capable of Incantation, if I was a descendent of the goddess of magic, then I could do it. Right?

There was only one way to find out. And that was to *try*.

I asked for a volunteer to go with me to the town library. It was the first place I thought of to start looking for the type of books I needed.

Micah jumped at the chance to drive me. Nathan promptly snuffed out Micah's joy by saying that he would do it instead. I overlooked the grudging tone of his voice, and viewed it as a step in the right direction.

About halfway there, I reluctantly accepted that being alone in a car with Nathan for twenty minutes was not going to turn out as I would have hoped. He wasn't into small talk. And quite frankly, with all the shit going on in my head, I wasn't feeling up to it myself. So I confronted our problem head on.

"Are you going to be mad at me forever?" I asked him.

His eyes flicked to mine briefly before returning to the road. I might have been mistaken, but I swore there was a hint of a smile threatening to break through in there somewhere.

"You know why I didn't tell you?" I asked, and continued when he didn't respond, "Because of *this*. I knew you would look into it too much, exactly like you're doing now."

"Look into it too much?" His eyes were fixed on the road, but, at least, he was talking. "You're acting like it's nothing. In our world, dream sharers are a big deal. They're soul mates."

"Because that's what you've been told?"

He shrugged. "It's the way it is."

"And what if I don't want it?"

He smirked, actually smirked, and I felt a rush of heat start in the roots of my hair as my temper boiled. "When it comes to soul mates, I don't think you get a choice," he said.

"Just like I don't get a choice about being a Skotadi, right?" I fired back. His grip on the steering wheel tightened, and I knew I'd gotten through to him. Just a little. "You're helping me fight *that* predestined path I'm supposed to be following without having a choice. You claim to believe I can fight it, but this? This you accept without question, without a fight?"

His jaw worked like he was about to say something. As

always, he bit his words back at the last second.

"Don't you see it?" I groaned. "Don't you get it? I don't want Micah! I'll *never* want Micah! Regardless of what he might think, he is not, and never will be, my soul mate. Not if I have anything to say about it. I just thought, out of everyone, that you would be the one on my side."

To that, he finally turned to look at me. "I'm always on your side."

"Really?" I hadn't meant for my voice to be laced with such contempt. It just came out.

Just as quickly as the question passed my lips, Nathan was hitting the brakes and pulling the Tahoe sharply to the side. I bounced in my seat as we came to a skidding stop off the side of the road. Nathan turned in his seat, leaning half way across the console, toward me.

"You think this is easy for me? Seeing you with Alec? Seeing the way he and Micah *both* look at you, and now knowing that, after everything we've been through, you might actually end up with Micah?" A hand scraped down his face. "My God, Kris. I'd rather it be Alec."

"I'd rather it be *you*."

His head tilted slightly at the impact of my words. He looked conflicted, and I could hardly blame him. Hell, I was confused, too. But when I tipped my head forward, narrowing the already small gap between us, nothing felt more right.

"Kris…"

My eyes lifted from his lips to his eyes. They were clouded and I knew, deep down, he wanted this as much as I did.

However, his self-control was better than mine. It always had been. Hell, *most* people had better self-control than I did.

At the sound of his voice, I realized that I had totally misread the moment. He hadn't been about to kiss me, like I had stupidly thought. My chest tightened as I wondered if he ever would again, after everything Micah had dropped on us.

I pushed back into my seat with a heavy sigh—a move that rivaled a three-year-old's temper tantrum. "Is it ever going to happen, Nathan?" I murmured softly.

"What?"

"Me…you. Us?"

There was a hesitation before he spoke, and I refused to look at him, afraid to hear his answer. "We got a lot more to worry about right now than what's going to happen between us," he eventually said.

I shut my eyes, trying to block his response from sticking. It wasn't at all what I'd wanted to hear. I flinched when I felt his knuckles rake across my cheek.

"Kris, I…"

"I need to know what I'm fighting for," I murmured. I opened my eyes and looked at him. Really looked at him. "If I have a reason to fight it."

It wasn't just turning Skotadi that I was referring to this time, and he knew it.

"I want you to fight it." He cupped my chin in his hand, making sure that I maintained eye contact with him. "'Cause I'm going to be here, with you, if that's where you want me to be."

"That's where I want you to be," I whispered.

He stared intently into my eyes as if searching my soul for any doubt. He wouldn't find it.

Finally, he nodded once. "Okay." He hesitated again, and this time, I thought maybe he would kiss me. Then, he dropped his hand, releasing me, and leaned back into his seat. "Now that we've got that figured out…"

I would hardly consider it *figured out*. Not if this whole soul mates thing was as big of a deal as he thought it was. But it was nice to know Nathan was behind me, and would support me. That there was a chance of *us* becoming a reality.

While we'd reached the conclusion that we weren't just going to sit back and let it happen, we still didn't know how to stop it. We didn't know how to stop anything. Yet. But I hoped to fix that soon.

Maybe there was a spell to break a soul mate connection? I smiled to myself, thinking about Micah's reaction if I were to ever ask him that question.

"What?" Nathan asked softly. His eyes were on me, watching me.

"Just imagining the look on Micah's face when I tell him I plan to break our connection."

Nathan snorted. "I don't think he'll take it too well."

That was an understatement if I'd ever heard one.

"I told you," Nathan muttered.

"What?"

"That there was more to his story than he was giving us."

I had to agree that Nathan had been right about Micah from the start. While I'd suspected he was hiding something, I'd never imagined anything like this. Even as Nathan and I shared knowing smiles and the broken pieces of whatever relationship we had were mended, I couldn't help but wonder what else Micah may have been hiding.

And what kind of blow it would have on the future that I wanted.

CHAPTER 13

While Nathan and I were gone, Richie and Gabby had returned with a load of boxes from the warehouse. They'd been placed in the basement, to be sorted through later.

That was where I was now, sitting alone in a circle of glass jars filled with weird liquids, objects, and minerals that I was trying to identify and find the meaning behind their use in Incantation. Mostly, I wanted to know if any of it could be used to help Alec and me.

I had snuck downstairs after everyone had gone to bed. I didn't care about the lost sleep. That's how determined I was to fix everything. Well, two things really—mine and Alec's unwanted Skotadi destinies, and my connection to Micah.

After a few hours, I really thought I was getting somewhere. I had just started to get an understanding of the use of certain minerals and objects in Incantation—and there were a lot of healing and protection uses that sounded promising—when a creak on the floorboard above me pulled my focus out of a book.

I tilted my head to listen, and heard a clear footstep, followed by another creak. Someone was in the house, moving slowly. Stealthily.

It didn't make sense for any of the others to be walking

around like that, even to go to the bathroom. My first reaction was fear. That led to the question of who, or what, was sneaking around upstairs.

I set the book down, maneuvered carefully around the glass jars, and crept as quietly as I could on the wooden steps. I stepped lightly, the whole time fearing that I would hit a squeaky board and alert the prowler to my presence. By the time I reached the landing, I realized I had been holding my breath the entire time, and inhaled deeply, shakily. It did nothing to ease my fear.

The basement door was cracked open. From behind it, I could hear movement in the living room. Making sure to stay hidden in the shadows, I poked my head around the corner.

Who I found was Alec. Since the living room has been serving as his bedroom, it wasn't surprising to find him there. But it was surprising to see him slinging his packed bags over his shoulder as he headed for the door.

I stood frozen until the door shut behind him. Then reality hit me and I ran after him. He was halfway to the driveway before I hit the deck, the door slamming shut behind me.

"Alec!" I called after him in a loud whisper.

He stopped and turned. Moonlight seeped through the tree canopy, illuminating him in a magnificent light that nearly took my breath away, and in that moment, I knew I was approaching a crossroads I wasn't prepared for.

Heart thundering, I descended the steps and crossed to where he stood, waiting for me. From the look on his face, I didn't need to ask, but I did anyway. "What are you doing?"

"I'm leaving," he said simply, and though I'd expected them, the words nearly knocked my knees out from under me.

"Why?"

Alec's gaze drifted to the house behind me. "I can't stay here anymore, not with the way things are going for me. I'll kill him and deep down—deep, *deep* down—I don't want to do that."

Two months ago, I would have assumed he was talking about Nathan. Now, for once, Alec's hatred was not directed at him, but at Micah. Unfortunately, the only one out of all of us that really *needed* to live.

If only he weren't so damn annoying, he'd have better odds at survival.

"You don't have to leave, Alec. I'll help you."

Alec shook his head at the ground before looking at me. His eyes, when they met mine, were sad. "It's too late for me, Kris. It's getting harder to control. I'm serious when I say I might kill that kid. I don't want to do anything to ruin your chance of getting through this."

Okay, so he had given this some thought. And he was determined. I needed another angle. "Alec, I don't *want* you to go," I pleaded, my voice bordering on desperate.

He held a firm stance in front of me, and I realized he wasn't going to be swayed. "I left a note under your pillow, Kris. I wrote down the address where you can find me. Don't tell anyone else where I'll be, but I'll be there for you if you need me."

The gravity of his words hit me. Like a train. He was really leaving. "Alec, don't. Please." I was all out begging now, but didn't care. He couldn't leave. I couldn't bear to see him go.

It was more than just needing his help, and him needing

mine. It was so much more. Surely, he knew that.

He hesitated to take in the likely pathetic sight in front of him. In two strides, he was in front of me, a hand cupping the back of my neck.

"I hope you find a way, Kris," he whispered. "For you."

"No. I want to do it for you, too."

Alec shook his head sadly, and then we were both talking, at the same time and over each other, but his words still hit home and I flinched with the finality of them.

"You've got a lot of people fighting to help you, Kris—"

"—I'm fighting for you—"

"—you can do it, but I can't help anymore—"

"—Let me help you—"

"—I'll only hurt your chances."

I leaned closer to him, forcing him to look me in the eyes. "I need you. Doesn't that matter?" I shoved my palms into his chest, pissed off at him for leaving, and pissed off that I couldn't hold back my tears anymore. "Does that matter?"

When he didn't respond, I shoved again. "Huh?" Again. "Does that matter to you?" Again. "'Cause you matter to me!"

His hands came down on mine, halting my physical attack. "Of course it matters. You're *all* that matters to me! And that kid in there—" He jabbed a finger toward the house. "He can help you, but not if I kill him first!"

"I…" What could I say after that? He was right, of course. About some of it. Not the part about leaving though. That can't happen. "I'd rather take my chances than let you leave. We can get through this, Alec. Together, we can do it."

He paused. His eyes held mine, and for a moment, I thought he might reconsider. "You really think that?"

There was a flutter in my chest at his words, so full of hope. "I really do."

He shifted to look me evenly in the eyes. "Then come with me."

My throat constricted. This was it. The crossroads. The moment I had been dreading for a long time. The moment I had to tell Alec that my heart had chosen…and it wasn't him. I could never do what he was asking. I could never go with him. Not when my heart belonged with Nathan.

"I see," he scoffed. He lowered his hand to waist level. "Micah." He moved it up a few inches. "Me." Finally, lifting his hand above his head, he spat, "Nathan."

"It's not like that," I murmured.

"Yeah, it is. And it's okay. I've come to expect it." It wasn't anger, but hurt, that I heard in his voice. It wasn't right. It didn't fit him.

And I hated that I was the one that caused him pain. "Alec, please…"

Sadness and regret lined his face as he leaned in to press his lips to my forehead. He lingered there, as if coming to terms with his decision. His throat jumped and I wondered if he was fighting back his own tears. His voice, when he finally spoke, was thick. "Goodbye, Kris."

* * *

As promised, Alec had left me a note with an address, as well as an explanation of where the Tahoe could be found in town. Apparently, he'd driven it to the bus station. From there, it was anyone's guess as to where he'd gone. Only I knew, and I would honor his request to keep it that way. I briefly considered telling Nathan, and plead with him to go and drag Alec back, but I suspected neither of them would appreciate that.

Alec was gone.

Business went on as usual. Callie seemed to be the only other one taking his absence hard. Three days after he'd left, I found her crying in our room. She didn't bother to hide her tears as I approached.

"He was like a brother to me," she whined.

I sat on the bed beside her, wrapped my arms around her shoulders. "I know. Me too."

"He's really not coming back?" It was about the tenth time she'd asked me that question, and each time she looked at me with renewed hope, like something had changed. Each time, I shattered that hope.

"No, Callie. He's not."

She blew out a puff of air and wiped her nose with a wad of toilet paper. "It's not like he *died*." She tried to laugh at herself, but ended up crying harder. I sat with her silently, fighting back my own tears as hers slowed.

"I'm going to miss him," she murmured, and it sounded like she had finally come to terms with the fact that he wasn't coming back.

Now, if only I could.

It was hard knowing that I knew where he was, knowing that I could go to that address and he would be there. It was even harder knowing that, really, I couldn't just do that.

Not when everyone else I cared about—Nathan, Callie, and even that annoying little prick, Micah—were here. I couldn't leave them. They were all I had left. My other friends, Gran, my home with Gran…all gone.

"Callie?"

"Huh?"

"Don't you miss home?" Unlike me, Callie had a home to go back to. She had other choices. Better, less dangerous choices. She had parents that loved her.

"Yeah, of course."

"Don't you want to go back?" I asked her. Not that I didn't want her here. Because I did. She was my best friend, but that was also why I wanted what was best for her, and I wasn't so sure being here was best for her.

"No," she said without hesitation. "I want to be here, to help you."

"What about your parents? Your sister?"

"If I go home now, my parents will know I haven't been in Italy, silly. I'll be grounded for the rest of my life, so really, I'm in no hurry. I've called them a few times to check in. They think I'm having the time of my life."

"Wouldn't you rather be on that trip, actually having the time of your life?"

"Kris," Callie said forcefully, making me look at her. "I want to be here. You're not going to make me leave, especially now that Alec's gone. Unless…" Her eyes lit up in excitement. "You think he might have gone back to Boone?"

"I don't think so. He didn't have anyone in Boone. He only went there to find me." It was where we had met, where we had first kissed, where it had all started. But there was no reason for him to go back there. And, well, I knew he wasn't there.

"You're right," Callie mumbled. "He'd probably go back to where he was from. Where was that again?"

My stomach churned. I didn't want Callie to start guessing about Alec's location. I couldn't tell her where he was, and I wasn't a good liar.

"Out west somewhere," I said hastily. I stood and extended a hand to her before she could ask for more details. "Come on, Callie. Let's go do something fun today. Get away."

I could really use a break from studying the books and going through the boxes in the basement. And I doubted Callie would argue against taking a break from drill-sergeant Nathan. We both needed it, and we needed each other, even if just for a few hours today.

"Let's talk one of the guys into taking us into town. Maybe go shopping? Catch a movie?"

"Sounds good." She hesitated. "But I want you to be the one to tell Nathan I'm playing hooky."

As it turned out, he was fine with it. Really fine, actually. So fine that he suggested making a day out of it, and even mentioned needing to stop by the mall himself. I was curious as to what he needed, but he walked away before I could ask. Of course, once Micah heard about the trip, he wanted to come. That meant

Gabby and Richie were coming too.

The six of us clambered into the Tahoe for a much needed day of distraction. For the time being, we were like one big, happy family. Minus one very important member. Several times throughout the day, I caught myself thinking about the one that was missing, and wondering if he was okay.

* * *

In the days that followed, I locked myself in the basement and threw myself into the books. The unused pool table had been turned into my makeshift desk, and was now covered in books and notes. Over time, I learned a lot about the unique qualities associated with certain materials and objects, how they could be used to perform a spell, and what kind of spells they could be used for.

I learned everything but how to actually perform a spell.

Not that I hadn't tried…sort of. Granted, most of the spells emphasized confidence and a strong belief in what you were doing to be successful. I severely lacked both. Honestly, I felt like an idiot the first time I tried to make myself invisible. After staring at myself in the mirror for thirty minutes, standing perfectly still, holding an opal stone in my tightly clenched fist, I gave up.

The next night, I cast a spell for success. I've yet to see the proof that it worked.

I didn't know what I was missing. Maybe I couldn't do it. Maybe Micah was wrong. Maybe I didn't have it in me to pull this off.

That was assuming I ever found the spell I was looking for. I doubted it was titled *How to Convert Kala Into Skotadi*, so I paid special attention to spells that had anything to do with conversions, healing, spirits—stuff like that. I dog-eared a bunch of pages to come back to later. If anything, I could try them later—once I learned how to perform a spell.

And that was all based on the assumption that I carried the bloodline of a magical goddess. I sure didn't feel like I did. But then, I didn't really feel like the other things I was supposed to be either. Except maybe the fighter thing. I was always down for that, but part of me wondered if my interest in fighting had more to do with Nathan than the actual desire to fight.

Things with Nathan have been…good, since our talk on the side of the road. He hasn't shown me that kind of emotion again, but he hasn't been avoiding me either. In fact, we've started sparring again, usually once a day for an hour or two in the morning.

He has also expressed an interest in what I've been doing down here, and seemed to think that I might be on to something. Most evenings, he's been sitting with me, flipping through some of the books and acquainting himself to the world of Incantation.

In fact, he would usually be down here by now.

I glanced at the clock on the wall. I'd been at it for three hours straight.

I stretched and the sound of my back cracking reminded me of the sound bubble wrap made when twisted. As I gingerly got to my feet, I couldn't help but think I looked like Gran always used to when she got up from her chair after a long knitting session, shuffling and hunched over on her way to the bathroom.

Good God, I needed a break.

I ascended the stairs gingerly, straightening my back a little at a time until I felt closer to my age again. As my foot scraped across the landing, I heard frantic whispers to my left, in the kitchen, followed by a loud crinkling noise. More whispers.

I froze. It sounded like Callie.

What was she up to now?

The last thing I expected to find when I emerged from behind the basement door was a *HAPPY BIRTHDAY* banner stretched across the length of the kitchen. Callie was busy securing a balloon to one end of the banner, while holding onto what had to be a hundred more. Nathan was setting a yummy-looking cake on the kitchen table, and was the first to notice me. He grimaced, and I got the impression that I was crashing my own party.

Nathan nudged Callie into turning around. She looked momentarily disappointed before adopting a bright smile. Perfectly timed together, as if they had practiced it, she and Nathan wished me an over-the-top, "Happy birthday!"

Micah was standing by the counter, his back to me, and looked over his shoulder. "Happy birthday," he added belatedly.

Even Gabby and Richie were there. Granted, they stood in the corner, by what appeared to be an assortment of liquor bottles and sodas, and didn't look up as I approached. But they were there. That was huge. For them.

Surprised wasn't a strong enough word for what I felt.

Unexpected? Definitely. Happy? Seeing the look on Callie's face as she rushed me, a mountain of balloons flapping behind her, bouncing off each other and everything in her path, yeah, I was definitely happy.

I caught her as she threw her arms around my neck, gushing something about me having the best birthday ever. I had to knock a few balloons out of the way to see her face when she withdrew.

"We didn't quite get finished," she explained in a rush, "but it'll only take a minute to tie the rest of these up. Presents are wrapped. Cake is finished." Callie paused, dropped her voice an octave. "Nathan baked the cake."

My gaze slid over Callie's shoulder to Nathan, who was drilling a hole into the back of her head like she'd just given away a secret he'd rather not have shared with the entire household.

I didn't bother to hide my grin. So he could bake? Personally, I thought it only made him even hotter.

And presents? Had I heard her say presents? Sure enough, stacked neatly on the kitchen table, next to the cake, were a few wrapped gifts.

"This is too much," I told Callie. Especially since *I* hadn't even remembered that today was my birthday.

"Never. Not for my best friend." She slung an arm around my shoulders and escorted me the rest of the way into the kitchen. "Here. Cake first. We're hungry."

The cake wasn't anything fancy, but looked delicious with its white icing glittered with multi-colored sprinkles and the words *Happy Birthday Kris* drawn in purple glaze. Nathan had done a nice job. I looked up at him, eyebrows raised. He shrugged and lit the 1 and 8 candles planted in the center.

"Make a wish," Callie instructed.

So much to wish for, how could I possibly pick only one?

I wished for this adventure we were on to have a successful ending. I wished for the war between good and evil to end, and for everyone to go on to live happy lives without fear. I wished for my best friend to find her happily ever after, and for me to find mine as well. I wished for Alec to come back. I wished...

I didn't mean to, but right before I made my silent wishes and blew out the candles, I glanced in Nathan's direction. He was watching me closely, with a barely detectable smile, and I couldn't help but wonder if he had any idea what my last wish had been for.

CHAPTER 14

I had to give it to them. The party had been a good idea. We'd all needed the break. But, after an hour, I needed a break from the break.

It seemed wrong, somehow, to be celebrating when we had no reason to celebrate. Not really. Alec was gone. We were crawling our way toward the answers we sought, and it seemed impossible that we would find them before it was too late. I could barely stand to be in the same room as Micah anymore, and my whatever-you-wanna-call-it with Nathan was…stalled, to say the least.

All of that, plus the addition of Callie's strongly concocted margaritas was why I now stood outside, alone on the back porch, staring up at the stars like they held the answers I needed so desperately to find.

They sparkled down at me, but nothing inspirational materialized before me.

"Thanks for nothing," I muttered miserably.

"Talking to yourself now?"

I hadn't heard the patio door sliding open, but when I looked now, I saw Nathan closing it behind him as he joined me on the porch.

I turned forward and smiled as he stepped into my periphery. "Just complaining to the stars."

He mirrored my stance, positioning himself against the railing on the opposite side of the stairs from me. Silence filled the space between us, but it wasn't the uncomfortable type.

"They're bright," he observed after a moment.

"Sure are."

Were we really standing there, making small talk about the stars? But then, the little things always seemed so much more significant when Nathan was involved.

"You okay? Is the party too much?" Nathan asked. "It was Callie's idea."

I smiled. Of course it had been her idea. "No. The party's great. I just needed some air."

Out of the corner of my eye, I saw him shift his weight from one foot to the other—Nathan's version of fidget. I never grew tired of seeing him squirm around me. It only served as a reminder that I seemed to be the only one that could make him nervous.

"Thanks for the gift, by the way," I said with a smile.

While Callie's and Micah's gifts had been great—an assortment of girly accessories and a gift certificate to the hair salon in town to touch up my highlights which, according the Callie, needed some serious attention—Nathan's gift, a beautiful leather-bound journal, had been downright touching.

He had to have known how much it would mean to me, had to know that I'd been without the journal I'd had since I was a little girl since I'd been forced to leave it in Boone. Only I didn't know *how* he'd known. Again, one of the many things Nathan just happened to know about me.

"No problem," he replied.

"What made you think of it?"

He shrugged. "I know you've been without your old one. I thought you might like to have something to write in again."

Finally, I turned to him, my eyes narrowed. "You knew I had a journal?"

He hesitated as panic flashed in his eyes. "Yeah. I've seen you with it. You've had it since you were a kid." He glanced at me quickly, before looking away, facing forward.

I didn't hide the fact that I was studying him as he avoided my eyes. "Did you ever read it?" I asked quietly.

His head tilted toward me, one of his almost-smiles barely visible. "No. I never read it." He met my gaze as I continued to stare, my wary expression letting him know I wasn't sure whether or not to believe him. This forced him to add, "I didn't. I swear."

I shrugged like I didn't care one way or the other, though the thought of him seeing anything in that journal terrified me. No, *embarrassed* would be the right word.

"It's all about you," I said like it was no big deal. His throat jumped, but he said nothing. I hoped it wasn't because he'd already known that. "It was more like random thoughts about who you were, and what you were doing in my life. I'd probably get a good laugh out of reading it now. Maybe now that I got those questions answered, I'll have more appropriate teenage-angsty things to write about instead."

Never before had I wished for a teenager's mundane life

more. It would be nice to only worry about boys, clothes, and conquering firsts. Not life changing truths and a future I had no control over.

"The cake was good," I said cheerily in an attempt to alter the direction of the conversation. With a smile growing on my face, I added, "I didn't know you could bake."

I decided to leave out just how hot I thought that was.

"It came out of a box," Nathan returned drily.

"Still good."

"You make a wish?"

"Several of them. *Big* wishes. It would be nice if one of them came true," I grumbled.

His shoulders rose and fell with a heavy breath, and I was sure he'd guessed what at least one of my wishes had been. He turned so that he was facing me directly, leaning up against the railing. The entire width of the steps separated us, and I could feel every inch of that separation. His brief grin was gone now, and he opened his mouth to say something.

"No excuses, Nathan," I interrupted. "Just give me that for my birthday. Please?"

"I wasn't," he said as he took a step forward, closing the gap between us. One hand cupped the back of my neck, tilting my face up to his. He paused long enough to read the answer to his unspoken question in my eyes before he lowered his lips to mine.

Like the last kiss we'd shared, this one was soft and gentle, as if mirroring the delicate state of our relationship. A raw, unreleased passion simmered beneath the surface of his forced composure, and I wished for it to break free. It was a want that physically tore at every cell in my body, and I wondered if he would ever give in completely, like I wanted him to.

Even as our lips locked into their perfect fit together, even as my knees grew weak beneath me, even as my pulse thundered in my ears from the wonderfulness of it all, I craved more. I used my body and my mouth to indicate how much more I wanted from him.

Nathan responded the way I'd hoped. His tongue parted my lips and he pushed the kiss deeper, faster, needier than ever before. A moan rose in my throat as I clawed at his back, pulling him closer, wanting to feel as much of him as I could.

Pressed between him and the wooden post at my back, I finally unraveled a layer of Nathan I had been waiting to find. I'd known he was passionate—from his words, from his outlook on life—but I hadn't known him physically passionate until now.

We kissed, alternating between soft meaningful brushes and deep exploration driven by an insatiable hunger. For the first time, we eventually withdrew on our terms. Not because he had a moment of clarity and not because we were interrupted, but because we were both too winded to keep it up.

His forehead pressed to mine as we both caught our breaths.

"Huh," was all I could manage for the time being.

"Huh?"

I opened my eyes. His were still closed, but I saw a smile teasing his lips.

"Now that's what I call a birthday wish come true," I whispered, earning a full, dimpling-inducing grin from him.

He leaned back, his eyes holding mine. "I might not be able

to make them all come true…"

I wondered if this was it—the moment Nathan would forget about his hang-ups, his fear, and all the reasons he had in his head for us to not be together. While I hoped, I didn't ask. I couldn't handle to hear his answer. Not now. Not on the heels of that kiss. I didn't want to ruin it.

"We should get back inside." Though he said the words, he gave no indication of moving anytime soon. His hands still had a firm grip on my waist.

"We really should."

He smiled.

I smiled back.

Finally, with a shake of his head, he retreated a step, freeing me from my Nathan and porch railing sandwich. Taking my hand in his, he led me to the door.

"Callie made another batch of margaritas." He hesitated, slowing his steps. "I think that was why I came out here in the first place."

The way he said it came out sounding like a question, and I found myself laughing in response. "Forgot why you came out here, huh?"

"Hmm. I guess I did." He looked down at me then, and it took all the willpower I had not to jump him. Callie's party-voice cutting through the glass door acted as a bucket of cold water, giving my willpower the extra boost it needed.

Nathan seemed to remember that we had a party to get back to at the same time I did. He broke the magnetism between us first, turned, and slid the door open. "Come on, birthday girl," he said, ushering me in ahead of him.

And just like that our moment was over.

The margaritas were flowing. Callie was animatedly talking to everyone, obviously doing her best to keep the festivities alive in my absence. She didn't bat an eye when Nathan and I returned together, though I knew she was curious.

She wasn't the only one.

From his perch on the counter, Micah glared at Nathan. When his gaze shifted and he caught me looking at him, he didn't bother to conceal his anger, or his disappointment.

Apparently doors and windows weren't enough to block Micah from reading me.

* * *

I went to bed thinking of Nathan, but Micah filled my dreams.

A gentle breeze stirs my hair. My senses are on overdrive as I'm hit with the sting of saltwater and heat, and pick up the sound of water crashing behind me. I spin around to see the most beautiful beach I'd ever seen in person. Or in a dream.

Micah stands facing me, his bare feet ankle deep in the crystal clear blue water. His grin welcomes me to his dream world.

He has spun some nice settings for us, once he started getting good at controlling them, but this one…

"A little over the top, don't you think?" I shout to him over the sound of waves crashing.

He grins as he motions for me to join him. "Come see for yourself. Water's nice."

He's right. It is nice. I stop to enjoy the feel of the sand between my toes as the water swirls over my feet. For a moment, I forget…everything.

"I was getting a little sick of the cold and snow," Micah volunteers.

"No complaints here," I say. "I wish I could manipulate my dreams like you can."

"Maybe someday." He doesn't sound so sure, and neither am I. I'm not the dream walker here. He is. For some reason, I'm just able to join him. He's the prophet. This is his dream.

My dreams, when they're not shared with Micah, are much, much darker. Things like car accidents, blood, and death are the norm for me.

But it's too pretty here and I don't want to think about that right now.

"Come on," Micah says, taking my hand in his.

And I let him. I'm distantly aware that things would be different in the real world, but in the dreams…things are different between Micah and me. We can talk and be together and have fun. And I don't despise him.

In fact, I kind of like him.

He seems to know that when he grins down at me and squeezes my hand tighter.

"You know," he muses, "we should probably work on your ability to block your mind."

"Why?" I stop to dig my toes in the sand. There's a smile on my face when I look up at Micah.

"Or at least teach you to block me until our connection is finalized," he amends. "That way, when you're making out with Nathan, I don't have to know about it."

And there it is. So much for serenity and nice dreams.

I pull my hand out of his. I manage to keep my temper under control, though my head feels on fire. "Maybe you should keep your nose in your own business."

"This is my business," *he returns quickly.* "We're connected, so your business is my business, and vice versa."

"No, Micah. You think we're connected—"

"You think I can do this with everyone?" *His arms grow wide as he gestures to the dream world we are immersed in.* "Only you, Kris. Because…"

"I know. We're supposed to be soul mates. Yeah, yeah, yeah."

"We are soul mates. I can feel it."

"Well, I can't." *I hesitate, uncertain where to go from there. My words, though I know they are hurtful, spill out of me like I cannot control them.* "And I don't want that. I'm not just going to let it happen."

"Let it happen?" *he smirks.* "Not like you can stop it."

"Well, I'm going to try."

I've never seen Micah react with such a raw emotion as that statement induces. His face drops and for a second—only a second—I feel bad.

"Doesn't it bother you that we get no choice?" *I ask him.* "Being forced to feel a certain way about someone? What if you meet and fall in love with some wonderful girl?"

"That's not going to happen. You're the only girl for me, Kris."

I spin away from him with a loud groan. "You only believe that because you think you have to, Micah." *I stop and stare at the waves crashing, almost wishing for the ability to dive in and get tossed around. It had to be better than standing here, doing this, with Micah.* "We shouldn't be forced into this."

"I don't feel like I'm being forced," *Micah murmurs.* "I would choose *this even without a predestined connection."*

"You don't know that. You don't even know me."

"Yes, I do." Micah closes the distance between us quickly. *"More than you know."*

He surprises me, then. Big time, when he leans forward, grips my chin, and brings his lips down on mine. I hesitate, only because I am stunned stupid, before shoving him away.

He presses his face close to mine. *"A part of your soul wants this, Kris…"*

"No!" I shove him again, harder this time, and the sand, the water, the gentle breeze fades from around me.

CHAPTER 15

I was on my feet before the lingering smell of saltwater faded from my dream-sense. Only one thing was on my mind as I stomped across the room and flung the door open. Micah's room was just down the hall from mine and, within a matter of seconds, I was barging inside.

With a quick glance across the room to Gabby's sleeping form, I crossed to Micah's bed. He was stirring, coming out of the dream. When his eyes opened and landed on me, on my furious face, he started to sit. I saw the excuses and reasoning for his actions form behind his clouded eyes, but I didn't give him a chance to voice them.

My fist slammed into his chest, driving him down onto the bed. Keeping my voice barely above a whisper, I snarled, "Don't you ever, *ever*, do that again, do you hear me?"

For the first time ever, I saw fear in Micah's eyes as he looked up at me. He didn't immediately answer, and I didn't give him the chance to form an excuse-ridden reply. I turned and walked out of his room. My temper was boiling over, and I knew I'd better get far away from him.

Before I did something stupid.

Just outside my bedroom door, he caught up to me, unaware

of the danger he placed himself in. Grabbing me by the elbow, he spun me around. "Are you really this upset because I kissed you? Or because you kissed me back?"

"I did—" I hesitated. Just like I had done when he'd kissed me. I hadn't *really* kissed him back, but I hadn't stopped him either. Not right away. "It was a *dream*, Micah," I hissed between my teeth. "I'm not really me in my dreams. I'm a different girl. The real me would never kiss you, and you know it."

"Not yet, maybe. But it's coming. That version of you that will want to kiss me? She's coming. I can feel it, and I know you can, too. That's why you're panicking, sticking your nose in those books all day long, hoping to find a way to prevent it."

"No." I was a heartbeat away from punching him in the face, and even though he had to know that, he didn't back up.

He stepped closer, pushing me unwillingly against the door. "We'll see. How you feel about me in the dreams will become a reality, Kris. It's a part of the connection. You won't be able to avoid feeling that way about me."

I scoffed. "If I don't kill you first." For the first time, I was serious. I didn't care that the kid was some almighty savior. I couldn't stand him, and would prefer to have him out of my life.

The thought of wringing his neck was starting to give me enjoyment.

"We'll find a way to stop you from turning Skotadi," Micah responded confidently. "You won't kill me."

"I won't have to be a Skotadi," I threatened viciously, pushing him away from me.

Before he formed a reply, the door opened behind me and

Callie stepped into the hallway. It only took her a quick glance between Micah and me to see what was going on.

"Come with me," Callie said, grabbing my arm and tugging me after her, away from Micah.

Even as the bathroom door shut behind us and Micah was forced out of my sight, I still shook in anger. When everything started to go blurry, I knew I was in trouble.

Or Callie. Perhaps she was the one I should have been worried about, being locked in a bathroom with me—the girl who was quickly, after one standoff with Micah, losing the battle over the evil raging inside of her.

I suddenly knew exactly what had happened to me that day I'd punched Nathan in the nose. I knew because it was happening again. Anger, so much anger, blurred my vision.

I wanted to hurt someone. Anyone would do.

"Kris?" Callie turned with a washcloth extended to me. When I didn't immediately take it, the frown on her face deepened. "Kris? You okay? Your eyes…"

I looked down at the floor to shield them from her. My hands hung clenched at my sides.

"Here, Kris," she said, sticking the cloth under my nose. "It might make you feel better."

I swatted it out of her hand, something that sounded similar to a snarl rising in my throat. She bent to pick it off the floor, and I thought about how easy it would be to snuff out her life right then and there.

Quick. Easy. Fulfilling.

My hands shook as I tried to keep them down, at my sides,

but it was as if someone else were moving them for me, toward an unsuspecting Callie. As she stood up, I lifted my gaze to meet hers, and saw her eyes widen in fear.

I briefly wondered if it was the excitement of seeing her fear of me, or the sudden intense need to do something to give her a reason to really fear me, that drove me to black out.

When I came to, I was floating. I heard voices—two familiar voices—around me. One, the deeper one, above me and close. The other one softer, and farther back, but getting closer.

I was moving, I thought. Something big and sturdy had a hold of me and I was moving. I squirmed, trying to move on my own, but the grip on me tightened.

"Easy, Kris," the deep voice—I now recognized as Nathan's—said. "You're fine. Just getting you into bed, okay?"

A moment later, I was set down on something soft, and I opened my eyes. As they came into focus, they fixated on Callie. Then on Micah standing at the foot of the bed.

With one look at him, my desire to ensure a violent end to him was rekindled. I don't know what the others saw in my face in that moment, but their reactions were brisk and severe. Callie gasped, and she and Micah both took a step back, while Nathan pressed my shoulders into the mattress.

"Kris!" He shifted to block my view of Micah, lowering his face to mine so I had nowhere else to look than at him. "Focus on me, Kris. Not him. Focus! Micah," he called over his shoulder, "get the hell out of here. Now!"

In my periphery, I saw Micah move to the door and as much as I wanted to jump up and run after him, I wanted him to leave even more. I would be glad to see him gone.

The door opened before he reached it, and Gabby and Richie rushed inside. Their initial reactions when they first saw me mirrored those of Callie and Micah. Then their expressions changed and, instead of fear, I saw hatred and vengeance.

They didn't hesitate to charge. Nathan sprung from my side, placing himself between me and them. Micah managed to grab ahold of Gabby from behind and wrestled her toward the door. That left Nathan to take on Richie one-on-one. Callie took Nathan's place, between me and the struggle, as my final defender.

While Richie was a trained Kala, he was not a natural fighter like Nathan. They traded a few blows, and I winced as one of Richie's fists found Nathan's face. Despite that, it was a brief scuffle, with Nathan gaining the upper hand and forcing Richie out the door with Gabby.

"Lock it. Keep them out," Nathan ordered Micah before returning to my side.

With just the four of us in the room now, Nathan turned his undivided attention to me. From the wary look on his face, I knew he wasn't sure what was happening to me. Not like I did. I knew exactly what was happening.

I was dangerously close to slipping over the edge, to the side I had been fighting against so hard, for so long. The impulses that Alec had spoken of were happening to me, right now, and I couldn't push them down. Couldn't control them.

Surely the others, especially Nathan, had to have the same suspicion.

If they didn't realize this, they were idiots.

But then, easy prey.

Stop!

I shook my head to push out the malicious thoughts before they took hold of me. Even so, they were right there, brewing, pushing to break through. I couldn't—I wouldn't—let them.

"What happened?" Nathan asked me softly. When I didn't immediately respond—I couldn't for fear of losing control again in a moment of weakness—he turned to Callie and repeated the question.

"I don't know," she replied. "I heard her and Micah out in the hallway, arguing. She sounded like she was ready to kill him. I took her to the bathroom to calm down. She was shaking…"

Nathan's eyes lifted to Micah, where he stood against the door with his arms crossed. He didn't need to ask Micah. The question was visible in the rigidity of his jaw.

Micah shuffled his feet before answering. "She got mad at me. It was like a lit fuse, escalated into something else entirely."

"Why was she mad at you?" Nathan asked harshly.

Micah shrugged and glanced between Nathan and me like he was afraid he would soon have two people in the room wanting to rip his head off. He had a right to be nervous.

"I—uh, I kind of kissed her," he stammered, then added hastily, "In a dream."

Nathan glared. His mouth opened, and what he had been about to say in response, I'll never know, because Micah's mention of the kiss brought the surge of anger back. I shot up, intending to launch myself across the room at him. Nathan caught me mid-leap, pushed me to the mattress, and held me there. My body shook with the need to break free and finish what I'd started, but Nathan's hold on me wouldn't allow that.

"Kris!" Nathan yelled, lowering his face so that he was all I could see. "Pull it together! You can fight this! You need to fight this!"

He shifted his weight, kept me pressed down with his forearm across my chest, and used his free hand to brush away the hair that had fallen in my face. Looking up at him, I saw the raw fear in his eyes, and knew that it matched mine.

I was scared. Terrified. I didn't want this.

I had to fight it. I wasn't exactly sure how to do that, but Nathan's encouragement gave me the strength to try. The simple act of his hand gliding softly down my cheek was giving me the willpower I had previously lacked.

I could do it. I would do it, with his help.

My breathing slowed, steadied. I saw him nod his head.

"Good, Kris," he murmured. "You're doing great."

Breathe. Just breathe. One at a time.

Nathan's blue eyes broke through to me—the real me—and I started to believe that I could do it. I *was* doing it. The demons were quieting.

But not gone yet.

My eyes were locked on Nathan's, but that didn't prevent me from catching a glimpse of Micah in my periphery as he stepped closer to the bed, apparently having thought that the danger had passed. As my eyes shifted to him, the anger surged once again, and my body went rigid as the battle for control of it raged inside of me.

A high-pitched ringing sounded in my head as nothing but thoughts of violence and blood and Micah's painful death took over. In the distance, I heard Nathan's voice as he shouted at Micah, but I couldn't make out what he was saying as everything—Micah, Callie, Nathan, the room—faded from around me.

Micah waits for me, the quickly dissolving black abyss all that separates us. As I grow closer to him, I try to shout to him, to tell him to run, to get as far away from me as he can. Not because I hate him, but because I know of the danger I am to him.

And because I care for him. He is my soul mate, but we cannot be together. It is for the best, but I know he refuses to see that, to believe that. His love for me is all that matters.

His smile widens as I near, and I know that he cannot hear my warning. Nor would he likely listen to it.

Tears are streaming down my face by the time I reach him, and only then does his smile fade. Not because he realizes the danger I pose, but out of concern for me. He is blinded by his concern, by his love, for me.

It blinds him to the knife as it pierces his chest. As his white shirt turns red with blood, his eyes remain on mine, pained and mournful as he realizes too late what I am.

Together, our eyes drop to the knife, and my hand on the handle. I should be surprised to see that it is my hand, but I'm not. I had known my role in Micah's demise. It was he who was taken off guard.

Only then do I hear my own screams.

The scream didn't follow me, and I awoke quietly, surrounded by darkness. For a moment, I thought I was still stuck in the dream, or in some in-between world, until the room came into focus around me. It was only dark because it was still night.

Or night again? My muscles were stiff, as if I had been asleep for days. Callie slept peacefully beside me, and I watched her for a moment as I stretched my achy muscles and collected my thoughts.

It was me who had turned Micah's shirt red. I was the one who killed Micah in the dream. I knew that I had been created as his one true nemesis, for that very purpose. But to see it...

I would not let his devotion and blind love—or what he thought was love—for me get him killed. I had to find a way to stop it. Not only my fate, but everyone's, relied on Micah surviving me.

The bed shifted as someone sat beside me. I rolled my head to see a shadowy outline hovering over me. Nathan's face came into focus as he leaned closer.

"You okay?" he whispered.

Of course, he had never left. I smiled despite the lingering heaviness of the dream, and the reality of what it meant. "I think so." I kept my voice low so as not to disturb Callie. From years of sleep overs, I knew that she was a deep sleeper, and this was no exception.

Nathan's hand lifted slowly, to tuck a chunk of stray hair behind my ear. I loved it when he touched me, even something as simple as that. His tender side was something I would never grow tired of. Probably because I didn't get to experience it often.

"Do you remember anything?" he asked.

Aside from the horrible dream, which was crystal clear in my memory, most of the events from the last several hours were mostly a blur, with spots of clarity here and there. And those spots, I wished I could erase.

"Some of it." I shifted, only to be reminded of my stiff joints. "How long have I been asleep?"

"A day."

What I recalled had happened twenty-four hours ago? I sighed warily. No amount of time would take away the flashes of memory in my head.

"Start from the beginning. What do you remember?"

"I remember being mad at Micah. I wanted to hurt him. Callie took me to the bathroom to calm me down..." What I remembered then was something I immediately wanted to forget. I sprang up in a panic. "Oh, my God, Nathan," I said a little too loudly. I cast a look over my shoulder at Callie. She hadn't moved. Looking back at Nathan, I couldn't keep the panic out of my voice. "I nearly hurt Callie. I *wanted* to hurt Callie!"

Nathan gripped my shoulders, pressed his face close enough to mine that I could see the tiny silver specks in the blue of his eyes. "But you didn't," he said firmly. "You fought it. That's when you blacked out, wasn't it?"

I nodded numbly. "I think so."

"The same thing happened when you fought the urge to hurt Micah." He wasn't asking; he was stating a fact. "You fought it, Kris. You can fight it. You need to keep doing it."

"Nathan, I—"

"No, you listen," he interrupted gruffly. "We've gotten this far, we're this close, and you can't give up now. I'm not going to lose you now."

I'm not going to lose you now. Despite the tone with which he said it, his words wrapped my heart in silky sentiment. It was the best kind of combination of tough-Nathan with tender-Nathan. Not the distant, dismissive one that boiled my blood, but the one I had fallen for.

If I'd had any lingering doubts, the look of utter determination in his stormy blues crushed them. I loved those eyes and…yes, I was in love with him.

"Say it," he demanded. My heart nearly stopped beating as I wondered when Nathan had developed the ability to read minds. "I want to hear you say you're not going to give up," he clarified, saving me from burying my head in the pillow in mortification.

"I won't," I said softly.

"Won't *what?*"

Geez, he really meant business. I sighed and tried again. "I won't give up."

Only then did he loosen up enough to give me one of his almost-smiles. It was perfect—the moment, the setting, the soft shadows around us. If it weren't for Callie sleeping beside me, it would have been the ideal moment to tell him how I now knew I felt about him and that I would do *everything* in my power to keep my promise to him because of that.

As it was, Callie's soft snore sort of ruined the moment. And, well, Mother Nature had something else in store for me anyway.

Nathan must have seen the grimace on my face. "What's wrong?" he asked.

"Nothing," I said quickly, then amended, "I just, well, I really have to go to the bathroom."

At least I'd found a way to turn the almost-smile into a full-on grin. With an amused nod, he stood, giving me room to slide out of the bed.

I was slightly mortified to see just how little I was wearing. I really hoped it had been Callie that had taken off my clothes and slipped nothing but an oversized t-shirt over me. As much as I would welcome a little skin exposing encounter with Nathan, I'd prefer it to be when I was conscious. Fortunately, my expanded bladder made it possible to overlook my lack of attire.

"I'm going with you," Nathan said as he followed me out of the room. When I shot him a curious look over my shoulder, he added drily, "Not *in* the bathroom. I just don't want to leave you alone yet. I don't trust Gabby and Richie."

Nor did he probably want to risk me having another run-in with Micah. As I took care of business in the bathroom, I wondered how much of that had to do with Micah's safety and how much had to do with Nathan's reaction to hearing why I'd been so angry with Micah in the first place. Did knowing Micah had kissed me, even if it was only in a dream, bother him the way it bothered me? I'd felt wrong when it happened, like I had betrayed Nathan by letting it happen. Technically, I had no reason to feel that way. Nathan and I weren't together, even if I wanted that to be the case.

But did he feel that sort of tie to me that I felt to him? I knew I wouldn't like to hear of him kissing another girl—dream or not.

By the time I finished and washed my hands, I found another reason to hate Micah. For not letting me hear Nathan's response to hearing about the kiss. Fortunately, it wasn't enough to send me into a Micah-hating Skotadi-driven killing spree. Regardless, I splashed some water on my face to cool myself down. Just thinking about Micah had a way of rising my blood pressure.

As I blotted my face dry and looked at myself in the mirror, what I saw immediately chilled the blood running through my veins. I leaned closer just to be sure, but there was no mistaking the tiny golden specks in my eyes. Contrasted by the black of my pupil, they stood out like tiny flames burning in the night. I'd once thought of Skotadi eyes as tiny portals to hell, and seeing the same flicker in my own eyes now only made that link all the more justifiable.

I would dig my own eyes out if I thought it would help. Instead, I screamed, and the only word that came out of my mouth was Nathan's name. In an instant, he was in the room, cradling me as my knees threatened to give out under the weight of those two gold spots.

"It's happening," I sobbed into his chest.

He attempted to lift my face to his, but I wouldn't let him, ashamed of what he would see in my eyes. Of course, he was a lot stronger than me, and ultimately succeeded. I reluctantly met his gaze and saw, from his lack of reaction, that this was not the first he had seen the gold flecks.

His jaw was rigid with determination. "We don't know what's happening."

Despite his assurance, the hope I had been holding onto crumbled. Despite his arms wrapped protectively around me, I knew that my fate would ultimately find me. Despite the words I'd spoken only moments ago, I feared that I would end up breaking my promise to Nathan.

Despite being a fighter, this was one fight I feared I would eventually lose.

CHAPTER 16

I was surprised to find myself alone when I awoke in the morning, but not as surprised as I was by the smell of bacon that immediately hit my nose. If anything could stunt the despair brought on by the events of the last thirty-six hours, it was bacon.

Something about turning into a monster must have jump started my appetite.

After slipping on a pair of mesh shorts I found lying on the floor, I ambled my way to the kitchen and its tantalizing aromas. The array of food I found there was nothing compared to the deliciousness of the other sight before me: Nathan slaving over the stove, cooking.

So, he could bake *and* cook. In my opinion, nothing was sexier than a hot, tough guy that could toss around evil creatures effortlessly, and still knew his way around the kitchen. I paused in the doorway to savor the moment.

Catching a glimpse of me when he turned, Nathan paused and smiled with a hint of bashfulness. "Cooking breakfast," he said with a shrug.

"I can see that. It smells good." Glancing around me, I asked, "Where's everyone else?"

Usually, when someone decided to make an actual meal, the

rest of the house hovered like vultures, waiting for their opportunity to scavenge. To see no one, with the smells wafting from the kitchen, was unexpected.

"Actually, it's just us," Nathan answered as he turned back to the stove. I tried to interpret the undercurrent in his tone. Anxiety? Reluctance? Maybe timid, but why?

"Where did they go?"

I saw his shoulders rise and fall as he stood with his back to me. "To get more supplies and food. Stuff like that."

I wandered farther into the kitchen, maintaining a casual charade despite the flip-flopping in my stomach. "So we're alone?"

Because I was watching him closely, I caught the way his movements froze briefly before he continued flipping the bacon. "Uh-huh." I detected an air of dismissiveness in his voice, like he was purposefully trying to be tough.

"You afraid to be alone with me?"

That question spun him around to face me. "Why would I be afraid of that?"

"Oh, I don't know," I sang. "Maybe because I'm a closet Skotadi, who apparently can snap at any moment."

That earned me a chuckle. "No. I'm definitely not afraid to be alone with you because of that."

Was there another reason that he would be afraid of me? The way he worded it, the way he said it, and the way he stood like he was prepared to run any second made me wonder. Was it simply being alone with me in this intimate setting that scared him?

"Why don't you go shower and get dressed," he suggested as he turned back to the stove. "By the time you're done, breakfast should be ready."

'You scare the shit out of me, okay?' he had told me a few weeks ago and suddenly it all made sense. He was nervous simply being alone with me…and it wasn't because he was afraid of what I could do. Well, maybe he was afraid of what I might do, but not because it was harmful to his well-being. Perhaps harmful to his self-control.

Good knowing that he struggled with it as much as I did.

That fact managed to put a smile on my face as I followed his advice and took a much needed shower. When I emerged, the sun was shining bright, and I slipped into a pair of jeans and the cutest shirt I had. Nathan was just finishing up when I joined him in the kitchen.

It was already a turn on to know that he could cook at all, but I nearly gave him something to really be nervous about when I took a bite and discovered that he could not only cook, but cook well. On top of that, it was nice to have an enjoyable moment with just the two of us again. This wasn't the first time I'd missed the days it had just been Nathan and I, the days we'd spent in the cabin in the woods, but this moment brought about a pang in my gut I'd never felt before. For the first time, I wished for the ability to go back and relive those days, when things were tough, but easier than now, before I'd known the truth, before I had impending doom on the horizon.

What if we never got to enjoy another moment like this?

Far too soon, we finished our plates and started the cleanup.

But then, that was nice, too. As I stood at the sink, Nathan brushed by me over and over again as he cleared the table and the stove, bringing me the dirty dishes to clean. We didn't talk, but it was a comfortable silence, and preferred over the many heavy subjects we otherwise would have conversed about.

I almost forgot about the events of the day before. Until I lifted the knife out of the soapy water.

I was immediately thrust back into the dream, looking down at the knife in my hand as it sliced through Micah. Though it had not been this knife—but a diamond-coated knife—in the dream, the emotion behind my actions gripped me. Though Micah was not here, there was another Kala here, and any Kala was as good as another.

I slanted my eyes in his direction as he wiped the stove clean. With his back to me, it would be easy. I could kill him before he ever knew what happened.

It was as if someone else's hand lifted the knife in the air, poised and ready, and I struggled against the impulse to rush forward, to attack. My arm quavered in rebellion, the knife rattling in my hand.

The hesitation was long enough for Nathan to turn, to find me standing there with the knife raised. With one look into his eyes, the struggle over control of my body ceased. I opened my hand and the knife dropped to the floor with a clatter.

Nathan looked from the knife to me. His mouth opened, perhaps out of shock, or perhaps to say something, but I didn't stick around to hear what.

I ran to my room, shut and locked the door. I backpedaled

until the back of my knees touched the edge of the bed, and I sat down, unable to support my own weight any longer. Dropping my head into my hands—the same ones that a moment ago had not belonged to me, but to a dark force trying to overcome me—I screamed.

The scariest part was that I knew what I had been about to do, but those seconds when the knife had been in my hand were only a blur. I barely remembered. All I knew was that I had been a heartbeat away from stabbing Nathan.

Though I probably should have expected it, I was startled by a knock at the door. A moment later, Nathan's voice carried through.

"Kris? You alright?"

I shook my head with a scoff. I'd nearly attacked him, and he was worried about me? Typical Nathan. Too blinded by his own need to help me to realize what I was becoming.

"Go away, Nathan," I returned loud enough for him to hear me through the door.

He knocked again. "Let me in."

"No!"

There was a thud and the door shook, either from a kick or a dropped shoulder. "I'll break the door down, Kris," he threatened. "It would be much easier for you to just let me in."

When I didn't answer, another hit vibrated the door, and another. I didn't doubt that he would manage to break it down. I didn't want him to. I didn't want to see him, didn't want to face what had nearly happened.

I didn't want him anywhere near me, for fear of what I might do.

Then again, it would be nice to finish what I started...

"Nathan, stay away! Please!" I pleaded, gritting my teeth as I struggled with my inner demon.

With another hard hit, the door crashed open. Nathan appeared in the doorway, and the demon won. With a snarl, I launched myself at him. He was quick, but not quick enough, and my arms encircled his neck.

It took him longer than it should have to gain the upper hand on me, most likely because he was trying not to hurt me in the process. I used that knowledge to my advantage, and managed to grab the knife he always carried with him from its sheath around his waist. Diamond-coated. Perfect. Just one scratch...

At the sight of the knife in my possession, he responded with the ferocity I'd come to expect from him. Life or death. He wasn't gentle in trying to rip me off of him now. My legs wrapped around his hips as he tried to restrain my arms, and we toppled over together. My head hit the floor hard, briefly stunning me and allowing him to pin my arms down, the knife held ineffectively in my hand above my head.

"Look at me, Kris!" he demanded.

I shook my head violently in refusal. He leaned down so close I had no choice but to look at him. His eyes burned into mine, pleading, desperate. Familiar, those eyes I could look into all day long. Eyes that belonged to someone I knew to my core that I had fallen in love with.

My hand wavered. The knife slid from my grasp and fell to

the floor.

I melted under Nathan's weight as I found my true self once again. His grip on me softened, and his hands slid up my forearms, across my wrists, until his fingers intertwined with mine. We lay like that, with his thumbs tracing delicate circles on my palms, until both our breaths slowed, steadied.

Only then did the reality hit me. A tiny quiver that started in my lips spread outward until my entire body was trembling, not from an internal struggle for control, but from a wave of emotion too powerful to contain. Wordlessly, Nathan shifted and guided me up until I was resting on his lap, his arms wrapped securely around my middle, and I buried my face into the warm spot between his neck and shoulder as the tears came.

He was one of the reasons I was fighting this battle, and was the one person fighting for me even more than I was fighting for myself. Protected in his arms now, I remembered why I could not give up. He believed in me, and I must believe in myself.

But never again would I put Nathan in danger, nor would I let him endanger himself for me. This had been too close, and I feared it would only happen again. I had to do something to protect the ones closest to me.

The question was what?

* * *

When the answer came to me later, I danced around it, toyed with it, tried to find another way. Ultimately, I knew it was the only thing I could do to keep everyone I loved out of harm's reach. Out of *my* reach.

I waited until I was sure everyone was asleep. I'd packed my bags after dinner, stuffed them under the bed. They and the books I'd been studying were all I took with me now. I half expected Nathan to be positioned outside my bedroom door, standing watch for Gabby and Richie, but he wasn't, and I slipped outside without meeting resistance. I felt guilty, but had no choice but to take the Tahoe.

There was only one place I knew I could go, and I punched the address into the GPS.

I drove through the night, and didn't stop until the sun started to rise. I managed to get a few hours of rest in a hotel outside of St. Louis, before setting off on the second leg of my trip. I hoped to be where I was going by nightfall.

It took longer than I'd anticipated, mostly because I struggled just to stay awake the last few hours. I got a second wind when the Rocky Mountains appeared in front of me, and I knew I was close. Shortly after midnight, I pulled to the curb in front of a white ranch house on a nicely maintained, tree-lined street. The GPS announced that I had arrived at my destination, and I couldn't have been more relieved.

Several cars were parked along the curb in front of the house, in the driveway, and even a few were angled awkwardly across the front yard. When I turned off the engine, I heard heavy base coming from inside the house, and knew that this was the right place.

A party. I would expect nothing less of Alec.

My nerves slowed me when I reached the stoop, and I had a

fleeting thought that maybe Alec wasn't there. Or maybe he was too far gone to help me. Or for me to help him.

There was only one way to find out. I couldn't go back now anyway, so I knocked on the door.

A tall, tanned, extremely good-looking blonde that looked like he belonged on the beaches of Malibu, not the mountains of Colorado, answered the door. He took one look at me, and raised his eyebrows in intrigue. Even with several feet separating us, I could smell the alcohol on his breath. Or maybe it was the house itself that reeked. It was hard to tell.

I groaned inwardly, but put on my sweet face. "Is Alec here?" I held my breath as I waited for the guy to tell me he didn't know anyone by the name of Alec.

Instead, he mumbled something that sounded something like, *"It figures"* before turning to shout, "Hey, Alec! Girl at the door asking for you!"

He walked away, leaving everyone with a clear view of me as I stood in the doorway. A cluster of scantily clad, heavily made-up girls looked up from a game of poker being played on the coffee table. Someone, though it was hard to tell who with all the people crammed into the room, whistled from the back. Smoke filled the small space, and I suspected not all of it was cigarette smoke. I had been to my fair share of parties, but this one made them all look like an eight year old's birthday celebration. I wanted to run and hide from all the curious stares.

Then I saw him, working his way through the crowd on his way over to me. He passed Malibu Guy, and laughed at something he said. When he looked up and saw me, his smile faltered. By the time he reached me, his face had morphed into a mixture of disbelief and anger.

"Kris? What are you doing here?" Alec barked and grabbed me by the elbow to usher me outside. He shut the door behind him, blocking us from view of all the nosey onlookers.

I dug the letter he had written me out of my jean's pocket and held it out to him. "You told me to find you if I needed your help."

"What is it?" he asked. "Boy problems?"

The harshness of his voice brought me up short. I opened my mouth, but clamped it shut without a response.

Alec spread his arms open. "Well, Kris? What do you need?"

I have never seen Alec this way. Well, I have, but never with me. I shook my head, unable to believe the way he was looking at me. Like he was irritated with me. Like I was bothering him.

Like, despite what his letter said and what he had said to me before he left, he didn't want me here.

"Nothing," I finally managed to choke out. I backed away from him, edging closer to the steps. "Nothing at all. Forget it."

I turned and raced down the stairs. I had the keys ready, and unlocked the Tahoe as I hurried toward it. I barely had the door open when someone reached from behind me and pushed it shut.

I spun around to see Alec, jaw clenched, advancing on me. "Dammit, Kris. What are you doing?"

"I'm leaving." I shoved against his chest to push him back so that I could get the door open again. He grabbed ahold of my shoulders, pushed me up against the side of the Tahoe, and that was when I saw them. His eyes. The specks of gold shining dimly, only visible because we were in the dark.

"Alec?" I asked tentatively.

"What?" he sneered. His grip on my shoulders tightened, and I gritted my teeth against the sharp pain. His hands trembled, and I recognized the signs of his inner struggle as he fought what was likely an overwhelming urge to hurt me even more.

The Alec I knew, the Alec I had come here for, eventually won the battle, and his hold on me loosened. His hands lifted off my shoulders and he pressed them against the Tahoe on either side of me, trapping me. But not in a threatening way.

His eyes weren't shining anymore.

"Are you okay?" I asked softly.

He nodded silently, and I heard him take a deep calming breath. "I think so."

"I'm sorry," I started. "I shouldn't have—"

"No," he interrupted sharply. "You shouldn't have come here."

I dropped my head as I blinked back the tears, and tried to pretend his words hadn't just stomped on what was left of my heart.

Alec stepped closer to me, close enough to rest his chin on top of my head, and he sighed heavily. "It's not that I don't want you here," he murmured into my ear. "It's just…I'm getting worse. I can barely help myself right now, let alone you."

"I'm getting worse too, Alec," I said. "That's why I came here."

His heavy breath tickled my ear. "Dammit." There was a long pause before he shifted to look down at me with a grin.

"And I thought it was because you missed me."

I returned a small half smile. "Well, maybe that, too."

His smile faded, his eyes leveled on mine, and only then did I realize how close he was standing to me. It was way too close, especially with the magnetism that I felt toward him. And our history. Pressed against the side of the Tahoe, within kissing range of Alec, was dangerous. He must have seen the fear in my eyes because he took a sudden step back, giving me the space I needed to clear my head.

"Alright," he said with forced cheer, and placed an arm around my shoulders to guide me toward the house. "Now that you're here, I'm not about to let you leave. Come, meet some people, have a drink, and submerse yourself in denial right along with me."

CHAPTER 17

Alec's friends knew how to party.

The house was being rented by the kid that had answered the door, whose name I learned was Tenner. Alec had lived with him for a year before he'd been sent to Boone by the Skotadi on his mission to lure me into the Skotadi life. Tenner was human, and completely in the dark. All Tenner knew was that Alec was fun, and got a lot of girls to come over. For those reasons alone, he let Alec move back in.

Why Alec had returned here baffled me at first. But he claimed it was easier to be around humans. Less desire to mangle them, he'd explained. While being surrounded by a houseful of Kala that he had been programmed to despise had become unbearable, humans he could handle. I supposed I understood his reasoning.

I had to admit, I hadn't had a desire to rip anyone's head off all night. Even getting eye-balled by ninety percent the girls in the house didn't bother me. I figured they were merely curious about the girl that had managed to steal all of Alec's attention without blatantly coming on to him. Based on the attention we were receiving, we must have made quite the scene.

As the bottles of beer dwindled and the crowd thinned, the

heaviness of the long drive started to take its toll on me. I started to feel every one of the five hundred miles I had driven, and that separated me from the people I cared about.

More than anything, I missed Callie and Nathan. By two in the morning, I was ready for a comfortable bed and a pillow to wallow my sorrows into.

It amazed me that, despite his wild lifestyle, Alec's room was kept immaculate. His bed was made, with navy blue satin sheets, and no clothes—neither his nor any random girls' clothes— littered the floor. While crisp and clean, I noted that it also lacked personalization. It was only a room, somewhere for him to sleep. No pictures, no mementos from happy occasions.

Only a room.

He retrieved my bags from the Tahoe, and I changed into mesh shorts and a t-shirt in the bathroom across the hall. On my way back, I could hear voices in the living room, but the lingering partiers were definitely taming down. There was no way they could keep me awake at this point anyway.

I found Alec sprawled on the bed when I returned, and stopped in the doorway, eyeing him curiously. I had been so tired, I hadn't even given a second thought as to what the sleeping arrangements would be. Seeing Alec laying on his back, his arms propped behind his head, and staring up at the ceiling stirred something in me I had thought was dead and buried.

Oh, shit. There was no denying the flip-flop in my stomach at the thought of sharing a bed with him. One, because I knew what Alec was capable of. Two, he was good at it. And three, I *was* attracted to him. I knew where my heart belonged, and that was with another, but nothing could lessen that raw pull I felt toward Alec.

I realized that was probably why I had done my best to avoid him and situations like this one in the past. Because I hadn't wanted to give Nathan any more reason to insist that I needed to 'figure out my feelings for Alec.' I'd known they had been there. Buried because of my stronger feelings for Nathan, but there. That was what I worried about as I approached Alec now.

"Stole the Tahoe, huh?" he said casually, his eyes still lifted to the ceiling. I could just make out the curve of his lips as they tipped into a grin.

"I wouldn't exactly call it stolen," I returned.

"Oh?" He rolled his head toward me. "So, they knew you took it and came here?" There was a smirk on his face, like he knew the truth, but asked anyway.

I sat down on the edge of the bed, close, but not too close, to him. I attempted to establish a distance from him by avoiding eye contact. "Well, no," I murmured.

"No one knows where you are?" He sounded surprised, though from the look of his growing grin, I figured I had just confirmed what he had been hoping.

"No."

"Not even Nathan?"

"Especially not Nathan." I hadn't intended for there to be a tone to my words, but based on Alec's reaction, I must have given something away.

His eyebrows raised curiously, and there was no mistaking the suggestive tone in his voice. "Trouble in paradise?"

"Alec," I chastised.

"What? A guy can't be hopeful?"

I finally looked at him and our gazes locked, reminding me why I should have stuck to my plan to avoid eye contact. I knew he was teasing, but I also knew Alec well enough to know that there was always a hidden truth to everything he said. Usually those meanings were romantically infused innuendos.

As he had once told me, *"I'm a guy, surging with testosterone. What do you expect from me?"*

I have come to expect his flirty nature like I expect the sun to rise every day. Just because I anticipated it didn't mean I knew how to handle it. Avoidance had been my go-to in the past, and was what I opted to go with now. He had more than likely come to expect it, and didn't push me now.

"What happened?" he asked me, his tone serious again, having dropped the flirty direction he had been going.

"Same as you," I said. "Horrible dreams, urges, and this desire to hurt people that I don't want to hurt."

He nodded along, completely empathetic, and I realized that he was the only one I could truly open up to, because he *knew*, like no one else could. Micah might have been able to read my mind, Nathan might have been the one I opened my heart to, but Alec was the only one that knew what I was really going through.

And after months of bottling it up, I was glad to have someone to share my troubles with.

"It's been going on for months," I continued, "only I didn't realize it until recently. Little things would make me mad that normally wouldn't. My temper was slowly getting worse. The day

I left..." I trailed off and hesitated, the next words catching in my throat, "I nearly killed Nathan."

Alec's eyebrows shot up in the air. "Really?"

"All I saw was a Kala that needed to be destroyed, and nothing else mattered. There was this battle raging inside of me over control of my body, a battle between me and this evil version of me."

I was relieved to see Alec nod along with my description like he understood exactly what I meant. It made me hopeful that I wasn't completely losing it, that what I was experiencing was to be expected, and maybe Alec had a way to help me deal with it.

"Anyway," I continued, "when I snapped out of it, I realized what I had almost done. I don't want to hurt him. Or Micah. And the dreams I'm having about hurting Micah..."

Alec sat up to place a hand on my shoulder when I trailed off, unable to finish. "I know, Kris. I know, and I'll do what I can to help you. I'm fighting the same urges. I don't know how much I can help you, but I'll try. I've got a few tricks that help me sometimes. They might work for you, too."

I grinned despite the severity of the situation we found ourselves in. "Kind of like the blind leading the blind?"

"Something like that." Alec swung his legs off the side of the bed and stood with a yawn. "I'll let you get some sleep. See you in the morning."

I hesitated briefly before asking, "Where are you going to sleep?"

"The couch. Right next to the poker chips and empty beer bottles."

I grimaced. "I'm sorry, Alec."

I felt bad that he was giving up his room for me, but Alec merely shrugged. "Don't be," he said. "I'm glad you're here."

"Thanks."

I smiled, and he turned to leave me alone in his room. Never thought I would live to see that ever happen.

* * *

Not surprisingly, I was the first to rise in the morning. Alec was still asleep on the couch and Tenner was nowhere to be found. Fortunately, no stragglers were passed out on the floor.

I decided to be a gracious guest by making a large pot of coffee. As expected, the aroma wafting from the kitchen served as an effective alarm clock, and I heard Alec stir in the living room. However, I hadn't expected him to saunter into the kitchen wearing nothing but an expensive-looking pair of silver checkered boxer shorts.

He didn't seem to mind one bit, or notice my mouth dropping open, as he rubbed his eyes on his way to the coffee pot. "We could've used you around here a little sooner," he murmured. "I've been trying to figure out how to work this thing for weeks."

It sounded like a joke, but I didn't doubt his remark carried with it some honesty. Alec never had been very domesticate— aside from having a clean room, of course.

As I stood with arms crossed, pondering how he couldn't have figured out how to use a coffee maker in all this time, Alec approached me. He was wide awake now, his gaze steady as it locked on mine. I backed against the counter, cautious, as always, of his advance.

As he grew closer, I stiffened, wondering what his intentions were. He stopped in front of me, close enough to see the flecks of gold in his eyes. Even though I knew what they symbolized, I couldn't help but notice that they brought out the jade hue in his eyes, and made them all the more alluring. My gaze dropped to his lips as they curled into a sly grin, and I looked away quickly. He stepped forward and our arms brushed. I pulled mine back, and placed my hands safely on the counter behind me.

Despite our already close proximity, he angled closer still. My breath caught in my throat when I realized that he intended to kiss me. I braced for it, and all the while my mind swirled with what I would do.

Kiss him back? Stop him? Tell him…

Tell him what?

I was more than likely in love with someone else. Someone who may never reciprocate my feelings. Someone who I had left in order to join Alec. Someone I may never have the opportunity to be with, but that I would always want.

A chuckle from Alec interrupted my impending panic attack.

"The coffee cups are in the cupboard behind you," he murmured. He reached around me, pressing his body against mine in the process, and produced two mugs. After a brief but purposeful hesitation, he stepped back and handed one to me. His eyes twinkled when they met mine, before he turned away.

I found my breath again, and inhaled deeply to steady

myself.

"It's a real shame," he said as he crossed the small kitchen to the coffee pot.

"What?" I croaked.

Fortunately, Alec kept his eyes down, focused on pouring his coffee, as he spoke. "That you supposedly want another guy, even though you're so damn attracted to me."

I gulped. Because Alec wasn't looking at me, he missed the panic in my eyes. Because, dammit, he was right. I was attracted to him, on some deep primal level. Especially at times like this. Times that it would be so easy to give in to that attraction.

Alec wouldn't fight it. Not like Nathan.

It would be so easy with Alec. But, he wasn't Nathan. What I felt for Nathan went beyond attraction. It was all that, and so much more.

My mind was made up. Nathan was the one I wanted. Alec knew that. He also knew a part of me would always want him too…and he was toying with that part now. Really, it wasn't fair.

"Stop, Alec," I said, managing barely more than a whisper.

Now, he turned to me, and took several steps in my direction. I had never moved from my previous sanctuary, pressed up against the counter, and that was where he cornered me yet again.

"You really want me to?" he asked softly. He was close enough that I felt his breath tickle my cheek.

I nodded, though weakly and not at all convincingly. To Alec, it was more than likely an open invitation.

His grin grew like he knew how weak I was in that moment,

and I didn't doubt that he was about to capitalize on that weakness, but by some miracle, Tenner picked that exact moment to make his entrance. He announced his presence with a loud, overdramatic yawn as if to let us know he was there, and that he knew damn well that he was interrupting something.

Alec reluctantly backed away. Before he turned, I saw that look on his face—that one that said he knew he would eventually get his way. And that made me nervous. Because if there was one thing I had learned about Alec since I've known him, it was that he often got exactly what he wanted.

From the quick look that Tenner shot him, it was clear that Tenner knew that much about Alec as well. The look Tenner cast in my direction was one of curiosity. To mask the growing heat on my cheeks, I turned to get another coffee cup from the cupboard, and handed it to Tenner. I met his gaze with far more composure than I felt, daring him to make a comment.

He didn't.

With his back to us as he prepared his cup of coffee, he spoke to Alec casually. "You remember we were supposed to go snowboarding today? Probably our last chance before the snow melts."

Alec groaned. "I'm way too hung over."

Tenner glared at Alec like he was an imposter. "When do we *not* go snowboarding hung over?"

"True." Alec rolled his head side to side, then looked at me. "You up for it?"

Tenner turned to me. "You board?"

I shrugged. "Not really. Alec took me once."

"She's not bad," Alec added.

At that time, it had been about the most fun I'd ever had. Granted, I'd had a huge crush on Alec at the time. And we'd been skipping school, which only added to the fun. But to consider myself a snowboarder after one day of falling my way down the mountain was a stretch.

"You know Chelsea will be there," Tenner said to Alec in a warning tone.

Alec blew out a puff of air. "That could be a problem."

"Who's Chelsea?" I asked.

Alec started to wave off the question, but Tenner volunteered the answer hurriedly. "Alec's latest admirer. They hooked up when he first got here, and now she won't leave him alone. She doesn't quite get that Alec doesn't do relationships."

Alec nodded along as Tenner spoke, then said, "Thanks, man."

"Just keeping it real." Tenner looked at me pointedly. "She happens to be my girlfriend's best friend, so she's around a lot."

"Yeah," Alec scoffed. "Maybe you should get a new girlfriend."

At that, a model-tall, skimpily dressed brunette bounced into the kitchen. "I heard that," she said to Alec, before planting a kiss on Tenner's cheek. She took his cup of coffee, apparently having just claimed it as her own, and turned to me. "So, this is her?"

I immediately disliked her.

"This is my friend, Kris," Alec responded drily. I got the impression he didn't much care for her either. "Kris, this is Sara, Tenner's obnoxious girlfriend."

I smiled at her, at least attempting friendliness. She ignored me, and turned to Alec. "I didn't realize you had *friends* that were girls."

"I don't," he answered quickly. He glanced at me, then amended, "Well, except for you. And Callie. But that's it!"

Alec crossed to where I stood, and reached behind me to grab another mug from the cupboard. In the process, he wrapped one arm around me and gave me a gentle squeeze. I took it as a silent apology for the last two minutes. Just before he stepped back, I swore he pressed his lips to the top of my head, but it all happened so fast I couldn't be sure.

Looking up and seeing the subtle snarl on Sara's face as Alec presented the mug to Tenner, I was glad for what Alec had done. Regardless of our strained relationship, seeing that girl's dislike of his affection toward me somehow made all the trials worthwhile.

I suddenly couldn't wait to meet her best friend.

CHAPTER 18

About halfway through my first run down the mountain, I suffered a moment of regret. I quickly learned that the mountains outside of Boone didn't compare to the mountains in Colorado.

What had Alec been thinking, being so sure I could handle this?

While I'd eagerly agreed to immerse myself in denial, just for one more day, I could have thought of a hundred better things to do for fun than face planting into hard packed snow all day long.

At least Alec stayed with me the entire time, even if he did more laughing than encouraging. By the time I gimped my way down three beginner's courses, and saw no indication of things getting easier, I headed straight for the lodge.

"Where are you going?" Alec called after me.

"To get x-rays done of all my broken bones," I answered over my shoulder.

I heard him chuckle as he glided up beside me. Raising his goggles up and placing them on the top of his head, he gave me a smile, and his eyes gleamed a dazzling green in the reflection bouncing off the snow. "You were just starting to get good," he argued.

I stopped and looked at him. "Not even close, Alec."

He relented with a shrug. "Yeah, you do kind of suck. I'm

due for a beer anyway." He leaned down to unstrap his boots from the board, and fell in beside me.

"It's not even noon yet," I said.

"Okay," he drew slowly. "Hot chocolate then?"

As I thawed out next to one of the many fireplaces scattered around the enormous lodge, Alec tracked down some hot chocolate. I saw him approach after a few minutes, with Tenner and Sara. A girl with tight golden curls and a very expensive looking snowboarding suit with matching pink boots was with them, and had her eyes set coolly on me.

Alec flashed me a fake smile visible only to me. "Look who I found," he crooned.

"Chelsea?" I whispered to him as he handed a cup of hot chocolate to me.

A tight lipped, eyebrow raised expression on his face was my answer.

There were others that joined us eventually, as they came in off the mountain, and before long, the loud obnoxious crowd had claimed their own corner of the lodge, having driven away the families with children and older couples. Drinks flowed freely. A lot of flirting was taking place all around me, but the most nauseating display was happening right in front of me. Really, this Chelsea girl had no shame. Nor could she take a hint.

Alec had rolled his eyes more times than I could count. He'd barely paid attention to what she was saying half the time. It was obvious to everyone but her that he just wasn't interested.

I actually felt a little bad for her.

Twenty minutes later, after one doe-eyed hyena-laugh too

many, I got up from my seat and grabbed Alec's shoulder. "I'm ready to give it another shot."

"Really?" He looked eager. Too eager, and I knew it had nothing to do with snowboarding.

"We're kind of in the middle of something here." This came from Chelsea.

I should have ignored her, let Alec handle the situation, but at the fake, high-pitched sound of her nasally voice, I was only reminded of how much I despised girls like her.

"It didn't really look like that to me," I returned. Turning to Alec, I asked, "Where you in the middle of something?"

His lips turned in as he tried in vain to mask the grin on his face. For the first time ever, I saw Alec at a loss for words.

"What are you doing here?" Chelsea spat. "He dumped you. Move on. Stop being so pathetic."

Oh, so that's what was going around Alec's circle of friends?

I faltered, surprised by her assumption. From the slight shake of Alec's head and the look of confusion on Tenner's face, I knew that he hadn't told anyone that. Sara glared up at me from behind Chelsea's shoulder, and I figured the two of them had come to that conclusion on their own.

Only then did I notice that the low rumble of voices around us had dropped a decibel as they turned their attention to the impending cat-fight. My cheeks warmed under their stares, and I briefly considering tucking my tail and bolting.

Fortunately, Alec saved me from further humiliating myself.

"Actually," he drew slowly to pull all the attention to him. "She dumped me, and she's here because I want us to be friends.

And maybe I'll wallow around a little until she takes me back." He turned to me then, upping the act by placing a hand over his heart. "I'm not really sure how to do that because I've never been dumped before, but I'd do anything for you, baby."

I hadn't expected all of that, and stared at him dumbly before I realized that his *'friends'* were watching me, waiting for a response. Adopting a flirty smile, I took Alec's hand in mine. "Anything?"

He faltered, eyes dropping to my mouth. His throat jumped as he stepped closer to me, keeping up the charade. "Anything."

Or maybe it wasn't a charade?

It was real nerves that rendered my voice useless now. Something about this, though it was all an act, was hitting a little too close to the truth. We shouldn't be doing this, especially not in front of others, who had no idea just how complicated the history between Alec and me was.

We needed to go. Now.

Tossing a glare over my shoulder at Chelsea, I walked away. I heard Alec calling out goodbyes to Tenner and a few of the guys behind me before he followed.

We didn't go snowboarding again. The car ride home was quiet. Only made tolerable by the music filling the tightly charged space between us. I didn't know what had happened back there, and didn't know if I wanted to know. If Alec wanted to talk about it, he didn't say anything.

The moment we walked into the house, I attempted to make a beeline for the bathroom. Alec grabbed ahold of my hand to stop me. When I spun around, I found him just a tad too close for comfort. That twinkle in his eyes certainly didn't help.

"I know what happened back there," he said.

I didn't need to ask what *'back there'* was in reference to. But in order to avoid a conversation I really didn't want to have, I played dumb. Alec wasn't fooled.

"You know what that was all about?" he asked me. When I didn't respond, he continued, "You were jealous."

"I was not," I responded automatically.

"Could've fooled me."

"I was not jealous." I hesitated, thinking about my words. *I hadn't been. Not really. However, another feistier part of me may have been, and that part was getting louder and more prominent every day.* "I can't control what Skotadi-Kris does most of the time."

"Blaming it on your alter ego?"

"Well, yeah, I am."

Alec grinned as I attempted to snatch my hand from his grasp. He wasn't about to let go. Not yet. He had more to add, and he pulled me closer. "I like knowing at least a part of you wants me."

This time when I pulled my hand away, he let it go. "I'm going to shower," I announced with enough force to let him know I considered this conversation over. He was too close to a truth I wasn't ready to acknowledge.

"Is that an invitation?"

I stifled a laugh, and shot a glare over my shoulder as I walked away. "Not in a million years, Alec."

I hurried to the bathroom, needing to put distance between

the two of us fast. I couldn't be certain, but I was pretty sure, in that moment just before I shut the door behind me, I heard him mutter something that sounded suspiciously like, "We'll see about that" under his breath.

* * *

The days passed uneventfully. For the most part.

Living with Alec, frequently alone since Tenner was gone more than he was home, proved to be my greatest test. He grinned, he flirted, he tempted. He did what Alec did best, but this time, he didn't get the girl. I knew what he was thinking: *Not yet*. He wasn't the type to shy away from a challenge, and I had a feeling he was only biding his time.

I busied myself as I had before, reading the books on Incantation I had brought with me. When I wasn't doing that, Alec helped me work on my control. He'd learned some tricks along the way and shared his methods with me.

Basketball. That worked for me. When I felt my temper rising over the raised toilet seat, constant visitors dropping in unannounced, or stares from girls who didn't understand my relationship with Alec, I thought about basketball. Anything to do with basketball. It was my innocent distraction.

Alec's was snowboarding. When he'd first suggested that to me, we'd learned that thinking about snowboarding only fueled my anger. A broken lamp had been the outcome of that trial.

I hadn't lost it—really lost it—since I'd been here. He was right. Being surrounded by humans was easier. If I could stay in

Alec's room, busy myself with reading, and avoid his more annoying visitors, I would be okay. For a while longer anyway.

It was nighttime that worried me. That was when Micah pulled me into his dream worlds.

During the dreams, I was fine. I liked Micah then. It was when I woke up, and I remembered how I really felt about him, that I got mad. He knew the dreams were my weakness and tried to use that knowledge to trick me into telling him where I was. So far, I hadn't slipped, but I'd been close to changing my sleep patterns so that I could avoid sleeping at the same time as him.

Then I found something in the spell book that looked promising. I made Alec drive me to the rare gems shop in town to pick up a black tourmaline crystal. Apparently, it had a blocking effect on psychics, so I figured it was worth a shot.

I put it under my pillow that night before I went to bed and, for the first time in a very long time, I experienced Micah-free sleep. When it happened again the next two nights, I was convinced it wasn't a coincidence.

I'd done my first successful spell. Feeling good after that, I threw myself into the spells with more confidence and the belief that I could do it.

I found a list of stones and gems that were thought to have other blocking and healing abilities. I wondered what the chances were that they could help. Could they sort of…block my soul from turning evil? Or heal the souls of those that had already been changed?

I hadn't a clue as to what they might be capable of, but after the success I'd had with the tourmaline crystal, I was excited to try others. I decided it wouldn't hurt to get them…and see what happened.

I opened my notebook to make a list of gems I wanted to look for, only to discover that I had no more blank pages left. Every page was filled with my notes. Tossing the notebook to the side, I glanced around the room, hoping Alec had something I could write on.

I zeroed in on the small computer desk in the corner of the room. I moved a few of Tenner's books out of the way, uncovering a thick blue folder. It wasn't what I was looking for, but my hands lingered. Hoping to find a few blank pieces of paper inside, I flipped it open.

I immediately spotted my name sprawled across the top of the first page, in Alec's choppy handwriting. Every cell in my body turned to ice as I continued reading, flipping through the pages like they were on fire.

Adoption…protection…murders…disappearance…

My life looked up at me from the pages in my hand. Things I'd known, things I'd never known. Things I didn't know how, or why, Alec had filed away in a folder in his room.

My blood boiling now, I gathered up the papers and marched out of Alec's room. He was in the living room, watching television. I tossed the file on the coffee table in front of him. Pointing to the scattered papers, I demanded, "What is this?"

He looked up slowly, calculating his response. "Kris…"

"You have a file on me, Alec!" I yelled. "Why? What is this all about? And you had better start telling me the truth, or we're about to find out which one of us is stronger."

He took a deep breath, and thought about his words carefully. "After I left, I started wondering about some of the things Micah mentioned before, about you being descendent of Hecate. When I came here, I didn't have anything else to do, so I started looking into some of his theories."

"And this is what you found out?"

He nodded. "I have a few Skotadi friends who haven't turned on me," he explained cautiously, like he was afraid one wrong word would send me on a rampage—with him as the target. "I had them dig into your past."

"I was adopted by my family when I was six months old? That's what you found out?"

I'd known from the day I first started development that my family, that had been murdered when I was three, could not have been my birth family. They'd been human, incapable of having a hybrid baby. But seeing the truth in print felt like a knife twisting in my gut.

He nodded solemnly. "The orphanage you were adopted from…" He searched for the paper with the information he was looking for. Finding it, he handed it to me. "It's a Skotadi-run orphanage. It's where they put the kids born to Skotadi parents, so that the parents can return to the field without having to worry about raising kids. It's the same orphanage I was placed in."

The thought left a sour taste in my mouth. Those poor kids. Dumped in an orphanage by their parents so that they could continue to fight this silly war. While that didn't make any sense to me, something else had me even more confused.

"If it was a Skotadi-run orphanage, why did they let me get

adopted by some human family?" It was how they had ultimately lost me after all, when Nathan came along.

"Well," Alec said slowly, and I knew that he had the answer, but was hesitant to share it with me. "The family that adopted you was apparently one of the many human families that are in alliance with the Skotadi. They do things like this to help the Skotadi out."

"Humans in alliance with the Skotadi." I said the words slowly, digesting them. Ultimately, I decided I didn't like the sounds of it. "Why would any human want to do that?"

Alec shrugged. "I don't know. There's got to be something in it for them, but I can't guess what. The fact that humans are working with the Skotadi is a heavily guarded secret, too. They don't want anyone knowing about it."

I had the nagging suspicion that this had something to do with the kidnapping of humans we had witnessed in West Virginia, and I really didn't like where my thoughts were headed.

"Alec, those girls they took…"

"I know. I was thinking the same thing."

"Incantation? Could they be using Incantation to…" I trailed off, struggling to complete the thought. It was too much, too horrible, to fathom.

"Force them?" Alec paused to read the aghast look on my face. "That's the only explanation I can come up with."

Sick, sick bastards…

But was that all? Was that the only reason they were using the humans—to help them raise their abandoned Skotadi children? Or was there something far worse, far bigger than that going on?

The Skotadi's words played over in my head again.

They are our pawns…

Only the beginning…

What were they planning? What were we missing?

"There's more," Alec murmured, breaking into my panicked thoughts. I stared at him and waited. "Ninety-nine percent of the Skotadi have gone through that orphanage at one time. They keep records on all the kids. They keep files on *everything* there. If anyone has the details of your creation, it's them. If we can find your file, we'll know exactly who you are, where you come from, and what makes you so different from me."

"And who my creators were." If I were really descendent of Hecate. And if I were, maybe I could find clues to help me break the unwanted soul mate connection she'd handed down to me.

Knowing the details of my creation might help us determine how to put an end to everything, once and for all. Explain the link I have to Micah, tell us if his theories were right. While a part of me wanted to continue living in denial, a bigger part of me wanted to get to the bottom of everything, to know who I was and where I came from. Especially if that information might help us.

"We have to find those files, Alec."

"I was looking into it when you showed up," Alec said. "I meant to tell you about all of this. I just got distracted, and I guess I didn't really know how to tell you."

"It's fine." I brushed it off with a wave of my hand. "But we can't waste any more time."

Alec nodded hesitantly.

"What's wrong, Alec?" I asked.

"Aren't you afraid of what we might find?"

Of course I was. In fact, I was downright terrified. But this was too important to run away from.

Instead of answering Alec, I asked another question of my own. "Where is this orphanage anyway?"

Alec grimaced, and I imagined he was about to tell me that it was in the Himalayas or some impossible location like that. If it was going to take us awhile to get there, we needed to start making plans now. Surely, he realized the importance of that.

"Alec, how far is it?" I pressed.

He sighed heavily and met my gaze with a hint of reluctance. "About an hour outside of Aspen."

My mouth dropped open. Really? Could it really be that easy?

An hour away. The buried secrets of my past, the truth about who and what I was, were so close. And I was ready to uncover them.

CHAPTER 19

Alec wasn't exactly eager. Not like I was. In this case, he was the calm, collected, calculating one, and I was the spontaneous daredevil ready to jump into the lion's den without considering the consequences. It was a little weird—our roles being reversed.

"We're not doing this tonight," he repeated for the fifth time since we'd left the house. His hand hesitated over the Tahoe's door handle, and he looked at me, waiting.

"I know." He didn't move, didn't look away, forcing me to add, "I got it, Alec. We're just scoping it out. I promise I won't try to talk you into breaking in tonight…again."

At my promise, he finally got out and rounded the front of the vehicle to meet me on my side. He had pulled off the side of the road half a mile from the orphanage, hiding the Tahoe behind a large snowbank where no one could see it. The road dead ended at a gate. Beyond that lay the orphanage.

We walked the remaining distance. Not on the road, but rather a few yards inside the line of trees that surrounded the property. The lights of the orphanage supplied us with just enough visibility as we approached. From what I could see, it looked like a small college campus. Five wings branched off of a large central building, like a large star. Each wing branched off into two or three more wings. The place was huge.

"How many kids are housed here?" I whispered to Alec.

He shook his head. "Thousands."

I scoffed. "Sick, selfish bastards."

Even in the dim lighting, I could make out Alec's smile as he glanced down at me. I shrugged as if to say, *well, it's true!*

A gate kept us from waltzing right up to the front door, not that we were going to do that anyway. However, as I took in the high fence wrapped around the entire property, I was curious as to how he planned to get in. The fence wasn't something I would want to scale, not with the barbed wiring at the top.

We stopped, still hidden in the trees, several yards from the fence. Alec was looking at the building, placed back from the fence line about a hundred yards. He was the picture of calm.

"Alec? How are we going to get in?"

He glanced at me. "There are ways."

"Considering we're about to do something highly dangerous, with a good probability of getting caught, maybe you should elaborate on these ways."

His arm shot out in front of me, as he pointed along the fence line behind me. "Down there about fifty yards is a hole in the fence." His arm moved, directing me to the far left wing of the building. "Right there is a window that will be unlocked." His arm swung to the large central building. "In there are the administrative offices. The one we need will be the third door on the left."

I made a face like I might have been impressed. So, he had a plan.

"How do you know there's a hole in the fence?" I asked.

"Because I made it when I was fourteen," he answered. "Just like I jimmied the window to never lock." He smiled smugly at the look of awe on my face, and added, "I made a career out of sneaking out."

The mental image of a young, rebellious Alec got a laugh out of me. "How do you know the Skotadi didn't find the hole, or fix the window?"

He looked at me like he took my lack of faith in his plan personally. With a sigh, he grabbed my hand and pulled me after him through the woods, running parallel to the fence. He stopped at a precise location, pulled a heap of foliage away from the fence, revealing the hole he'd known would be there.

"Okay, okay," I said. "You're prepared for this. I get it."

He nodded his head, looking at the building. "Security will be lighter on the weekends. That's our best chance. I'm thinking middle of the night, when everyone is asleep. We should have only a few security guards to sneak past."

Sounded easy enough. "Saturday?" Two days from now.

"Sunday," he countered. "Sometimes the kids have parties on Saturday nights. We want everyone asleep."

I nodded as I took in the daunting building before me. In three days, we'd break in. In three days, I would know everything. Who I was, where I came from, what made me different.

I'd learned to expect the unexpected. This time, facing this uncertainty, I wasn't afraid. I was ready.

* * *

The drive back to Aspen was quiet.

I knew there was a chance of one or both of us getting caught on Sunday. As much as I hated that thought, I hated not knowing the truth about myself even more. Learning the truth could be vital to what we were trying to accomplish. Maybe knowing everything about my creation will help us to help each other. Help us fight our destiny.

We had to go through with it. For both of us. For both of our futures.

And if we both died in the process?

"We're doing the right thing, aren't we?" I asked Alec softly.

He nodded, and I was grateful to have that reassurance from him, but he didn't add anything. He was quiet, and the usual comfortable silence between us morphed into something awkward and unwelcome. I wished he would say something, anything.

"Alec?" When he glanced at me, I opened my mouth, but nothing formed.

"You know what, Kris?" he pondered. "I think we need to have a little fun."

I half scoffed, half snorted a laugh. "Fun?"

"Yeah, you know, before we attempt to pull off the world's dumbest break in."

"Okay, fun." His way of making me forget about what we were about to do. For now. "What do you suggest?"

I was a little hesitant to hear what he had in mind. I had learned over time that, with Alec, anything was possible.

He didn't elaborate, but I found out what he had planned when he turned off the main road a few moments later, and we pulled up to a dark, empty, red-brick building. A sign by the front doors announced a warm welcome to Mountain Ridge Elementary School.

"School? Never thought you were one to consider school fun," I said.

Alec chuckled as he got out of the car. Reaching into the backseat, he withdrew a small satchel and a flashlight. He tossed me the light. "Don't turn it on yet. Come on."

Even in the dark, he seemed to know exactly where he was going. As I followed him around the side of the building, I had to wonder how many times he'd done this—whatever this was we were doing.

In the distance, I could make out the shadowed shapes of a swing set, jungle gym, and see-saws. For a moment, I thought his plan was to frolic innocently in the playground. But then, Alec was Alec, and he never ceased to surprise me.

He stopped outside a big red door with the words 'No Trespassing' painted ominously across the top. Opening the satchel in his hands, he glanced at me. "Flashlight."

I provided him with light as he withdrew a few small gadgets. He turned and dropped to one knee in front of the door, and motioned for me to redirect the light as he inserted what looked to be a set of tweezers into the keyhole.

"You have a breaking and entering kit?"

"Got to be prepared."

I laughed. "How many times have you done this?"

"Here? Never, but wanted to."

"How many other places have you broken in to?" My voice approached hysteria, even if I did find it a little funny.

He shrugged without any indication of answering. I heard a soft click, and Alec shot me a smug smile as he stood and opened the door. He swept an arm out in front of him. "After you."

"This is wrong in so many ways," I muttered. With a final nervous glance at the playground—no angry security guard, thank God—I stepped inside.

"You know what, Kris? You're going to have a real hard time with this turning evil stuff," Alec said as he let the door swing shut behind us.

"I consider that a good thing." I spun around to Alec, only to realize I couldn't see him. With the door shut, we were standing in the dark with zero visibility. I felt his hand brush against mine, and I jumped.

I heard a chuckle. "You want to turn on the flashlight so we can, I don't know, maybe see? Or we can stand here like this. I don't care. It's kind of hot."

I promptly clicked the rubber tip of the flashlight, and jumped again when I saw how close Alec was standing to me. He grinned as he took my hand in his.

"Come on," he said, tugging me after him. "We're supposed to be having fun."

I shrugged like it was no big deal and let him lead me down the wide hallway. I could let loose and have fun for a little bit. With Alec. Alone, in an empty, dark school. Sure, nothing to it.

Alec pushed through a set of double doors and we entered a

room that felt large and open. The faint smell of sweat and rubber kicked me back to Boone, to dodge ball and volleyball games in gym class.

Alec flipped a switch, turning on a section of overhead lights along the far side of the large gymnasium. It was just enough light for us to see, but left most of the room in shadows.

Finally dropping my hand, Alec crossed to the rack of basketballs along the wall, grabbed one, and turned to me with a smile. "You're favorite sport."

I watched as he dribbled to the free throw line, and sunk a basket. It reminded me of the time we'd played HORSE on the playground in Boone. Right before he'd kissed me for the first time, right before Nathan came along and changed everything.

Apparently, Alec remembered too. "How about we finish what we started at that party," he suggested.

"We did finish," I said. "I kicked your ass, remember?"

Alec shook his head, his grin growing. "No, not that. I remember you mentioning something about playing for clothes." He paused, and met my eyes unflinchingly. "We never got to finish that."

"I'm pretty sure that was a joke."

Alec chuckled. "You have no idea how serious I was. Here." He tossed me the ball. "One-on-one. I'll even let you go first."

Having possession first had its advantages, and I had Alec shoeless, sockless, and shirtless before he ever got to touch the ball. Perhaps it was the fact that he was shirtless that rattled me enough to let him steal it. Or maybe I was afraid to find out if he was wearing anything under his jeans.

"This is not going the way I had hoped," Alec admitted as he finally took possession of the ball. "But things are about to change."

I smiled as I took a defensive stance. "We'll see about that."

A few minutes later, Alec was much happier as I was forced to remove my last sock, and we were both barefoot.

"One more shot," he said with a laugh, "and I get to see some skin."

I gulped when I realized the tough spot I was in. I didn't want to take anything else off any more than I wanted Alec to. Either way, no matter who won this next shot, things were about to get a lot more interesting.

I should walk away. *Now*.

"Check." He bounced the ball to me. I held onto it a second, briefly debating my next move, before I returned it to him with a returned, "Check."

Alec could play, I had to give him that. I tried, hard, but he beat me to the basket, floated the ball over my head, and scored.

"It's really not fair considering how much taller you are than me," I whined.

Alec ignored my complaints as he dribbled toward me. His mind wasn't on the logistics of the game at the moment. His eyes wandered over me expectantly. "Well? What's it going to be?"

I lowered my eyes, unable to meet his. My pulse jumped and a bead of sweat trickled down the back of my neck—and it wasn't from the physical exertion. Pants or shirt?

Shit. Pants or shirt?

I wasn't happy with either option. I considered telling Alec I didn't want to play anymore, and back out of this game with my clothes on. It was heading in a dangerous direction I wasn't so sure I was ready to handle. But I was no quitter either, and I wasn't about to back down to Alec. Not with the way he was looking at me, daring me to continue.

I decided to call his bluff, and force him to back down first…*if* that were even possible.

After considering my choices, I opted to remove my jeans. I was wearing the least sexy panties ever made, and my shirt was long enough to cover them up, so it wasn't like Alec would get to see much.

Regardless, he raised his eyebrows as I tossed my pants to the side. "Interesting choice."

I shrugged and took the ball from him. "Check."

I was on a mission this time, and Alec didn't stand a chance. It wasn't difficult, considering how distracted he was now. I easily slapped the ball out of his hands and made a run for the basket, scoring effortlessly. As I turned around triumphantly, Alec was already happily slipping out of his jeans. Luckily, he still had on a pair of boxers.

I kept my eyes on the ball to keep them off him. No matter how hard I tried, I couldn't ignore how aware I was of just how little clothing remained between us.

"I'm getting the next one," he taunted, spreading his arms out wide to block me. "You're not getting by me."

I made a move, but hesitated at the thought of scoring again, and forcing Alec to lose his boxers. The hesitation was enough for him to poke the ball away from me, and sink his own basket.

Catching the ball as it dropped through the net, Alec turned to me expectantly.

"I'm not taking anything else off," I said.

Alec shrugged, undeterred, and took a step toward me. "Okay. I'll do it."

My heart wasn't anywhere near my chest by the time he reached me. I tried to back away from him, but my feet were stuck, frozen under his gaze. And, maybe, a part of me didn't want to move. He gave me just enough time to stop him if I wanted, but I didn't, and his hands reached out and caught the hem of my shirt.

His fingers brushed against my skin and involuntary goosebumps prickled the surface of my stomach. Alec must have noticed because he smiled knowingly as he inched the fabric higher. His hands stopped near my ribcage, where he gripped me tightly. Though his touch felt incredible, I couldn't prevent the stiffening of my spine and the short puff of air that slipped between my lips.

Alec's eyes lifted to mine. "I won't if you don't want me to."

"I don't want you to," I said, unable to raise my voice above a whisper.

"Okay." He let go of my shirt, letting it fall, but his hands remained underneath it, and encircled around my waist. "And what if I were to kiss you?"

I tried to block out the way his thumbs tracing over the spot just above my belly button felt—because it felt amazing. Such a simple motion on his part, but it was doing a hell of a job at tearing down my walls.

"Would you want me to do that?" Alec asked softly.

"No." The word shook as it came out of my mouth, and didn't pack the punch I had hoped for.

"I don't believe you."

That made two of us.

Knowing I would be at his mercy if I looked into his eyes, I fixed my gaze on his hand as it trailed slowly up my arm and over my shoulder. The goose-bumps his touch left behind sent a shiver up my spine. A good shiver. Definitely a good shiver. Too good, in fact.

"Alec…"

His fingers brushed along the curve of my neck, coming to a rest under my chin. With one finger, he forced my head back. His eyes were aflame, not with evil, but with a desire that melted most of the rest of my resolve. I had to close my eyes to regain my composure.

"I know you want me to." His mouth brushed against my upper lip, teasing, tempting me.

Oh, I wanted him to kiss me. Physically, my body was responding to Alec the way he wanted it to, the way it has to him before.

But my body didn't know that my heart belonged to someone else.

"Tell me to kiss you, Kris." His hand stroked the side of my face, further fogging my thoughts and nearly making me forget the reasons why we shouldn't be doing this.

I opened my eyes at last, and realized, too late, how bad of an idea that was. He was close. Really close. It would be so easy, so natural, so right in so many ways to give in. I had only a small sliver of willpower left, and I held on to that with all my might.

"I can't," I choked. Alec flinched as if I had struck him. Though brief, and quickly covered by indifference, I saw just how much the rejection had hurt him. And I immediately felt horrible. "Alec…"

"It's fine." He backed away, offering me a half smile that only broke my heart even more, before stooping to collect our clothes off the floor. He tossed me my pants. "Looks like you won again."

"Alec," I tried again, but came up empty on a follow up. None of the words floating around in my head sounded good enough, or worthy enough.

Alec was the image of indifference as he slipped his shirt over his head. "I was getting cold anyway, and it's getting late. You ready to go?"

"Yeah," I offered meekly.

I snuck a few glances at him as we redressed. His expression remained blank, and he said nothing. I didn't like it. I didn't like knowing that I was the cause of Alec's suffering. I struggled to think of something to say to him, to repair the rift between us, but again, came up empty.

The thought was planted in the back of mind. I tried to push it away, but as we left the school in strained silence, that annoying voice in my head repeated what I was afraid of.

She, too, thought this rift might not be fixable.

* * *

The cascade of hot water was just what I needed to melt away the rigidness in my muscles. After a long, uncomfortable car ride, we had returned to find Tenner and Sara gone for the evening. To avoid prolonging the misery smothering Alec and me, I had formed some excuse about needing a shower.

I finished without having come up with a resolution.

I wanted Nathan. It was that simple. Alec needed to understand that. Most importantly, I needed to avoid temptation with Alec. Because, sometimes, various parts of myself were confused.

My heart knew what it wanted. Even if I couldn't have him, even if I might never have him…

"Ouch! Damn it!"

My hip caught the corner of the countertop and I stopped to briskly rub the sore spot on my side. Eyeing the scratch on the surface, and already seeing the start of a bruise underneath, I cursed under my breath.

Since when did I start cursing like Alec?

I dressed hastily and let my wet hair cascade loosely down my back. I was still mad—at the counter, at Alec, at everything and everyone at this point—by the time I yanked the door open.

The television in the living room was on some late night program. The crisp hiss of a beer bottle top being twisted off reached my ears, and I knew where I could find Alec.

I stood in the entryway for a moment as his eyes shifted from the television to me. His mouth parted to say something, but my quick tongue stopped him.

"Don't, Alec," I interrupted. "Just don't."

He shifted and, for the first time since I've known him, looked very uncomfortable as I crossed the room to him. His eyes remained fixed on me as I lowered to sit on the edge of the coffee table in front of him.

"Kris…" he started, and leaned forward until our knees touched. "I'm sorry about earlier. I just…" He trailed off, then shrugged in defeat. "Hell, I don't know what I was thinking."

"Shut up, Alec." I edged closer, wedging my knees between his. In one swift motion, I reached out and cupped his face in my hands. I didn't know what I was doing, didn't know why I was doing it, but it felt…right. Now, at this moment, it felt like the most natural thing in the world. "I was scared earlier. The way I feel about you scares me sometimes, but I…"

"What, Kris?"

I swallowed. *Here goes…* "I did want you to kiss me. And…I want you to kiss m—"

Alec's mouth was on mine, burying whatever else I might have said under his soft, yet hard, lips. Lips that wasted no time parting mine so that he could dive deeper. Into me. Into whatever reservations I might have had left until they were nothing but a bad memory.

Something happened to me in that moment I opened up to him. Something stirred inside of me. Something I hadn't realized, or wanted to admit, had been there. Until now.

Whereas other kisses might be sweet, or tender, or full of unspoken meaning, the way Alec kissed me now was nothing like that. It was as if he were kissing away a physical pain. And it pulled at a part of me that wanted nothing more than to cure my own physical ache.

When Alec's hands traveled up from my knees, across my thighs, and gripped my waist to pull me closer, I did the next best thing. Breaking the connection between us only briefly, I climbed onto his lap, before meshing my mouth to his again, as if that second we had parted had been too much.

If he was surprised by my boldness, he didn't let on. If anything, he kissed me with renewed urgency, and when his hands slipped under my shirt, I didn't stop him. Instead, a soft moan escaped my lips as I briefly came up for air.

I'd never made out with anyone like this before, but Alec made it easy, made me forget what I was doing, made me not care about the fact that his hands were inching higher, lifting my shirt up. When his mouth dropped to graze the sensitive spot just above my belly button, I forgot about everything but how good it felt. And that I wanted more.

Which was why it was very hard for me to pull away. Alec looked up at me, his eyes hooded and smoldering hot, with a question in them.

My answer was to take his hand in mine as I slid off of his lap. I wasn't sure what I was doing until I did it, and even then I felt as if I were trapped in a stranger's body. Yet, it felt right as I led him down the hall to his bedroom.

CHAPTER 20

It took less than a second of consciousness, lying quietly, alone in bed, for it all to come back to me. Faint rays of light peeked through the curtains. It was early, but there was no way in hell I was going to be able to go back to sleep after remembering what I'd just remembered.

It was as if I had been drunk, for crying out loud. I didn't do stuff like that—make out with guys, *heavily* make out. To the point that I was mortified to piece together the parts of last night that remained foggy.

I had been in Skotadi-mode. That was the only explanation. Why I did the things I did. Why I let those things happen. Why I could barely remember. From the moment I'd first kissed Alec, everything became sort of hazy, with only flashes of images that lit up my memory.

Alec had been willing. That much I knew. He'd let it happen. And I was pretty sure he hadn't been in Skotadi-mode.

I bolted out of bed, threw on a pair of baggy sweats, a t-shirt, and stormed out of the room. Alec was in the living room, and I made a beeline straight for him.

My open palm connecting with the back of his head, I thought, did a good job of demonstrating how pissed off I was, and he felt, rather than heard, the level of my anger with him. He turned to me with a puzzled expression on his face, and I tore into him, throwing my shaking body on top of his, pummeling him with my small, but hard, fists. He blocked several blows with his forearms before he managed to take ahold of my wrists.

His arms encircled me, and the only reason he was able to do so was because I had now completely lost it. When he sat up with me cradled in his lap, he couldn't even be mad about the red welt expanding under his right eye. Even though he was the one who had deceived me—at least that was the way I saw it—I let him hold me there, my face pressed into his neck, because he was also the only friend I had. His hand stroked my hair until I calmed down, and he didn't have to tell me the guilt I knew he felt.

Even so, my guilt was worse. Far worse.

I was mad at Alec, but I also knew he wasn't all to blame.

"You're back?" he asked softly, his mouth nuzzling my ear.

I nodded.

"And you remember?" I nodded again and he tipped my face back to look him in the eyes. He opened his mouth to say something, but the words never formed. He didn't have to say anything. I saw in his eyes how sorry he was—about more than what had happened between us. With him, it was more, so much more. It was a different kind of regret he suffered from.

"I can't do this anymore…" I started to rise, but he held me down. I didn't have the strength or the willpower to struggle.

"You remember the part where nothing happened, right?" he said to me.

I faltered. *Nothing happened?* But I remembered…

"I mean, we made out," he amended. "A lot, and it was awesome, but that was it, Kris. You don't remember that?"

"It's all kind of fuzzy," I murmured.

"Yeah," he said softly. "You had a Skotadi moment. That's why you can't remember everything."

I nodded my understanding and, this time, when I pulled away, Alec let me. I stood and paced to the other side of the room, as far from him as I could get. Even then, I didn't feel safe. No amount of distance from Alec ever seemed to be safe enough.

The boy had a piece of me firmly in his grasp. I knew that now.

Just like I knew that some of the pieces of last night that were coming to me in flashes were not what I would consider 'nothing happened.' Maybe in Alec's world. Not mine.

"How far did it go last night?" I asked him hesitantly, not so sure I wanted to hear the answer.

He shrugged casually. "Not far. I put a stop to it when I realized you weren't really you." He paused and grinned at me. "You were pissed."

I ignored that last statement, and pressed for what Alec was coyly keeping from me. "At what point did you realize I wasn't myself?"

He pulled his lip between his teeth as he pondered an answer, then just let me have it. "I started to suspect it when you took off all your clothes, and then started going for mine," he said.

"I…what!" And then it hit me. The memory. Yep, it had

happened. I had taken off my clothes. "Oh, my God."

"That's what I said."

"Alec!" I groaned. This was horrible. No, this was way beyond horrible. I couldn't believe I had done that. Well, technically, it hadn't been *me*.

It had still been my body though.

"What? Nothing happened, Kris," Alec insisted, then he added with a shrug, "I just have the ability to see you naked every time I close my eyes." With a grin growing on his face, he did just that. He closed his eyes, and his grin grew even more.

I snatched his pillow from the couch and hurled it at him. "Stop that!"

He laughed. "Take it easy. I've seen lots of girls naked."

"Not me!"

He cocked his head to the side with a smile. "Well, technically—"

"Oh, shut up, Alec!" I turned and stormed away.

I didn't make it to the hallway before he caught up to me. He grabbed my arm and swung me around. "Kris, wait," he said, his voice suddenly somber. "I'm sorry. Really. I'm an asshole. It's something I've come to expect of myself, but I shouldn't tease you."

I wasn't sure what I was more upset about. The fact that I had stripped in front of Alec, or that I had done something to validate Nathan's reasoning behind us not being together. He had given me the opportunity to decipher my feelings for Alec, and I did this. I ruined it.

The guilt was eating me up.

"On some level, I think I knew, and I should have put a stop to it sooner," Alec continued. "I guess I wanted it to be real, *hoped* that it was real. The last thing I ever wanted was to hurt you, Kris, and I'm sorry that I did."

"I'm just glad you pulled the brakes when you did," I offered weakly, then a thought came to me. "Why did you? If you wanted it to be real so bad, you could've…"

Apparently, I'd been game. And Alec was a guy. It couldn't have been easy for him last night, to make the call he'd made.

"I might be evil, Kris, but I'm not a monster. I wouldn't do that to you. I…" He trailed off, letting his next thought hang in the air between us. I could see that whatever it had been was still on his mind, and bothering him.

Or he was really confused.

"What is it, Alec?"

"Nothing," he said quickly, and not convincingly at all.

"You wouldn't do that to me because you…?"

He took a deep breath before his unfinished thought burst through, seemingly without his permission, "Because I love you." He paused like he was surprised by his own admission, seemed to ponder it a moment, and ultimately made up his mind—that yes, he did love me. He nodded his eventual acceptance, even if he looked shocked as hell.

The look on my face likely matched his. "Really?"

He shrugged. "I guess so." He sounded less than thrilled, and I suspected he'd never said those words to anyone. Ever.

"Since when?" He started to turn away, and I put a hand on his shoulder, stopping him. "Alec. Since when?"

"Since that night on the playground in Boone."

The night of our first kiss.

"Why didn't you tell me?"

"Seriously? Kris, I never had a chance. Nathan came along…" Alec shook his head and muttered under his breath just loud enough for me to hear, "I knew I should have left his ass locked up in that cell."

Oh, yes. Nathan. The one that had unintentionally stolen my heart from Alec. The one I had fallen in love with. The one that might love me too, but won't admit it. The one who had insisted all along that I had unresolved feelings for Alec.

The one I had deceived, by proving him right.

"I know how you feel about Nathan," Alec continued. "I also know what would have happened between us if not for him. As hard as this is for me to admit, I'm glad he came along, because he can give you a chance at the happily ever after that you deserve. I can't."

My mouth opened, an incompletely formed argument rushing forth, but Alec shushed me with a finger to my lips. "You deserve the best," he continued quickly, "and I'm not it. He is. He loves you as much as I do, even if he doesn't know it yet, and that makes him worthy."

He hesitated, long enough for me to muster words, though they were mumbled with his finger still pressed to my lips. "I would've been happy with you, Alec."

"Maybe." He shrugged. "It wouldn't have lasted. Eventually, we both would have been stuck, unhappy, in a Skotadi-run life neither of us wants. It's better this way, for both of us. I can see that now. I did a lot of thinking last night."

"Since when did you become a philosopher?" He gave me a small crooked grin that only made me sad to see. "Alec, I—"

"A part of you loves me," he interrupted. "I know that, and I think you do too. It sucks because the part of you that loves me is the part that we're trying to destroy." He paused and, this time, his grin was more Alec-like. "I'm a little conflicted about the whole thing."

My only response was a timid smile. Was he right? Was it only my Skotadi-side that had feelings for Alec?

He turned to walk away, leaving me stunned by his words. All of them. All of those wonderfully spoken, heart-breaking words. They'd torn a big piece of my heart to shreds. A far bigger piece than my inner Skotadi owned.

It wasn't just her that loved Alec.

"Alec," I called after him in a whisper.

He turned to face me. As I crossed the room to him, I was sure he knew what I was doing before *I* knew what I was doing. His voice was cautious. "Kris…"

I shook my head to silence him, then lifted onto my tip-toes to press my lips softly against his. He didn't pull me into his arms, he didn't touch me anywhere else. He did nothing but kiss me back gently, like he knew what this kiss really was.

I wanted to tell him that the part of me that loved him was not just the part we were trying to destroy, that it was more than that, but I choked the words back. Instead, a single tear slid down my cheek as a big piece of my heart said goodbye.

* * *

Living with Alec after that—knowing that he loved me—wasn't easy. It bordered on torture. Neither of us wanted to talk about it, and neither of us brought it up again, though sometimes I thought it might have been easier to clear the air.

If only I knew how to do that.

It wasn't like I'd changed my mind. Even if we might never be together, Nathan was still the one I wanted. I knew that, and Alec knew that.

And Alec accepted it.

I determined that having Alec's blessing was something I'd needed all along. Hearing him say what he had said, and knowing that he was willing to let me go despite loving me, sealed the deal for me. Nothing was there to hold me back. There were no more unresolved feelings or issues for me to work out.

There was only one big problem now. I had left Nathan. And considering that tonight was the night Alec and I planned to break into the orphanage, there was a good chance I might never see him again.

Alec parked the Tahoe behind the same snowbank as a few nights ago. We made the same walk to the fence in silence, the butterflies in my stomach multiplying with each step. Alec pulled back the same bushes covering the same hole in the fence, and I took a deep breath.

Here we go...

As I stepped forward to climb through, Alec grabbed my arm. "Kris?" I stopped and waited. "We're cool, right?"

"Of course."

Despite the reassuring tone of my voice, he looked uncertain. "You sure? All that happened…" He trailed off, grimacing as if the memory was painful for him. "After everything that I said, we're good? 'Cause I don't want to go in there with that between us."

"Alec…" I stepped closer to him, close enough to see the light in his eyes—only because they were that magnificent, not because they were surging. The words that came to mind didn't sound good enough, so for lack of anything worthy to say to him, I hugged him.

I pulled him in tight, wrapped my arms around his middle, and really, *really* hugged him. At first, he hesitated, then his arms enclosed around my shoulders, and he held me against him. It was better than words.

I considered letting go after a moment, but I didn't. It felt good there, snuggled against Alec's chest. I'd missed him the past few days, and I wanted to bask in this moment because it was the first that I realized that we really were going to be okay.

And I was scared, that after all that we had been through, to lose him now. When I felt closer to Alec than ever.

"Are we going to stand here all night?" Alec murmured in my ear, earning a laugh from me.

But I still didn't let go, and neither did he. "Maybe."

"Okay." I didn't know how it was possible, but his grip tightened. "I love you, Kris. And I mean that as a friend."

I smiled into his shirt. "I love you too, Alec." And I did. Just not the way he might have wanted me to.

Alec shifted, finally breaking the hold we had on each other. "Alright," he said gruffly. "I'm not saying goodbye to you tonight. That's not what this is. Got it?"

I nodded numbly. I hadn't realized it at the time, but it had felt a little like goodbye.

God, I hoped we got through this okay. Together.

"It's not too late to go back," I said.

"Yeah, it is." Alec grinned before turning to the fence. This time, when he pulled back on the bushes covering the hole, he held them back as I crawled through.

Coming to a stand on the other side, I glanced around nervously, expecting a spotlight to come out of nowhere and bathe us in light, or a pack of guard dogs to charge, baring teeth.

Alec joined me with neither happening. He took ahold of my hand and led me across the wide open yard toward the closest wing. Dropping to our knees beneath a window, pressed against the wall, we took the opportunity to look around.

"I don't think anyone saw us," Alec whispered to me.

"Where are we?" I asked. "What wing is this?"

"One of the dorms. Come on." He wrapped around the corner of the building, keeping his head below the level of the windows. I followed blindly. He seemed to know exactly where he was going, and stopped below a window halfway down the back wall. He stood to peek through the glass.

"Hopefully, they haven't installed a new security system since I've been here," Alec muttered to me.

Though he'd assured me that the window would be unlocked, I half expected him to find that it wasn't. But it was, and he lifted it without a problem. Except for the shrill screech about three-quarters of the way up.

He froze and we both hunkered down, cautious. His eyes flashed to mine with a silent apology. After a few moments, when no one came to inspect the noise, Alec clambered through the opening. Once inside, he turned to help lift me climb in. Together, we hunched down against the wall, and listened.

It was almost too quiet. Something about an unlocked window in any Skotadi-occupied building made me nervous. Seriously, how had they not discovered the tampered window in, what, five years?

I didn't want to think about the possibility that we were walking into a trap, and shut out the nagging voice in my head as I followed Alec farther into the room. I figured, from the shadowy shapes I could just make out in the dark, that we were in some sort of classroom. Alec came to a stop by the closed door, and waited for me to join him.

"There's a long hallway to our left. We'll be going past probably seven or eight dorm rooms. The administrative building is at the end," he explained to me in a hushed voice.

He started to open the door, and I grabbed his hand to stop him. "Will the office we need be unlocked?"

"Probably not."

"How do you plan on getting in?"

"Kris." He cocked his head to the side, and placed both hands to his chest, over his heart. "Your lack of faith in my breaking and entering abilities hurts. Don't worry. I got this."

With that, we darted into the hallway. Though the lights

were on, they were dimmed. I'd have preferred complete darkness, but this would have to do. I stayed close to Alec's side as he led the way. We passed eight doors that were thankfully closed. As we drew closer to the end of the hallway, I glanced over my shoulder to be sure no one came out of one of the rooms behind us.

Not that I had a plan as to what we'd do if that happened.

Finally, we reached the intersection. Alec peered around the corner, looking both ways, and motioned to me that the coast was clear. We hurried past another three doors, and came to a stop outside a blood red door with an ominous *Authorized Personnel Only* proclamation painted across the top.

Alec glanced at me before trying the door. Locked.

He wasn't deterred, and dug into his pants' pocket, withdrawing the tools he'd used to break into the school. Placing a small penlight between his teeth, he knelt down to start working on the lock. I took a stance beside him, and swept my eyes up and down the hallway.

It's almost too easy.

Not that I wanted to get caught, but I'd come into this sort of expecting to. I'd figured this to be a suicide mission, and was surprised that it was going so smoothly. Even so, there was a gnawing in my stomach that grew more pronounced the longer I stood there.

Alec cursing under his breath drew my focus down to him as he dropped the penlight to the floor. It wasn't because it slipped free; he'd tossed it out of frustration.

"What's wrong?" I whispered.

"Can't get in," he muttered as he stood.

"Now what?"

He looked down at me, his expression thoughtful as he contemplated our options. "We need a key." With that statement, he grabbed me by the elbow and ushered me back the way we had come. Instead of turning down the hallway toward the dorms, we continued straight, farther down the administrative wing.

"Where do you plan on getting a key?" I whispered harshly.

"It's probably best if you don't know."

Oh, shit, this can't be good.

We continued silently and quickly until we reached the intersection to another wing. Surprisingly, we hadn't seen any security guards along the way, and no one had seen us. But as we rounded the corner, something told me that was about to change.

On a large brass plate nailed to the wall of the hallway we'd just turned down were the words: *Faculty Wing. No Students Permitted.*

I pulled on Alec's arm, forcing him to a skidding stop.

"Are you crazy?" I demanded as forcefully as I could in a whisper. "We'll get caught for sure."

"Where else do you expect to find a key to—" Before he'd finished the question, I saw the answer register in his eyes. They twinkled as he turned me around. "Come on."

I happily obliged as we retreated back to the administrative wing. Whatever method of obtaining a key he had just thought of had to be better than breaking into a faculty member's room.

Before we made the turn out of sight, the click of a door

sounded behind us. I risked a quick peek over my shoulder as Alec picked up the pace.

Too late. An older Skotadi woman had spotted us.

"Hey!" she yelled. "Stop right there!"

Alec tugged on my arm, turning me forward, and forcing me into a run.

"Don't let her see your face," he muttered to me.

The second we rounded the corner, out of her sight, Alec let go of my hand and started checking doors. All locked.

I moved across the hall from him and checked two handles as we moved farther down the hallway. In the distance, the fast footsteps of the Skotadi were growing closer.

The third handle moved, and the door opened in front of me.

"Alec!" I called quietly. "Here!"

He darted across the hall toward me, pushed me inside ahead of him, and shut the door gently behind us. I heard him searching for, and eventually finding, the lock.

I couldn't see six inches in front of me. Though I couldn't see the room, it felt small, like the walls were close. The familiar scent of lemon and pine stung my nose, and I suspected we were in a janitorial closet.

Did all schools use the same floor cleaner?

I felt Alec brush by me, and heard shuffling nearby, almost as if he were searching for something in the dark. He wasn't making a lot of noise, but as I heard the clicking of footsteps in the hallway, I put a hand on what I hoped was his shoulder to quiet him.

He paused as the footsteps approached, and continued without slowing.

Out of the darkness, two hands cupped my face, and then I felt lips pressed against mine. Just as quickly as they appeared, they were gone. As were the hands.

"You're a genius, Kris," Alec whispered.

I heard a soft click, before light shone from his penlight. It was only enough to illuminate what it was directed at, and would not be visible under the door, in the hallway. Even from what little I could see, I realized I had been right. We were in a janitorial closet.

Alec was rummaging through the uniforms hanging along the wall. I heard him muttering under his breath, but I couldn't understand what he was saying.

"Alec?" I whispered as I joined him. "What are you looking for?"

"The maintenance guys will have keys."

Of course! Of all the rooms for me to find unlocked, it wound up being a useful one. I really was a genius.

I helped Alec search the pockets of the uniforms. When that search turned up empty, he spun around to shine the light around the room. Cleaning supplies and tools filled the cluttered space. Along the wall next to the door, was a peg board. With keys.

Alec snatched them. It was a big ring with dozens of keys in various shapes and sizes.

"I have no idea which one is for the office we need," he muttered. "It's going to take a while to try them all out."

And if someone spotted us before we could get in…

We looked at each other, the weight of our dilemma setting in. But we had come this far. There was no going back now.

"Now what?" I asked.

Outside, in the hallway, we could hear voices approaching, and Alec flicked off the flashlight.

"Probably just a few kids…"

"…snuck back into their rooms…"

"Waste of time…"

I stepped closer to Alec, dropped my voice. "How long will they look for us?"

"Not long. She didn't know who we were. They'll figure we were just a couple of kids sneaking around. Used to happen all the time. We'll just wait for them to give up the search."

I wanted to ask what we'd do if they decided to look in here, but bit my tongue because I didn't want to hear his answer. Of course, we would do what we needed to do. For survival.

I only hoped we could get out of there without testing the combat moves I'd loved to practice with Nathan. Real life wasn't as fun.

CHAPTER 21

No one invaded our hideout. The voices in the hallway moved away. For good measure, we stayed in the closet for an additional twenty minutes before Alec cracked the door open. His head swung back and forth before he stepped out into the hallway, and he waved for me to follow.

There was a chance that the security guards were on some sort of high alert now, so we needed to be extra careful. And super quick.

Our dash to the administrative office took barely thirty seconds. Finding the right key took a lot longer.

As Alec tried one, after another, after another, I kept watch. Each time he had to switch keys, the knot in my stomach tightened.

It was taking too long. If the security guards made rounds, surely one of them would be coming by soon. One of them would catch us—

"Got it!" Alec swung the door open and pushed me inside ahead of him. He shut the door and locked it behind us.

The emergency lights in the hallway did little to illuminate the room. I stood just inside the entrance as my eyes adjusted to the dark. Alec brushed by me, having already spotted what he was looking for.

"Over here," he said, opening the top drawer of a tall filing cabinet. There were two others next to the one he was going through, and I picked one. Opening the top drawer, I squinted at the files inside.

"Here." Alec tossed me another small penlight.

"What if the file's not under my name?" I asked. What if they knew me by another name? A name I didn't know?

"It's possible," Alec murmured as he shuffled through files. "Look at the pictures. Everyone will have a picture."

A solid ten minutes passed without either of us finding anything that looked remotely like a file on me. Shutting the third drawer, I sighed heavily.

It was pointless. There was nothing here. We weren't going to find out the truth about my background, about who I was. The truth wasn't where we were looking.

Alec moved to a desk on the other side of the room, and began rummaging through the papers on top, and then the drawers. I moved on to the last, and probably worthless, drawer in my cabinet.

It didn't open. I knelt down to get a closer look at it, and saw that it had a key hole on the front.

"Alec?" I called over my shoulder. "You find any keys that might fit a cabinet lock?"

I heard him rummage through a drawer. Finding what he was looking for, he came to my side and wordlessly dropped to one knee beside me. He had a small key in his hand, and slipped it into the lock. It clicked, and we slid the drawer open.

One manila envelope lay at the bottom of the drawer. I glanced at Alec before picking it up. My hands trembled as I lifted the flap and withdrew a thick stack of papers. There was no picture, and I avoided looking at the pages closer, suddenly afraid to know if it was my file.

I handed them to Alec, and walked away. With my back to him, I asked, "Is it me?"

My question was met with silence for what felt like an eternity before Alec's guarded voice reached me. "It's you."

"Well?"

"You want to see?"

I kept my back turned, shook my head. "You do it."

The only sounds I heard were from the shuffling of the pages as Alec flipped through them. After a few moments, I gained some courage and turned to watch him. He was standing, the papers strewn across the top of the cabinet, with the penlight in one hand, illuminating my history held in his other hand. His finger traced down as he read the lines, and came to a stop.

When his eyes lifted to mine, I gulped.

"You want to see this?" he asked.

"Just tell me what I need to know."

Alec lifted the papers in his hand. "This chronicles your entire life, including all the information on the searches they conducted after Nathan took you."

"Okay…"

"Apparently they put that Lillian chick in charge of finding you," he added, then hesitated like he was unsure how much to tell me. "They converted her for that specific purpose."

My heart sunk. I'd suspected it, and now I knew.

That meant they've been changing Kala to Skotadi for at least six years. How many others had been changed, like her?

Though alarming, that was the least of my worries now. There was something there Alec was afraid to tell me. Something that had caused those shadows in his eyes.

"You know you were created by the Skotadi," he started as if easing me in to bad news. "Hade's four demigods all contributed to your creation. A hybrid created with all four of their bloodlines was your father."

So not five as Micah had suggested. And not Hecate's bloodline. I supposed it should have made me feel better to know that I had no connection to Micah. But there was more. I could tell from Alec's guarded posture, and that made me nervous. "What else?"

"They have listed who your birthmother was."

My breath caught. *Birthmother?* I hadn't even given the idea any thought. I had always assumed that she was one of the demigods, but if Alec had said that all four of Hade's demigods had created my father, then who had my mother been? A poor, unsuspecting human?

Or one that they had forced into helping them?

Crossing to where Alec stood, I took the files from him, and read down the first paper. Apparently, my birthday wasn't what I'd always celebrated. According to this, I had turned eighteen months ago. My birthplace was some place I couldn't pronounce. Next to birthmother was the name...*Hecate.*

I lifted my eyes to Alec. "Hecate?"

He looked troubled, avoiding eye contact like he didn't know how to respond.

"Hecate's my birthmother? What…"

What does this mean? For a moment, I couldn't process anything. Somewhere, churning in my head, were thoughts. Bad, bad thoughts.

No, this can't be happening…

Alec's eyes finally met mine. He gripped my shoulders like he knew I was struggling to put it all together. "Your mother was a goddess, Kris."

It took several moments for his words to sink in, for me to register what they meant. If my mother was a goddess, then…

"Kris, you're a demigod," Alec said, piecing my scattered thoughts together for me.

I was a demigod. The demigod created by the goddess of magic. I was capable of manipulating magic—an Incantator. As a demigod, I was this world's strongest Incantator.

My eyes snapped up to Alec's, which were already on me, watching me carefully. "Am I the Incantator?"

He didn't answer.

"Alec?" My voice rose in panic. "Does this mean I'm *the* Incantator?"

He didn't get the chance to answer, if he were ever going to anyway. We both whipped our heads around to the sound of pounding on the door. The handle rattled as someone tried to turn it. A second later, a bright white light spilled through the window in the door and canvased the room.

"Come on," Alec whispered as he grabbed my hand.

The light washed over us briefly before we moved beyond its reach. But we'd already been spotted. There was a shout from the other side of the door. "In here!"

With no time to look for another way out, Alec lifted the desk chair and hurled it into the wall of windows. At that moment, the sound of shattering glass was heaven to my ears.

"Go." Alec guided me toward our escape route.

I looked out and recoiled. "Alec, it's like a two story drop."

The land below sloped down and away from the building, and though we were technically still on the ground floor, the ground on this side was a lot farther down.

Alec looked down and saw what I saw. "Shit."

With a furtive glance over his shoulder toward the door, where we could now hear multiple voices, Alec swung his leg over the edge. He gripped a hold of the windowsill and lowered himself down before dropping the rest of the way to the ground. He landed easily enough and waved up to me, motioning for me to do the same.

"I've got you, Kris!"

As I lifted my shirt and tucked the file that held all the truths of my life into the waistband of my jeans, the door burst open behind me. A single Skotadi rushed into the room as I quickly swung a leg over the ledge. I didn't have the time to get turned all the way around before he grabbed me. The second I lifted my face to his, I saw the recognition register in his eyes.

He knew exactly who I was.

He faltered briefly, enabling me to swing my other leg over the ledge. His hand still had a firm grip on my arm, and after his initial shock wore off, he started to pull me inside.

Below me, I heard Alec cursing and I imagined he was attempting nothing short of scaling the side of the building. He was too far below to be of any help to me.

It was all up to me.

I closed my eyes and thought of fire. Feeling the familiar tingling in my palm, I opened my eyes. The smile on my face alerted the Skotadi, a second before the baseball sized ball of fire exploded in his face.

He let go of me and staggered back, bumping into the desk. Behind him, two more Skotadi filed into the room. They looked from their companion to me, and charged. I had another ball of fire ready and rocketed into the center of the room, engulfing the desk and blocking them from coming any closer.

I swung around, grabbing the window sill, and lowered myself down as Alec had done.

"Come on. I got you," I heard him say.

With one last look at the Skotadi scurrying around the room, attempting to extinguish the now fully engulfed fire, I let go. Alec's arms encircled me, softening my awkward landing.

"Good?" he asked. When I nodded, he grabbed my hand and took off at a run.

I glanced over my shoulder as we rounded the side of the building, saw the orange glow from the fire, and permitted myself a little smile.

I did that!

The fence seemed farther away than I remembered and, even though we were running full speed, I swore it took twice as long to cross the open yard. With every step we took, I expected a small army of Skotadi to intercept us, but as we got farther and farther from the building with no one stopping us, I realized we were going to make it.

As we climbed through the hole in the fence, crossing to the other side, the sirens started behind us. They were a distant wail by the time we reached the car. No one intercepted us there either, and Alec peeled out onto the empty road. Stealing glances out the rear window, I assured myself that no one was following us.

Only after several miles were placed between us and the orphanage did I finally start to calm down. Barely.

I lifted my hand, watched as it shook uncontrollably in front of me.

"Hey." Alec grabbed my hand in his, gave it a gentle squeeze. "That was awesome back there."

Afraid to speak just yet, I merely nodded.

We didn't speak for thirty minutes, before I thought I finally *could* speak again.

"He saw me, Alec," I said. "That Skotadi recognized me."

Alec was silent for a long time. "We can't stay here," he finally said. "They'll be looking for us."

"Do they know where you live?"

"No."

Another long silence passed before I asked, "Where are we going to go?"

"I don't know," he admitted solemnly.

I wanted to suggest returning to West Virginia, to Nathan

and the others, but I didn't think Alec would go for it. On the other hand, it might end up being our only option. Where we would go wasn't as important now as just leaving. Our first priority was to get out of Aspen. Fast.

We dove into a discussion on our preparations to leave: what to pack, who would pack what so that we could do it quickly, what to tell Tenner. Fortunately, he was gone for the night, so we only needed to leave a note.

On the surface, I was preoccupied with our plans, but in the back of my mind, I obsessed about everything I'd just learned.

Demigod...

Incantator...

I was both. All rolled up into one gigantic wrecking ball waiting to be swung at the world. The more I thought about it, the more sure I was. But I didn't accept it. I'd never accept it.

While I knew I was right, I held onto a small sliver of denial.

"You know," Alec said, breaking through my thoughts. I hadn't realized until then that we had both fallen silent. For how long? I wondered. "You're probably the most pure, potentially strongest, demigod to ever exist?"

Despite the dim lighting inside the car, I knew Alec got a good shot of my narrowed eyes and tight lips.

"You'll be capable of things that none of us could dream of doing," he continued in an eerily calm voice, not seeming to notice that his words were rattling me to my core.

Didn't he think I already knew that? Did he think it was cool? Because I sure as hell didn't.

I didn't want to be this. Any of this. I sure as hell didn't want to be capable of doing things others could only dream of. Especially when that meant destroying everything and everyone I loved.

"It's why you're developing faster than me. Than Micah. Why your specialties are coming in faster, and stronger, and better than—"

"Enough already!"

He shot me a perplexed look before facing the road again. He didn't say anything as he turned into Tenner's neighborhood and pulled to the curb in front of the house. His hand moved to the door but paused when he saw me sitting motionless in my seat.

"I don't want it," I croaked, swallowing the tickle in my throat that warned me of the tears not far behind.

Alec shifted so that he was now leaning across the console. With one hand, he turned my face to his. His eyes were clouded, with no trace of the ornery Alec I knew. "I know. I'm sorry. I shouldn't have—"

"Everything is spiraling out of my control," I murmured. "I'm powerless to stop it."

"Maybe not." I heard the hopefulness in his voice, but it didn't rub off on me. "Look, Kris, we'll find a way to get you out of this mess. I know we will. But right now, we have to go."

I nodded, taking a deep breath and preparing myself, once again, to run. I was so tired of running.

The springs under my seat creaked as Alec leaned onto it, placing one hand just to the side of my thigh. I felt his breath on my cheek just before he planted a soft lingering kiss to my temple. "I'm not going to let anything happen to you," he said. "We'll get through this, okay?"

"Okay."

"Good." He reached across me to open the car door for me, since I was apparently incapable of doing anything to help myself at this point. "Now, come on. Get out."

As soon as my feet hit the pavement, I was good. For the most part. Sure, I was overwhelmed, and confused, and scared, but that wasn't going to go anywhere. Now, I had to focus on getting out of Colorado and away from the mob of Skotadi likely already searching for us.

Alec met me on the sidewalk and I gave him a look that let him know I was okay. He grabbed my hand, and this time, I had no reservations about it. If anything, I welcomed his touch, as it was the only thing grounding me at the moment.

It was a short walk from the car to the front porch. As we approached, a dark shadow in the shape of a man rounded the side of the house, walking toward us.

"Alec," I whispered.

"I see him." He squeezed my hand, and together we turned, walking quickly back to the car.

A second shadow was waiting for us there. As it stepped forward to intercept us, Alec braced, ready for attack, or ready to attack.

Not me. I knew that shape. I would recognize it anywhere. As he stepped closer, close enough to see his face, my pulse accelerated out of excitement and fear. I wanted to run, but I wasn't sure if it was from him, or to him.

To keep from doing either, I planted my feet firmly on the ground, and asked, "What are you doing here?"

He didn't answer as he took a step closer. I sensed Alec relaxing beside me, and knew the moment he also realized who it was.

"Took you long enough," Alec muttered.

I turned and gaped at Alec. "What? Did you—? Did you call him?"

Alec looked equally appalled when he looked down at me. "Seriously, Kris?"

A voice behind us demanded my attention. "No. We found you." I turned as Micah joined us on the sidewalk, with Callie beside him. Micah kept his eyes on me warily, like he would a momma grizzly with a few cubs, as he motioned to Callie. "We figured you were with Alec, and Callie remembered that he was from Colorado. The closer we got, the stronger I felt your presence. It was like a map that led us straight to you."

"Wow, that soul mate shit sure is something, isn't it?" Alec muttered, but I ignored him.

I backed away from Micah, putting as much distance between us as I could. When he took another step closer, I turned to run, and crashed into Nathan. I turned again, and backpedaled into the street, away from both of them.

"Stay away," I said to no one in particular, but looking at Nathan.

"Kris, it's okay," Micah crooned.

I shook my head rapidly. No, no, it wasn't okay. It was so far from okay.

"Stay away from me!" They didn't understand who I was, what I had learned tonight, what I would be capable of. How dangerous I would be to both of them. Unless…

I remembered the discussion Micah and I'd had about Incantation. That had been weeks ago, but I remembered there being something off about the way he'd looked at me at that moment. And the day in the warehouse, when we'd found the Skotadi's room and he mentioned Incantators. There had been this way he'd looked at me then, as if we'd shared a secret I wasn't even aware of.

I hadn't been aware until about an hour ago.

"Did you know?" I asked Micah. Perhaps it was the harsh tone I used, or maybe my eyes were surging, because I was pissed, so pissed, but Micah looked too stunned to do much more than gape at me.

"Did you know what I was?" I growled, and this time, I knew my eyes were burning.

"Not right away. I figured it out."

"When?"

His eyes lowered to the ground, a sign I took as an admission of guilt. He'd known long enough that he could have, and should have, told me.

"How could you not tell me?" I screeched. It took all the willpower I had left to not rip his damn head off. I didn't even let him answer before I turned my attention to the next victim of my rage.

"Did you know?" I asked Nathan between clenched teeth.

I'd never imagined a moment in which Nathan would

actually look intimidated, especially not of me, but in this moment, he sure was close. And he was hesitant. That was all it took for me to lose it.

I wasn't sure if I was more heartbroken or angry. "How could you?" I looked back and forth between the two of them, the two who had known the truth before me, and had kept me from it. I was mad at Micah, but Nathan? His deception just hurt.

Nathan had been quiet this whole time, but after seeing the devastation on my face, jumped into action. Before I could move out of the way, he was standing in front of me. His hands came down on my shoulders, holding me in place. "I didn't know, Kris," he said softly. "Not until a few days ago, when Micah told me."

I tried to turn my head, with a steely glare intended for Micah, but Nathan's grip shifted to my chin, preventing me from doing so.

"It doesn't matter," he continued.

"How can you say that?" I shrieked. "I'm spiraling out of control, Nathan, and it's happening so fast I can't stop it. I won't be able to stop it. You...you can't stop it! I'm a demigod...and I'm the Incantator!"

"Maybe being the Incantator is a good thing?" he suggested. "Being the one that brings an end to our kind? Maybe it's not as bad as it sounds. Maybe it means an end to the war once and for all? Maybe it means we'll all be freed of our duty to fight it?"

I shook my head against his suggestions. How could he be so naïve? Of course, the Incantator wasn't going to be something good. There was a reason they were taught to fear this person—

to fear me.

"Kris..." It was Micah's voice, closer now, which induced that familiar churning inside of me. Stronger than before. Stronger than ever. Again, I attempted to stare him down, but Nathan stopped me.

He took my hand in his, and with a warning glare of his own tossed in Micah's direction, steered me off the street and around the side of the house. Out of sight of Micah...and Micah out of sight of me. I would have been grateful, if I weren't so afraid of being alone with Nathan.

I tried to step around him, to put a safe amount of distance between us, but he pushed me up against the side of the house and forcibly held me there. My eyes lifted to his.

"What are—"

My inquiry was cut short by Nathan's mouth crashing into mine, and the question gave way to a tiny whimper against his lips, the reason he'd brought me here, the anger I had felt just a moment ago all forgotten.

A primal need took over. I hooked my fingers through the loops at the waist of his jeans and tugged him to me frantically, longing to feel him against me, and wanting him to feel me. A low guttural sound came from somewhere deep in his throat, and he gripped my waist, pushing me back until I was wedged tightly between him and the wall. Our bodies connected at all the right places, and not even a breath of air could slip between us.

He kissed me hungrily, deeply, like he feared it would be the last and he had to make the most of what we had. His hands slid from my waist, slowly trailed up my sides, and came to a rest wrapped up in my hair. With a gentle tug, Nathan tipped my head to the side so that he could bury his face in my neck as we both fought to catch our breaths.

I sighed with a smile on my lips. "Miss me?" I whispered teasingly.

He made an unintelligible sound just before finding my mouth again. He kissed me hard once more, before easing into a sweet, soft, barely-there touch of his lips against mine. Then he shifted to lean his forehead against mine, his eyes piercing when they fell on mine.

"You have no idea," he murmured huskily. Then he grinned, reminding me of how he could make my insides flip-flop with one look. Just as fast as it came, the grin faded. "Kris..."

He started to pull away to look at me better. I tightened my hold on him, prevented him from moving.

"Don't," I pleaded. The last thing I wanted was to fight. Not again, not after the night I've had. Nathan's kiss had temporarily stunted my aggravation and fear, and I wanted to keep it that way. Before I had to return to reality.

He peeled my hands off the back of his neck and held them at our sides. "I just want to know why."

I averted my eyes.

"Kris, why did you come here?" He shifted so that he stood in my line of sight, forcing me to look at him.

"I'm sorry," I offered meekly.

"Why?"

"It's not Alec, if that's what you're wondering." He had to know that. Had to know that he was the one I wanted, and would always want, even if my actions didn't always portray that.

His throat jumped. "It didn't look that way in the car."

He saw that?

I suddenly felt a weight on my chest, making it hard to breath. "It wasn't what it looked like," I gushed. "I literally just found out what I was an hour ago. He was consoling me. That's it."

"Then why did you come here?"

I dropped my eyes to the ground. I wanted to tell him, I really did, but I didn't know if I could. I was afraid of facing the truth, or his reaction to it. But, then, he had seen me that day. He knew what had happened, what had almost happened. Surely, he had to know that I was changing, and that was why I ran. Right?

"Kris." He said my name sharply, using a finger to lift my chin as he did. "Why did you leave?"

"I feel myself changing." I stared at him, every bit of confidence portrayed on my face fake. Truth: I was scared to death.

He saw through my charade, as always. Tenderness softened his features when he figured it out. "So you ran to avoid Micah," he concluded.

"And you."

"And me? Why?"

"Nathan, I almost killed you. I couldn't run the risk of that happening again."

He choked back a laugh. "You didn't—"

"Yes, I did. And it would have happened again. These episodes are getting harder to control. I know I can't hurt Micah because the future of humanity is at stake, but my heart and soul would be at stake if I hurt you. I wouldn't be able to breathe. Life would cease to exist…for me."

I saw the trace of a smile. "Exaggerate much?"

"Nathan, I'm serious," I whined.

"I know you are, but Kris, I'm not going to stay away from you, or let you run away from me." He enclosed me in his arms. "I want to help you. I want you to let me help you."

I rolled my head. He made it sound like it was easy. It wasn't.

He squeezed me tighter. "I'm not going to let you face this alone. You say life would cease to exist if anything happened to me? Well, I feel the same way about you, which means I'm going to be there with you every step of the way, and you're going to have to deal with it."

He felt the same way about me? That revelation should have put a smile on my face, but all I managed was a frown. "You're impossible to argue with," I muttered.

"Yeah," he agreed automatically. "The sooner you realize that, the better."

"And what about the next time I lose control?"

Nathan loosened his hold on me slightly as he pondered my question, and I could see that he was trying really hard to come up with a solution. Seeing the determination on his face nearly forced a smile out of me.

"Does Alec have any ideas? Suggestions?" he finally asked, with a hint of reluctance.

The smile was impossible to hold back now. "Seeking Alec's help, huh?"

Nathan shrugged like he wasn't happy about it, but knew Alec's assistance was necessary. "You're the one who came here for his help. He have anything useful to offer?"

"We've been working on some things."

"Then, maybe he should come back with us." He paused and I saw how much he hated to say those words, so much so that he felt the need to add, "Only because he can help you."

He looked at me and waited. For me to agree? For me to put up another argument? He looked as unsure as I felt.

"I'm scared, Nathan," I eventually said. "What if this doesn't work? What if we can't find a way to stop this in time? What—"

"Hey," he interrupted. "Don't think like that, okay? I need you to be positive. I need you to fight this."

"What if I can't?"

"You *can*. And I'm going to help. I'm not giving up, and I'm not going to let you give up either."

I dropped my head to hide the tears that sprung up in my eyes—from the hopelessness and fear that I felt, but mostly from Nathan's words. He was so sure I could do it. He was counting on me, and I didn't even know if I could count on myself.

"Kris," he said, lifting my chin and forcing me to look at him. With his thumb, he brushed away a tear that had slipped free, and then pressed his lips to my forehead.

The sweet and soothing gesture only brought on a body-wracking sob that I couldn't choke back. Nathan pulled me into his arms as a few more shook me, until I got them under control. Being in his arms again reminded me just how much I had missed him and just how much I had come to care about him…and love him. The more he did things like this, supported me as he was now, the more sure I felt.

The memories of what I had done with Alec, even if they had been done in a Skotadi state of mind, were eating me up inside. How could I have been so stupid? How could I have not controlled it, controlled myself?

Would Nathan understand? Would it even matter to him? It wasn't like we were together. Not really. Technically, we were both free to do as we wished.

Then again, I was sure my act of discretion with Alec would bother him, solely because of who it had been with.

Then again, he had been the one to suggest I explore the feelings he knew I had for Alec. Maybe he already suspected something had happened between Alec and me. Something worse than what actually did.

"Nathan..."

"Hmm?"

"I need to tell you something."

His expression was somber when he leaned back to look down at me. Surely, by my tone, he knew that I wasn't about to share good news with him. His fingers dug into my waist in anticipation.

Like he already knew...

I just had to do it. Like a band-aid. Quick and painful. "I made out with Alec," I blurted, paused, then like it would matter, amended, "Well, I didn't, not really. Skotadi-me did, but I remember it, so it's like I did do it."

His lips parted and I felt his heavy breath against my cheek, just before he shifted. Though fractional, I detected his grip loosening around my waist. I tried not to let the fact that he was pulling away bother me, and tried to get through saying what I had to say before I lost my chance.

"Afterwards," I continued quickly, "what I figured out only confirmed what I already knew, I just might not have realized that I knew." I paused, and jabbed a finger into his chest once, hard. "And, you know what? I blame you for that, because you insisted that I didn't know."

"Kris—"

I shook my head rapidly, silencing him. "You can't tell me anymore what I should feel, what I should do, because I know what I—"

My poorly prepared speech was cut off, in a good way, as Nathan's lips crashed into mine, stifling whatever words were next. Not that they would have mattered with the way I had been rambling. And all thought was lost to me now anyway. All I registered at the moment was that he was kissing me.

And boy was he kissing me. But it didn't last long. Apparently, he had things to say too, though I would have been just fine not talking. His mouth opened to say something.

A loud thud against the wall behind me shattered the moment, and his words slipped away.

"What was that?" I asked.

Nathan was already looking around the corner, toward the front of the house. "Sounded like it came from inside. They're not out front anymore. They must be inside."

"But what thumped?"

I hoped it hadn't been Micah's head, steered into the wall by Alec. Unfortunately, it was a real possibility.

Micah shouting for us from the front porch a moment later eliminated that fear. But then a new fear twisted my gut when I heard the panic in his voice.

Nathan hurried around the side of the house, pulling me after him. "What is it?"

"Skotadi," Micah answered, his eyes frightful. "I can sense them. A dozen or more, close, and coming fast!"

Nathan bounded up the steps two at a time. I ran after him, into the house, as Alec emerged from the hallway with several guns in his hands. He tossed one to Nathan, another to Micah. He looked at me and raised his eyebrows.

I held my hand out for the last gun.

Distantly, as if in another dimension, I heard the sounds of metal clanging and bullets dropping to the floor as the guys quickly loaded their weapons. I moved slower, on autopilot, as I tried to remember what I knew about guns. Not much, unfortunately, and what I did know was lost amongst all the panicky thoughts in my head.

This was it...

They were coming. A dozen of them.

The odds were against us. Again.

"Here." Nathan took the still unloaded gun from my hands and handed me his loaded one. I watched as he opened the chamber and smoothly glided the bullets into place. Finished, he turned to me, his unspoken question visible in his eyes.

"I'm okay," I said.

He looked uncertain, but nodded. "Stay with me."

That was a guarantee. I wanted no one other than Nathan at my side. And Callie…

"Callie!" I spun in a circle, searching for her. She was gone. Turning to Alec and Micah, I asked, "Where's Callie?"

"Snuck her out the back," Alec answered. "They don't know she's here. At least she can get away."

"The car's just down the street. If she can get to it, she'll be fine," Micah added.

"*If* she can get to it!" I snarled, and nearly hurled across the room at him.

If they caught her…

I couldn't fathom what might happen to her.

Nathan grabbed a hold of my arm. "She'll be fine."

Held back by Nathan, all I could do was glare at Micah. But he wasn't paying attention to me anymore.

"They're here," he whispered.

The room was deathly quiet as we listened, and waited. From behind me, glass shattered, and I spun around. I expected to see a group of Skotadi climbing through the windows, but instead watched as two black metallic objects rolled across the floor and came to a stop at our feet.

My first thought was grenades, and from the guys' reactions as they scattered, I suspected I might be right. Nathan grabbed my hand, pulled me after him. Just ahead of us, I saw Micah and Alec running for the rear of the house, toward the back door.

Nothing exploded. The devices hissed open, emitting a fine mist that filled the room within seconds.

Alec and Micah had nearly reached the door, but were moving slow, like they were stuck in an invisible pit of quick sand and sinking into the floor. My own legs had turned to jelly and my vision blurred as the room whirled around me. I felt Nathan's hand holding onto mine and I tried to squeeze it, to signal to him that something was wrong, but my muscles wouldn't work.

What was this mist? And what was it doing to us?

I wondered if this was it, if we were going to die, together but alone, on Tenner's cold kitchen floor.

Just as I came to grudgingly accept my fate, the back door opened, and a familiar face stepped into my line of sight. Familiar, but unwelcome. Especially since she had her evil claws curled around Callie's neck.

Why won't this bitch leave us alone?

Using every ounce of strength I had left, I lunged for Lillian, with every intention of inflicting serious pain, but my legs had other intentions. As they gave out from under me, a pair of strong arms caught me, and I was lowered gently to the floor instead of crashing to it. With a look over my shoulder, I saw Nathan's eyes droop shut.

I lifted my gaze, settled it on Callie and, as she faded from my sight, I couldn't help but wonder if it would be the last time I saw her.

CHAPTER 22

I was pulled back to consciousness by the sound of Nathan's voice. Disoriented and stiff, I lifted my head as my surroundings slowly came into focus around me.

I was in a room—a small, cold, poorly lit space that smelled like damp earth. I was reminded of the last time I'd been held hostage by the Skotadi. Everything, right down to the ropes binding me to the chair I was sitting on, was familiar.

As I looked around the room, I realized all of us were bound in the same manner—ankles tied to chair legs and hands pulled behind our backs. Four of us made a sort of square, all facing each other—Nathan to my right, Micah to my left, and Alec directly across from me.

Callie was missing.

"Kris?" I turned my head to the right, toward Nathan, and blinked. With disheveled hair and bloodshot eyes, he looked as rough as I felt. "Kris, can you loosen your restraints at all?" he asked me slowly, purposefully, as if he knew my brain wasn't working properly yet.

I strained against the rope binding my arms to the chair. Immediately, I knew there was no getting out of them. Same went with the rope around my ankles. In fact, I was pretty sure my toes were going numb.

"They're too tight," I told Nathan.

"What if you go all Skotadi-ish?" Micah asked quietly from his seat.

"I'll be one extremely pissed off, but still tied up, girl," I said, earning a snort from Alec.

"Her strength doesn't increase, moron," Alec piped in. "She's not The Hulk."

No one said anything for a long time after that. It seemed that I had been their last hope, and had left them all clueless as to what to do now.

"Wait!" I exclaimed when a brilliant idea came to me. I glanced back and forth between Micah and Alec with a smile. "Fire."

I could conjure fire…and burn the ropes.

I closed my eyes, pictured a fire building in my palm, nothing too big, nothing that would burn us all alive. Just enough to get free. The tingle never came like it should have, and I tried harder, squeezing my eyes tighter.

I'd done it under pressure before, at the orphanage. So why wasn't it working now?

I opened my eyes and glanced at Micah, hoping he had a suggestion.

He shook his head solemnly. "It's the charm." His head tilted forward, and I followed his gaze to the white stone dangling from my neck. "It's blocking you."

"I got one too," Alec said.

"We all do," Micah added. Nodding his head at Nathan, he

said, "Except for him."

"I'm the only one without super powers," Nathan grumbled.

We fell silent after that. If we couldn't use our specialties...

We were at their mercy.

I wondered what they had planned for us. For Callie. I wondered where she was, if she was somewhere better than us. Or worse?

"They're coming," Micah suddenly mumbled a warning.

Seconds later, the door opened, and Lillian entered with her entourage. Five of them filled the room, surrounding us from all sides. Lillian zeroed in on Nathan, and I tensed in my seat, fearful of her intentions. Nathan stared at her, appearing more angry than concerned, as she approached him.

"I told you I'd be the one to find you, baby," she said to him, the term of endearment sounding more like a taunt. She produced a knife—a sparkly, diamond-coated one—and traced the tip up his neck to his chin, forcing his head back to avoid being cut. I held my breath, watching helplessly as the blade grazed dangerously over his skin.

Just one prick, one scrape…

I wanted to scream at her to stop, but bit my protests back, not wanting to cause her to flinch and pierce Nathan's skin. Instead, I closed my eyes from the sight in front of me.

Considering how many people were crammed into the small room, it was chillingly quiet. The silence only reminded me of how powerless I was to stop Lillian.

We were all powerless. Even Micah, with his ability to heal diamond injury, wouldn't be able to help. Not strapped to the chair as he was.

We *had* to get free. Before Lillian killed Nathan. And that sure seemed to be her intent.

"It's a shame, really," she said, and I finally opened my eyes, hoping to see that she was done toying with Nathan's life. She wasn't. "Such a shame, what I'm going to have to do to you."

Her voice didn't sound regretful at all. I wondered if she felt anything, or if turning evil did away with the ability to feel emotions. I knew I never wanted to find out.

Nathan stared at her wordlessly, and I wondered what he saw. The girl he used to love? Could he see any of her left in that shell of a body?

"You really screwed up when you didn't kill me before," Lillian said to him quietly. "You shouldn't have hesitated, you know?"

"I won't make that mistake again," Nathan gritted between his teeth. Any more movement on his part and the knife would likely pierce his skin.

I silently willed him to keep quiet and still.

"You won't have another chance," Lillian responded ominously. I saw her cock her head to the side, but her face remained hidden from my view. "It really is too bad."

With impressive speed, Lillian lurched forward to press her mouth to Nathan's. As much of a surprise as it was to all of us, no one was more shocked than Nathan. He pulled back, but restrained to the chair as he was, there was only so far he could go. Her lips stayed planted firmly on his until she decided the dysfunctional kiss had lasted long enough. She gripped a handful of his hair as she pulled away, to hold him in place.

"Hmm…I've missed that," she said without an ounce of emotion. Surely, the woman was incapable of it. To not have some response to kissing Nathan was unfathomable to me, even if the kiss had been rather disturbing.

Nathan stared through her as if it had never happened.

Finally, Lillian stood and turned, as if noticing the rest of us for the first time. "Oh, I'm sorry," she sneered. Her eyes bored into mine, the gold ring around her irises glowing. "I'm sure you didn't want to see that."

I hadn't actually, but I wouldn't give her the satisfaction of admitting it. Besides, as disturbing as the whole thing had been to watch, I was glad the knife was no longer pressed to Nathan's neck.

"You're probably all wondering what you're doing here." She clasped her hands together, and the sound echoed around the room, chilling me to the bone. She pointed at Micah. "You," she said to him. "You are going to die tonight. And you—" She pointed at me with the knife, "are going to kill him."

I stared at the shiny blade in her hand, and felt the blood drain from my face when I realized I had seen it before. In my dreams. It was the very knife I killed Micah with in my dreams.

They hadn't been simple dreams, but a prophecy. And it was coming true.

It was going to happen. I would become the monster I'd feared I would. Despite all we had done to fight it, I would eventually fulfill the destiny I had been running from. The others—except Micah—didn't know what I knew. As Nathan and Alec voiced their disbelief, I shared a look with Micah. The despair in his eyes matched mine.

Even then, knowing what I knew from the prophecy and considering my dislike of Micah, I knew I could never kill him. Not really.

"It's not going to happen," I spoke above the others, addressing Lillian coldly. "You're wasting your time."

"*Biding* my time," she countered. "Because, you see, one of them will die tonight." She waved her arm around, motioning to both Nathan and Micah. "The choice of who is yours. The longer you take to decide, the more this one will suffer."

Her dark gaze fell on Nathan and, as if on cue, the giant standing by the door stepped forward. Before any of us knew what was coming, his fist shot out and connected with Nathan's face, snapping his head violently to the side. Blood sprayed from his nose, or mouth, or both—it was hard to tell.

A scream rose in my throat as I rocked in my chair. Despite my desperate pleas, the giant continued a vicious one-sided assault on a defenseless Nathan. He paused long enough to glance at me—to make sure I was watching?—just before he raised his knee and propelled it into Nathan's stomach.

Nathan crumbled forward, chin to his chest, held up only by the ropes binding him to the chair. From the way he was slumped, I suspected he might be unconscious, and I secretly hoped that was the case.

"Leave him alone," I begged.

With a harsh laugh, the big Skotadi grabbed a handful of Nathan's hair and lifted his head, forcing it back. My heart sank when I saw that his eyes were open.

"You want to see this?" Lillian asked. I knew she was talking to me, but I ignored her. All I could do was stare at Nathan.

I was forced to look away as the Skotadi's fist found its mark again, and again.

Lillian crouched in front of me, dangling the knife under my nose. "You can stop it."

I wished I could be like The Hulk, break these ropes, snatch the knife from her hand, and plunge it into her cold, unfeeling heart.

"I'll see to the end of you before this is over," I whispered menacingly.

Lillian's lips curled into something resembling a smile. "Stop," she ordered the Skotadi beating Nathan, but never taking her eyes off of mine. She looked smug. Like she'd somehow won.

"Kris."

I turned to the voice calling my name, to my right. Nathan—his nose bleeding, lip gashed, eye purple and swollen. Despite his physical injuries, and the pain he had to be in, his concern was for me. I couldn't imagine why.

"Don't," Alec mutter a warning. I wasn't sure who he was addressing, until he added, "She'll respond better to me."

My eyes shot across the room, finding his. From the grim look on his face, I realized what everyone else saw. My eyes. They must have been surging. My hatred for Lillian, my desire to see her destroyed, was fueling the rage, and the demon, inside of me.

Lillian shifted to block my view of Alec. "You want to kill me?" she taunted.

I refused to look at her, refused to let her urge me on. Yes, I wanted to kill her, but now was not the time. Now, I had to fight that desire with everything I had…before I turned my hatred for her on someone else in the room.

"Let it build," she sang, "and turn it on him." She swung her arm in Micah's direction.

From behind her, I heard Alec's voice, soft and calm. "Basketball, Kris. Basketball. You've done it before. You can do it again. You can fight it, and when you do, when the time is right, you'll have your chance with her."

At least Alec and I were thinking along the same line of thought. I would get my revenge, but at another time.

I squared my shoulders, and met Lillian's glare with a cold stare of my own. I wasn't about to let this bitch break me.

Her response was a frigid, knowing smile, like she thought she had me just where she wanted me. How gullible of her.

She stood and retreated, having given up this time. She called to the Skotadi and ushered them out the door ahead of her. Before shutting the door, she turned to me with a final message.

"We'll give you some time to think about your decision. Next time, it'll be worse." Her gaze fell on Nathan with those last few words, and I knew she had something terrible in store for him.

As the door shut, leaving the four of us alone again, I agonized over how much more Nathan could take, and how much more I could witness before I was forced to act.

And what exactly I would do.

* * *

They were gone long enough for Nathan to stop bleeding and for some of the swelling around his eye to subside. He sat up straight in his chair, quiet, but there. Sort of.

He lacked his usual air of confidence and determination, and that worried me.

If he lost hope in our chances…

I didn't want to think about that. Instead, I tried to come up with some sort of strategy while we were still together, conscious, and able.

One thing about his whole situation wasn't making sense to me, and I wondered if I had missed something important.

I understood that they had created me to kill Micah, but I'd always assumed that was only because they would need someone strong enough to kill a super-hybrid like him. Being helplessly strapped to the chair as he was now, anyone could take a coated knife to him. Why did it have to be me?

"I don't understand," I said, breaking the silence in the room. I turned my head toward Micah. "If they want you dead, why don't they just kill you? Why are they making me do it?"

Micah shrugged. "To fulfill the curse?"

"What?"

"Like Hecate is cursed to kill Asclepius if she ever reunites with him," he added, but he didn't sound so sure.

I shook my head. That made no sense. "Why would they create me to be your soul mate then? Who would kill their own soul mate?"

I hated that I was admitting to believing Micah's claims that we were soul mates. Hated it. I still wasn't completely convinced, but *if* he was right, why would they have done that?

Or maybe they didn't know Micah and I would be born with this link to each other. Maybe that was a defect in their plan. And maybe we could figure out how to use it against them.

"So that he would trust you enough to let you get close," Nathan muttered quietly. My head snapped around at his voice, and his eyes met mine reluctantly as he elaborated. "They hoped your Skotadi nature would take over, and when it did, he'd be close to you, and an easy kill."

Alec scoffed. "I'd say their plan has been working so far."

My eyes flicked to Micah's, and he met them with a wary smile, as if he knew the risk he had taken in getting close to me, and he accepted it. Even if that meant his own death.

I shook my head as I looked away.

"It's not because of the curse," Nathan added. Now, his gaze settled on Micah. "They know that if Kris does this, if she kills you, there will be no going back."

"They're trying to coerce me into going Skotadi?" I whispered.

"And *staying* Skotadi," Nathan added.

Sure, nothing like murder to seal a deal with the forces of evil, right? They knew my soul would never bounce back from that. *I* knew I would never bounce back from that.

If that had been their intentions—to get me close to Micah, so that I would ultimately kill him in a moment of Skotadi-rage, and never come out of that rage—then I was determined to beat them at their own game. There was a way, and I would find it.

They would lose. I would see to that.

I just hoped the cost wasn't too great.

* * *

It was probably two hours before they returned to beat on Nathan again. This time, we all knew what was coming, but it didn't make it any easier to watch. Or hear.

I kept my eyes closed most of the time, unable to watch the abuse he was taking, but I had no choice but to listen to each flesh-pounding, bone-cracking strike.

Lillian hadn't lied earlier. It was worse this time.

Tears fell faster and harder as my cries for mercy fell on deaf, uncaring ears. Only Lillian paid me any attention, and only to urge me to do something to end Nathan's suffering, urge me to do the last thing I could do.

Somehow, I funneled my rage down, buried it, as I stared unwavering through her. I didn't make eye contact, not because I was afraid of her, but because I was set on showing her that I would defy her.

"Do you want me to kill him?" she whispered to me. She cast a glance over her shoulder at the beating going on behind her. "I think another five minutes might do it."

"Stop," I seethed between clenched teeth, though my fierceness wouldn't matter. I couldn't do anything to her, not now, not tied up.

"You end it," she countered. "Do as I ask."

I gulped, fighting back the tears. How could I do this? How could I go on letting Nathan suffer like this? After all he had done for me…

But I couldn't kill Micah. I couldn't.

"Coward."

Through all the commotion, one word reached my ears. It came from across the room, and I looked up to see Alec glaring at the big Skotadi looming over Nathan.

For the time being, he stopped pummeling Nathan, but then, from the look in his eyes, I feared he would go after Alec next. "What did you call me?" he barked.

"A coward," Alec repeated unflinchingly, nodding his head in Nathan's direction. "It's so easy when he can't even defend himself. You've got him tied up. That makes you a coward."

The giant had been advancing on Alec as he spoke, but now turned his furious gaze back to Nathan. He took swift strides toward Nathan, angry determination in his eyes, and I wistfully wondered if Alec had managed to trick the Skotadi into letting Nathan loose. From the smug grin on Alec's face when he looked at me, I knew that had been his intention.

Too bad, from the looks of him, I didn't think Nathan would be able to mount much of an attack on his own. He could barely hold his own head up, let alone beat the Skotadi and rescue the rest of us.

I feared that Alec might have sealed Nathan's death by trying to help.

Part of me was relieved when Lillian blocked the Skotadi's path. "Are you really that stupid?" she demanded of him. "You can't let him go. *Ever.*" Her tone made it clear that she knew very well what Nathan was capable of, injured or not. She pointed a threatening finger at Alec. "You, shut up or you're next."

Alec's response was a smirk that suggested he didn't really care, and I shot him a warning with my eyes. It definitely wouldn't help us to have both of them hurt. With Nathan injured, we'd need Alec at the top of his game to make up for the slack.

If we ever managed to get out of this room.

For the time being, they were leaving us—leaving me with time to stew over my impossible decision—and we had to use that time to come up with some sort of plan. And if we couldn't, then what?

Kill Micah, or they killed Nathan? Ruin the world's hope of peace, or ruin mine? When put that way, the decision should have been obvious. Micah needed to survive this. For the better of everyone. If Nathan died, only my life would be ruined.

And if I killed Micah and released the Skotadi within, my life would be ruined anyway—with or without Nathan. Either way, I was doomed. But I wouldn't let everyone go down with me. They had a chance to live and be happy. I had to find a way to spare the ones I cared about most.

"Nathan?" I croaked, gazing worriedly at the top of his head. At my voice, he lifted his chin off his chest. One of his eyes was nearly swollen shut now, and the other was red with blood, but the fact that he was able to make some amount of eye contact was a relief.

"I'm fine, Kris," he said softly. Then, he contradicted his

words by lurching forward to spit a mouthful of blood on the floor. Rolling his head back, he tried to hide the pain I knew he was in. "I can go all day."

"No," I responded immediately. No, he couldn't. Not like this, and definitely not if it was going to get worse, as Lillian threatened.

"They're going to kill you," Micah said from his seat, as if scolding Nathan for letting them do such a thing.

"Oh?" Nathan glared across the room at Micah. "Would you rather Kris kill you instead?"

That response shut Micah up, for now, and if it weren't such a painful truth, it might have been funny. But I was in no mood to laugh.

"Nathan?" I said again, unable to force my voice much above a whisper. When his eyes reluctantly rolled to me, I spoke to him softly. "I can't let them do this to you."

His response was immediate and stoic. "You have to, Kris."

"Not if we can get out of here," Alec interrupted from his corner. I looked at him and noticed that his eyes were fixed on something beneath Nathan. As I followed his gaze, he asked, "See it?"

"What?" Nathan asked. He didn't have the view Alec and I had, and didn't see the shard of wood splintered from the leg of his chair. It hadn't been there before, and must have been caused by the most recent assault.

"By your right foot," Alec explained slowly, like he feared Nathan might have brain damage or something. "If you can get the rope on your ankle higher, you should be able to rub it against the splinter of wood there. Might saw through."

The splinter was about an inch above the ropes. As we all watched helplessly, a weak and bleeding Nathan pushed down on his toes, managing to raise the rope just enough for it to slide over the sharp piece of wood. He would have to work on it for some time, but it just might work.

Unfortunately, from the angle he had, he couldn't see what progress he was making, and had to rely on Alec to guide him through it—when to change direction, where to shift his foot, and when to saw away. After a few minutes, Nathan said, "It's getting looser."

That was the first time since I'd woken up in this room that I felt a glimmer of hope. We might make it. If he could get through, somehow get the rest of us free…

If anyone could do it, Nathan could.

Five minutes later, he proved me right, and slipped his foot free of its binds. Then we were faced with the problem of figuring out what to do next. It wasn't as if he could do much damage with one foot against a roomful of Skotadi.

"Can you break the splinter off?" Alec suggested.

Nathan blindly maneuvered his free foot against the leg of the chair. He glanced at Alec, who nodded. With a brisk swipe downward, Nathan broke the splinter from the chair leg. We all stared at it, amazed that this was working so far.

But then, I didn't know what we were going to do now. None of us could reach the splinter, and it would be in clear view of the Skotadi when they came back. In retrospect, breaking it loose might not have been smart.

Only Nathan appeared to have a plan. As he wrestled the sliver of wood with his foot, and managed to position it on top of his foot, I couldn't help but wonder what his plan was.

He looked at Alec pointedly. "Can you turn your chair around?"

Alec shuffled in his seat, managing to turn his back partially to Nathan. For Nathan, it was easier to scoot forward and meet Alec. Once they were lined up, Nathan lifted his foot and dropped the splinter into Alec's waiting hands.

After the successful exchange, they wordlessly scooted back to their positions. It had gone smoothly, and the Skotadi would have no idea that Alec was busy working on freeing himself behind his back.

All we had to do was wait for him to succeed. Hopefully before they returned and noticed that Nathan had one foot free.

* * *

We quietly discussed strategy as Alec worked. First, he would free Micah since he wasn't injured, then the two of them would free Nathan and me. After that, we only speculated as to what our next move would be.

There were no windows for us to sneak out of, and what awaited us outside the door was a mystery. Lillian was accompanied by four Skotadi that we knew of, but we couldn't be sure how many more were nearby. We didn't even know where we were. It could have been another underground compound that we'd have no way of knowing how to navigate, or a hut atop the highest peak of the Rocky Mountains.

The only thing we knew was that we had to do something.

I worried about Callie, and how we would find her. If she was nearby, at all.

She had gone through so much with me, suffered so much because of me. When we got out of here, I would find a way to get Callie back to her life, and keep her safe. That was a vow I was determined to see through, even if I doubted she would accept it.

She deserved better than this life—one of running and fighting and fearing the future. A girl like her should be looking forward to her future, not dreading it.

Not like I did.

Micah's warning interrupted my thoughts. A moment later, the door swung open and Lillian entered, along with her usual entourage.

I glanced frantically at Alec, who gave me a barely discernable shake of his head.

He wasn't through the ropes yet.

I felt Lillian's heavy gaze on me, and I turned my eyes away from Alec, but refused to look at her, despite her eyes boring into the top of my head.

"You going to make us do this again?" she eventually asked.

"You don't have to do this, Lillian," I said softly.

With a snort, she turned and waved her hand at the big Skotadi that had made Nathan his punching bag all night. As he closed in, I spoke to Lillian's back, "You used to love him, you know? You remember that?"

She spun to me, her face empty, eyes cold. "That was someone else. Not me."

"Only because the Skotadi changed you. Against your will, right?"

Her jaw set, and I knew I was on to something. I just wondered how far I could take it. "They helped me," she insisted.

"They used you," I returned, feeling suddenly brave. "To get to me. You were a pawn, and you still are."

"I'm a commander! And I am sick of waiting for you to do as I demand!" Her golden rings surged as she turned away from me in disgust. She held her hand out to the Skotadi standing by the door and he handed her a shiny black pistol. With her eyes leveled on me, she turned the gun on Nathan.

"No!" I screamed. "I'll do it! I'll do it!"

"I don't believe you," Lillian smirked and looked down the barrel of the gun at Nathan.

His eyes closed in anticipation.

"If you kill him you'll never get what you want," I threatened. "You'll have no leverage on me."

"No, but it would temporarily bring out your other half. The half of you that will happily do what I ask." She settled her sights on Nathan again. Her finger tightened on the trigger.

"I already said I'll do it!"

The blast was like a bomb going off, echoed through the room, striking my heart with a hollow dread.

No, no, no…

Nathan was still. So still that I wondered if I imagined the shift in his eyes. It wasn't until he finally blinked and lifted his head to Lillian, her smoking gun in his face, that I realized he was alive.

And Lillian had shot the wall behind him.

She turned to me expectantly. I knew I was surging—I felt it in every fiber of my body—and, from the look of triumph on her face, she knew it too.

"Cut her loose," she ordered the Skotadi closest to me.

My eyes remained on Lillian—the source of my anger—until the knife was placed in my hands. I turned it over, examining it, remembering how it had felt in my dream-hands. When I looked up again, I avoided Alec. I could feel his eyes on me, and knew that he would try to talk me out of doing what I had to do.

What a big part of me *wanted* to do. The other part of me was along for the ride as I slowly approached Micah where he sat restrained in his chair.

Should be easy.

So why were my hands shaking? Why were unwanted thoughts of freedom and love and happiness washing over me? And why was the boy sitting in the chair at my mercy smiling at me like he understood why I was about to kill him?

My hand wavered, and the knife dropped to my side.

"Do it." I glanced over my shoulder, saw Lillian hovering over Nathan with the gun in her hand.

Nathan was watching me with uncertainty, like he really hoped I had a plan. And Alec...the look he gave me meant something else. Something that I was supposed to understand. Something important.

His hand moved behind his back like he wanted me to see

something, but his hand was empty.

Empty, but *free*.

Lillian gave up her post by Nathan and crossed the room to me, the rage on her face growing with each step. "Do it now," she seethed, coming to a stop beside me.

Where she stood, it would be easy to spin around and catch her in the stomach with the knife. But then, I had another idea. A better one. One that trumped my desire to see Lillian evaporate into nothing.

I lunged for Micah.

CHAPTER 23

The knife sliced through the ropes around Micah's wrists. As he lurched forward and slammed a fist into Lillian's side, I dropped to my knees and slit the ropes at his ankles. He came to a stand as a stunned Lillian retreated a step.

Alec grabbed one Skotadi by the waist before he could rush Micah, while Nathan landed a kick into the stomach of another.

"Kris!" Alec shouted. "My ankles!"

I clambered across the floor on my hands and knees, avoiding the growing scuffle around me, stopping only long enough to sever Alec's bonds before moving on to free Nathan. I slashed the rope around his ankle first, then crawled behind him to saw through the rope at his wrists.

In a flash, he was on his feet and joining the fight.

It had all taken only seconds for us all to be freed, but we were still outnumbered, five to four, and though I had the diamond-coated knife, Lillian had a gun and…

And she had Micah lifted off the floor, pressed against the wall. Standing a safe distance from him, she held him there using nothing but a hand held out in front of her.

Levitation.

Lillian was levitating Micah off the floor.

Lillian was an Incantator?

"Oh, shit," I muttered.

A big Skotadi stepped in front of me, the jeer on his face exposing the rotten teeth in his mouth. His eyes were enflamed with fury. "You'll never be one of us."

"I'll take that as a compliment," I returned as I held the knife out in front of me. I met his eyes, daring him to make a move.

"She says we need you, but I don't think we do. I'm going to enjoy killing you...*the one*," he taunted, feinting to the right.

I didn't take the bait. Apparently, practicing with Nathan had paid off. I was in a real life fight, holding my own. Granted, the diamond in my hand was doing most of the work for me, but still. I was holding off a Skotadi three times my size.

Over the Skotadi's shoulder I glimpsed flashes of Nathan and Alec as they fought together, mirroring each other like they've been covering each other's backs for years. My heart swelled with pride for a moment before I glanced beyond them, to Lillian, who continued to hold Micah in the air, while barking out orders to the rest of the Skotadi.

What I gathered of her commands was that they were to spare me and Micah, but kill Nathan and Alec.

Preoccupied with watching them, she hadn't noticed Micah's hand moving slowly toward the charm around his neck. It looked as if every movement took a tremendous effort on his part, but I knew what he was trying to do. If he could get the charm off, he would no longer be blocked.

Same went for me.

I yanked at the charm from around my neck, breaking the

string, and tossed it at the Skotadi in front of me. It bounced off his chest and fell at his feet. He didn't look like he cared, and I wondered if he realized what the charm had been doing, if he knew what I was capable of without it.

My hand shot out with a blast of fire that hit him in the chest, showing him just what I could do. He stumbled backward, flailing at the flames that engulfed his shirt.

Behind him, Lillian half turned to me, while keeping one hand trained on Micah. He was closer to his charm, but not close enough.

"Take her out!" Lillian screamed.

I scoffed. No one was listening to her. One Skotadi was desperately trying to remove the shirt that was partially melted to his skin, two more were preoccupied with Nathan and Alec, and another was…gone. He must have been dissipated at some point.

It was me and her. The moment I'd been waiting for.

I felt the familiar tingling in my hand as I prepared a fire ball worthy of Lillian's face. As I raised my arm to launch it, Micah fell from midair, and Lillian turned the rest of the way around to face me. Both her hands shot out, sending an invisible wave that felt like nothing short of an atomic blast into me.

It rocketed me into the wall. My head snapped back, striking the concrete with a sickening crack. Stars swarmed my vision as I tried to hold on to consciousness. The fire in my hand extinguished, and the knife slipped from my hands, and distantly, I was aware of someone yelling my name.

* * *

A chair flying across the room…
Alec taking a fist to the jaw…
Nathan being dropped to the floor…
Shouts, from all around me…

Flashes of activity were interrupted by long stretches of darkness. I hoped the images were nothing more than remnants of a terrible nightmare, but when I finally blinked the black away, I saw that it all had been real.

Nathan lay on the floor in front of me, hands pulled behind his back as a Skotadi secured them with rope. Only when he was pulled to his knees and placed beside Alec did he see that I had come to. A soft shake of his head warned me not to move.

Across the room, Micah was blocked off by Lillian and two other Skotadi. The charm was still secured around his neck, and he looked…defeated.

What in the hell had happened after I blacked out?

Something bad, for Nathan and Alec to wind up as they were, and the Skotadi to have control of us again. The only advantage we had was that they thought I was still out. If I could take them—take Lillian—by surprise…

Unfortunately, thanks to my blurry vision and the throbbing in my head, I wasn't so sure I could conjure another fire ball. I needed to concentrate to pull it off, and that was hard to do with a concussion.

Regardless, I tried it, and winced at the stabbing pain that shot through my skull.

Yeah, that wasn't going to work.

All I had was the knife.

Keeping my eyes on Lillian as she spoke to one of the Skotadi, I slowly swept my hand behind me, searching for it. A sharp, burning pain in the tip of my middle finger clued me in to its location. I immediately pulled my hand back, but the damage had been done.

How could I have been so stupid?

I managed to keep my face blank as the realization that I'd just been cut with a diamond weapon swept over me. Nathan was watching me, his eyes pleading with me to stay still and quiet…to not do anything stupid.

Little did he realize it was too late for that. And when Lillian cocked the gun in her hand and took a few steps forward, closing the gap between her and the two guys I cared about more than anything in this world, I knew that *stupid* was my only option.

I was already injured with diamond. My fate had been sealed, but if I could save them before I succumbed to the diamond deliria, I would.

Lillian leveled the gun on Nathan, and I clambered to my feet with the knife in my hand. I had nothing left to bargain with…but myself.

"Lillian!"

Though she kept the gun trained on the back of Nathan's head, her eyes shifted to me. She looked surprised to see me awake.

"You want me to kill Micah?" I asked her.

"You've proven yourself worthless in that simple task," she spat.

"But you still need me. Don't you?" I lifted the knife in my hand, placed it over my forearm, never removing my eyes from Lillian.

In my periphery, I saw both Nathan and Alec squirm. One of them muttered my name, but my focus remained on Lillian.

"I'll do it, Lillian. I'll do whatever it takes to save them. I'm not afraid."

"You do it," she taunted, "and your boyfriend will be right behind you. Both of them. And you'll be around long enough to see them die."

"Or maybe you'll realize how badly you screwed this up when I take myself out of the equation, and you won't have anything left to fight for."

She scoffed. "You're not that important, girl."

"Oh no?" I pressed the knife against me, hard, but not hard enough to break the skin, and grinned when Lillian flinched. "I think maybe I am."

In that split second before I made my decision, my eyes found Micah's from across the room. I hoped, for the first time, that my thoughts were loud enough for him to read.

And then I slid the knife across the palm of my hand.

* * *

Someone yelled no, and suddenly there was a flurry of activity. Micah, already knowing my intentions, was the first to react while everyone else stared at me in shock. He broke free of the two Skotadi and wrestled a very stunned Lillian to the ground.

Their eyes had lingered on me a few seconds longer, but then Nathan and Alec were on their feet. Though their hands were still tied behind their backs, they were able to keep the Skotadi preoccupied while Micah fought with Lillian for control of the gun.

No one was paying any attention to me. Seeing an opening, I jumped on Lillian, pulling her off balance. She barely avoided the knife in my hand, but in the process, lost the gun. As I crawled across the floor after it, she lunged for me.

The moment my hands circled around the cold metal, I flipped around and pulled the trigger. My aim was off, and the shot hit Lillian in the stomach. Though it wasn't a kill-shot, she dropped hard.

I scampered to my feet, holding the gun out in front of me as I ordered the other two Skotadi to freeze. Nathan and Alec were both on the ground, beaten and worn, but okay. The Skotadi stepped away from them, hands held up in the air as they eyed me warily, stealing glances at their leader bleeding on the floor.

Yeah, I did that, thank you very much.

Micah was advancing on me. "Kris..."

I knew what he wanted to do, but I wasn't going to let him yet. "Cut them loose first," I told Micah, nodding to Nathan and Alec. Someone would need to keep the Skotadi in line while Micah worked his magic on me.

If he could still work his magic on me.

I was feeling...off. The room was starting to spin, I was

seeing double of everything, and my legs had turned to rubber. Someone needed to take the gun from my hands before I accidentally shot someone else.

The moment Nathan and Alec were cut loose, they were at my side. Alec took the gun, apparently recognizing the fact that I could barely hold it up anymore. And my legs…

They finally went out from under me and I dropped to my knees. Nathan went with me, cushioning my fall. "Kris…" He shook his head, face aghast. I could have been mistaken, but his eyes were glistening, almost as if he were on the verge of crying.

It was the deliria. It had to be the deliria.

"Out of the way," I heard Micah say. I looked over Nathan's shoulder as Micah approached, ripping the blocking charm from his neck. As he withdrew the vial he kept hidden under his shirt, his eyes leveled on mine. "Stay with us for five more minutes, Kris. Okay?"

Five minutes? I doubted I had five seconds, I thought, but slurred, "Yeah, sure."

"What are you doing?" Nathan asked Micah, his voice thick, shaky.

"Healing her," Micah answered quietly as he withdrew what he needed from the vial and held it in his hand. "I hope."

"You can do that?" Alec asked.

"Shh." This came from Micah as he closed his eyes, entering the state of meditation he was always harassing me about practicing.

My eyes fluttered shut, and I lost sight of them, but I was still there. I was distantly aware of being laid down, and my head resting on something hard, but soft. Legs, I thought. Nathan's legs. I felt his arm behind my shoulders, supporting me, as Micah held my diamond-cut hand in his.

As a warm tingle pulsated in my palm, then traveled up my arm, I wondered if it was Micah's doing or the diamond. If it was the diamond…

There was so much I'd never said that I needed to say, that I may never have another chance to say.

"Nathan…"

"Shh," came his response from above me, and his voice, whispering soft words that I couldn't understand was the last thing I would hear.

CHAPTER 24

I dreamt of the river, but unlike the other times I'd found myself on its banks, it was a peaceful experience. Lauren and Megan were there with me, as beautiful angels, and I didn't want to leave. It wasn't like our usual times together—they were dead now after all—but I was sent away with a message I swore to never forget.

Where there is free will, anything is possible…

I couldn't go where they were going, they had said. I had a destiny to fulfill. And it might not be as bad as I thought. That was all they told me, all they would give me.

Once I realized I wasn't joining them in the afterlife, we went our separate ways, and for the first time since their deaths, I wasn't sad. It was a bittersweet awakening, having to leave them, but when my eyes opened and fell on Nathan sleeping quietly beside me, the pain of saying my final goodbye waned.

The memory of my last actions rushed back to me, and I scanned the room for clues as to where I was. Wherever it was, it appeared safe. Perhaps a hotel room—and not a cheap slummy one either.

I couldn't be certain, but everything seemed…okay.

I lifted my arm from underneath the covers and traced a

finger over the new scar in the palm of my hand. It had faded and was barely visible now.

A smile spread across my face. Micah had done it. They all had done it. We had gotten out.

And Nathan lay beside me. Only a slight discoloration of the skin under one of his eyes remained as a reminder of the brutality he had endured.

Partially convinced I must be in another dream, I reached out to touch him, to trace a finger across his temple and down his cheekbone. The feel of his skin and the day old scruff on his jaw at my fingertips reassured me that he was really there with me.

His eyes fluttered and snapped open, and suddenly I was gazing into a sea of blue. He stared at me a beat as I smiled at him and then, as if suddenly realizing that he wasn't dreaming, he sprang up in the bed.

He hovered over me as I lay on my back, looking up into his eyes that were both terrified and relieved at once. As the seconds passed, they softened, as if he finally believed that I wasn't an illusion.

"How do you feel?" His voice sounded strained and wary, perhaps an indication of the hell I had put him through.

"I think I'm okay," I murmured.

With a heavy sigh, he dropped his head to my shoulder. He remained there as he gained control over his ragged breathing, his body shuddering above me.

"Nathan?" I ran my hand through his hair gently. I was halfway through my second pass when his head snapped up unexpectedly.

"What were you thinking?" he demanded, his voice full of emotion, but not anger.

"I had to distract them," I offered meekly.

"By killing yourself?" he croaked, and I realized that, to him, that may have appeared to have been my intention.

"Nathan, I—"

"Didn't I tell you we would get through this?"

I nodded and he lowered his head to rest his forehead against mine. His body still shook in tiny tremors, palpable under my hands when I put them on his shoulders.

"Don't do anything like that again," he ordered, then lifted his head to look into my eyes, and waited for me to agree with another nod.

I hadn't considered how my actions would affect him. Then again, I hadn't had much time to think about anything. It had been more of a whim, a desperate attempt, with a desperate hope that I could be saved, and only now did I fully understand how foolish I had been. And how my actions must have looked to him.

"I wasn't trying to kill myself." I felt the need to make him understand that. "I—I'd already nicked myself with the knife. I'd already been injured."

It was a little embarrassing admitting that, but he needed to know I hadn't done it on purpose. I didn't think telling him that I would have sacrificed myself anyway, to save him and Alec, would help my cause, so I kept that tidbit to myself.

"I knew Micah could heal diamond injury, and—"

"That was your plan?" His face dropped. "That was your

hope? That Micah could save you?"

"I guess so."

He shook his head in disbelief and shifted so that he was now propped up on his elbow beside me, facing me, but no longer hovering over me. He was still so close, but I'd preferred it when he'd been closer.

"And what if it hadn't worked?" he asked, his eyes raising to meet mine reluctantly.

I shrugged, feeling ashamed. The world would have been safer, but I hadn't stopped to consider the impact my possible loss would have had on others—on Nathan. From the haunted look on his face, I knew he would have been left devastated, and for that, I felt horrible.

"But it did," I offered. "Don't be mad."

"I'm not mad." He softened, looked down into the small space between us like all the world's answers could be found there. "I was just scared."

That I could understand, but I could also tell that he had more to add, and I waited patiently for him to organize his thoughts.

"I was afraid I'd never have the chance..." he started before trailing off. Unease clouded his eyes as he contemplated what he wanted, but struggled, to say. Finally, his eyes lifted to mine with determination. "I thought I'd never get to say to you all the things I should have said to you a long time ago."

My throat constricted as I waited. When those words didn't come fast enough for me, I forced a strained, "What?"

"How much you mean to me, how much I care about you,

how much…" His eyes flicked away as his throat jumped. They leveled on mine again as the next words made their way to my ears. "How much I love you."

I stared, unable to do anything else. It was just too much…so unexpected…so…

He loved me?

"I've been an idiot," Nathan continued. "I've loved you all along, Kris. It just took me this long to accept it, and to realize that it's what I want. You're what I want. And then, there was Alec… And I thought that if I pretended to not care, that it would make it easier if you chose him. I realize now how stupid that was, that I was practically pushing you to him, but I'm done being stupid now."

For a man of few words, there were times, like this, that he managed to blow me away. I managed a smile, but words were lost to me. Fortunately, Nathan wasn't done yet, which gave me time to collect my own thoughts.

"And I don't care what happened with Alec. It was all my fault, because I didn't fight for you like I should have. From now on, I'm going to fight," he continued. "I'll fight for you—and not just for your life or your future, but for your love."

For the first time in a very long time, happy tears welled up in my eyes. I placed a hand on his stubbly cheek, forcing him to stop and listen to me. "You already have it." His brow pulled together like he didn't understand, or couldn't believe, what I was trying to say. Just to make sure he understood, I added, "Nathan, I'm in love with you."

His eyes squeezed tight as if he were in pain, and he shook

his head in disbelief. "I don't deserve you," he muttered.

I would have voiced an argument, if not for Nathan angling close enough to stunt all brain function. A ghost of a smile graced his lips just before they found mine.

That kiss sealed our words with a tender promise. His mouth moved delicately over mine as if he were taking special care in savoring the moment. My heart swelled with the emotion I had grown used to restraining. Now, in letting it flow freely, my body responded ten-fold. My hands trailed up his arms, which were taut from holding his weight as he shifted over me. His upper body blanketed me, but when I cupped the back of his neck, I tugged him even closer.

That move sparked a change in the way Nathan kissed me. Tenderness and purpose gave way to raw desire. My hands moved over his back and shoulders as if wanting to touch him everywhere at once. None of it seemed enough. Finding the hem of his shirt, I slipped my hands underneath the fabric until they were flush with his skin. The muscles that, until then, I had only seen in my imagination, were at my fingertips, and felt even more magnificent in real life.

Fueled by love, and a previously restrained desire, this kiss quickly transcended all other kisses we have shared—both physically and emotionally. I knew it, and I'm pretty sure he knew it, too. As expected, he was the first to recognize the heady direction we were heading.

"Okay…okay…" Nathan murmured as he pulled away, albeit reluctantly. His chest heaved against mine as he caught his breath. Though it took visible effort, he pushed off of me.

Scooting back a few inches for good measure, he propped up on one elbow to look down at me.

"We get to do more of that now, right?" I asked wistfully.

His lips curled into a smile, wide enough to produce both the sexiest and most adorable dimples I had ever seen. "I sure hope so. But, for now, you stay over there."

That was fine. I rolled my head so that I had a perfect view of him, and that was enough for the time being. I was curious, but I didn't ask why he insisted on maintaining the six inch gap separating us. To me, it was a form of torture. I considered that being close to me might be a form of torture for him, so I decided not to press the issue if that was what he wanted.

We were together, and that was what mattered. Now that we had that established, and we apparently weren't going to make out again anytime soon, I figured we'd talk.

And I had a lot of questions. Starting with how I ended up here—wherever *here* was?

"What happened? After I blacked out?"

Nathan grinned. "You're two favorite people rescued us."

My two favorite people? His sarcasm had been apparent, so that could only mean…

"Gabby and Richie?"

He nodded.

"How?"

His grin grew. "Apparently, the Kala had a tracking device placed on Micah, in the event that they ever lost him. When we left to come find you, Gabby and Richie notified the Kala. They tracked him, sent practically their entire army. The Skotadi didn't have a chance."

I paled at his mention of the Kala. A chill whipped down my spine at the thought that we weren't rescued and safe, but rather held hostage, by the Kala now.

Nathan must have seen the fear register on my face. "Don't worry," he reassured me. "Micah was very convincing in persuading them to help you. He wouldn't let them near you until they understood what you did for him, and got them to agree to help."

The Kala were going to help us? All of us? Belatedly, I realized I hadn't seen anyone but Nathan yet. What about the others? I knew Micah would be okay, but what about Alec?

"Alec too?" I asked.

Nathan nodded. "Apparently, they realized the advantage of having all three of you on their side."

That was the most reassuring news I'd heard in a long time. Surely the Kala knew about the Skotadi's plans. They'd probably been working on stopping them for years, and maybe had some theories about how to prevent the conversions. They had to know more than we did.

"And Callie?" The question hung up in my throat, and I steeled myself for his answer.

"Callie's fine."

Oh, thank God. I would have never forgiven myself if anything had happened to her.

"So now what?" I asked Nathan.

"When you're able, we'll go to the base, start dissecting the whole conversion process." Nathan hesitated, and his posture told me that what he had to add wasn't something I would want to hear. "They got Lillian."

My brow furrowed. "Got her?"

She wasn't dead?

"Captured her," Nathan amended. He eyed me warily as I registered what he'd said, like he knew I wouldn't be happy about it.

I wasn't. I sat up a little straighter in the bed. "Why?"

"They're planning to study her, learn from her, to figure out how the Skotadi changed her and use what they learn to help you and Alec."

My heart sank. So the Kala didn't know more than we did. While I couldn't ignore the value of having her in captivity, knowing she was alive, and near, worried me.

"Security is tight on her, Kris," Nathan assured me. "She's already been sent to the base with most of the Kala army. Only a few stayed behind, to escort us to the base once you're okay to travel."

I pushed back the covers, but Nathan's hands on my shoulders prevented me from getting up.

"Not yet, you're not," he said.

"We need to get to the base," I argued.

The sooner we got started the better. My inner demons have been growing stronger by the day. I didn't have time to spare, and neither did Alec.

"We will, soon. Just get some more rest," he pleaded. "I'll tell them you're awake, and we'll make the arrangements to leave. But I want you to stay in bed until then."

I dropped my head to the pillow with a sigh. I was ready to go, but knew better than to argue with Nathan when he had his mind set on something.

"Besides," he said with a growing smile. "I think there might be someone else who would like to see you."

Before I could ask, he slid off the bed, crossed the room to the door and stuck his head outside. Muffled voices from the hallway reached my ears, but I couldn't tell what was being said or who was saying them.

A smile lit his face when he turned back to me. "I'll be back, okay?"

I nodded and he started to duck outside, but not before he was practically run over by a girl half his size. She practically shoved him out of the way as she hurried toward me. Showing no concern for unseen injuries, she threw herself onto the bed, and me. As her arms encircled my neck, I heard a soft click, and looked up to see the door closed and Nathan gone.

"You've got to stop scaring me like this," Callie said.

"You've got to stop squeezing me like this," I wheezed. Only then, did Callie loosen her hold and leaned back to give me a once over.

"You look like hell," she said with a teasing smile. "But I'm glad you're okay."

"I'm glad you're okay," I returned. "You are okay, right?"

She waved a hand dismissively. "Yeah, yeah, yeah. No evil creatures of hell can get me down."

Despite the flippancy of her words, I detected a hint of unease in her eyes. Something that I rarely saw in Callie.

"What did they do to you, Callie?" I asked softly.

Her eyes skirted away. "Nothing, really."

"Callie."

At the warning tone of my voice, she sighed. "Alright, fine. You'll hear about it eventually anyway." Callie took a breath, preparing to tell the story that, from her demeanor, I guessed she had repeated several times already. "They put me in this dark room, strapped me down. That Lillian chick came in a few times, and did some weird ritualistic voodoo shit, said some chants, and then that was it."

"She's an Incantator," I said.

"Yeah, I sort of figured that out."

"What was she doing?"

Callie shrugged. "Not sure. I heard her talking to the others about *life forces* and *immortality*, but I was so out of it, I didn't really understand everything they were talking about."

"You told the Kala about this?"

"Yeah, like a hundred different times. I think they keep expecting me to suddenly remember something important, but I got nothing." She shrugged and paused as a wide smile spread across her face. "Some of those Kala guys are *hot*, by the way."

I giggled. Good old Callie—boy crazy as always.

"Sure wish I could stay," she mused offhandedly.

It took me a moment to register what she'd said. When I did, I raised my eyebrows in a silent inquiry.

"I'm going home," Callie said. Whereas many would have said those words with cheer, Callie was nothing but mournful. "They won't let me come wherever you're going. Something to do with rules about humans."

I swallowed the lump that had formed in my throat. I was going to miss Callie and the thought of moving on to the unknown without my best friend by my side terrified me, but even that was out shadowed by the relief I felt at knowing she would be safe. As long as the Skotadi didn't give her any trouble. I would have to talk to Nathan about getting her some Kala protection. Just in case.

"They're sending me my own private body guard," she said, as if she'd read my mind. "Actually three of them. Can you believe it?"

"Really?" The Kala were sending three of their own to watch over my best friend? I wondered how much of that had been Micah's doing.

"Jared, Tony, and Austin are their names," Callie said. "And Jared?" Callie's eyes widened as she fanned herself. "Holy hot!"

"I'm going to miss you," I said, laughing to hide the tears welling in my eyes.

Callie nodded. "And I'm going to be in so much trouble when I come back from Italy early with three hot guys following me around."

We both laughed at that. Something told me that Callie would be fine. She'd always handled attention from boys just fine. Having three of them around would be more like a dream come true for her. Dealing with her parents, explaining where she'd been the past two months, if not in Italy, would prove to be a bigger problem.

Callie sobered first and fixed me with a fierce look. "You're in good hands, even without me."

"I know."

"I'm not talking about Nathan," she said. "Well, I am. But not just him. Micah, too. He didn't leave your side for days. Whatever he did, it drained him, but he wouldn't give up on you, not until he knew you were going to be okay, and only then did he finally collapse of exhaustion. He's still sleeping it off."

I smiled sheepishly. Though I'd expected Micah to wield his diamond-injury healing abilities, the amount of dedication that Callie described surprised me. Especially after the strained direction our friendship had taken. His commitment to saving me was sobering, and I didn't know if I would ever be able to thank him enough.

Callie stayed with me and we chatted and hugged and said goodbye over and over again. Each time, it was too difficult for her to turn and walk away, so she stayed and the cycle repeated itself. We had at least an hour together before the door opened and a Kala that I didn't recognize entered. From his posture, we both got the message that it was time for her to go.

Before she left, she flashed me a secretive wink and leaned close enough to whisper, "What did I tell you? *Hot*."

Callie and I separated in the most fitting way for our friendship—with laughter. Even so, my heart beat a little weaker as she disappeared from my sight. The only thing that soothed the pain was the appearance of Nathan in the doorway in her place.

* * *

It took four days to reach the Kala base.

Before we left, I'd asked Nathan where it was. His answer had been so unexpected, I thought he'd been playing a joke on me. As we approached it now, I realized he had been serious.

We'd crossed into Mexico two days ago and had continued south until we reached a small village along the coast of Costa Rica. From there, we'd boarded a boat. Nathan had said that Skotadi knew the Kala were in the area, but didn't know which island they inhabited. According to him, Skotadi often tried to intercept them on the mainland, but we'd passed through without incident, and now sped toward the island that was to be my new home.

For now. I wasn't so sure how I felt about island life. Nathan had left the base to live unprotected on his own in Boone. I couldn't help but wonder what had driven him to choose that over living in what appeared to be paradise.

Surrounded by the bluest water I have ever seen, it looked more like a scene on a postcard than an actual real-life place. Beyond the white sand beach, amongst the palm trees, a community was built, with an assortment of large structures built of wood and stone. It covered the area of a small college campus, and disappeared into what appeared to be nothing short of a jungle that encompassed the rest of the island.

Exotic was the best description I could think of to describe what I saw. Looks could often be misleading.

I figured I would learn soon enough what it was like. As the boat slowed and pulled up to the dock, I felt a pang of anxiety over the unknown.

Nathan took my hand in his as we followed the Kala soldiers off the boat and along a narrow trail into what appeared to be the heart of the village. I still felt uneasy, and a quick glance over my shoulder confirmed that I wasn't the only one. Alec looked as if he expected them to pull weapons and kill us all before we brushed the sand off our shoes.

The Kala that met us in the village stared, but no one showed aggression. With each step, my nerves settled and I started to look forward to living here with anticipation.

This was where it would all change. I knew this was where we needed to be, where the remaining pieces would fall into place, and the crossroads with the path to a better destiny awaited.

As we followed the wide walking trail through the village, I noticed that several more Kala had assembled to catch a glimpse of us. Being surrounded by so many unfamiliar faces was a little unsettling. I reminded myself that they were merely curious about us—the new arrivals, and the Skotadi stepping onto their shores.

Out of the crowd, I thought I heard my name called. I squeezed Nathan's hand tightly and his head tipped down to mine. From the blank look on his face, I knew he hadn't heard it.

I had to have imagined it. No one knew me here.

Then I heard it again, and I saw the recognition flash across Nathan's face at the same time I realized that I, too, knew that voice. It came again, this time calling Nathan's name, and we both looked up simultaneously, scanning the faces in the crowd.

It couldn't be her. It wasn't possible.

Was it?

We heard her again, closer, and Nathan's grip on my hand tightened as he pushed our way through the crowd, drawing us closer to the voice still calling our names. I knew it now. I absolutely *knew* it, but I still braced myself for disappointment.

And then I saw her, dwarfed by Kala who were much bigger and taller, her small frame straining to see around them as she stood on her tip-toes. When she saw us, she pushed through the remaining crowd with a strength unimaginable for her age.

Not until her warm arms were wrapped around both Nathan and I at once did I allow myself to believe it.

"You're alive," I breathed. "You're really alive."

Gran released me to give Nathan a kiss on the cheek, then she turned and cupped my face between her hands. "It will take more than a few Skotadi punks to get me down, sweetheart." Turning back to Nathan, she winked. "I told you she was special."

"How..." Nathan trailed off, at a complete loss for words.

Gran patted her grandson on the back, and I feared that he might fall over. Stunned stupid, only the slightest touch from her caused him to sway unsteadily, forcing me to grab ahold of his arm.

Gran took in our joined hands and the way we stood together, and a knowing smile graced her lips. "Well, then...I see you've finally come to your senses, Nathan." She looked back and forth between the two of us, and I knew that she was happy to see us together.

Perhaps I hadn't mistaken that conversation I'd had with her last year—when I'd thought she might be trying to hook me up with her grandson. If only I'd known then that it was Nathan, I would have encouraged her.

But then, the way it had all come together had been a hell of a fun ride. One I planned to keep enjoying for a long, long time.

"Come on," Gran said, placing a hand to each of our backs to guide us through the growing crowd. "Apparently, we have much to catch up on."

EPILOGUE

The living quarters on the island reminded me of a college dormitory. At least, that was what I told myself as I looked around my room.

It's not a jail cell. Not a jail cell.

It didn't look like one, with a nice bed, large closet, and a desk. I even had a balcony overlooking the island. From the fourth floor, it was breathtaking. I'd seen views like the one I had in travel brochures for expensive vacations I knew I could never afford.

No, the room was exquisite. The problem was that it *felt* like a jail cell. With the Kala guard stationed outside my room, it was hard not to feel imprisoned.

I couldn't leave my room without her. She reminded me of Gabby, except bigger and scarier. I didn't doubt they picked the most menacing female Kala they could find to follow me around.

I was told I must have an approved Kala with me at all times—Micah, Nathan, or the formidable Kim. Because boys weren't allowed in the girls' sleeping quarters, except for fifteen minute intervals—and they did keep track—I was stuck with her as my shadow almost everywhere I went.

Alec had one too, which I learned when I walked over to the

boy's quarters. I knew exactly which room was his from the muscled Kala standing outside, and knocked on the door.

The door swung open, and Alec's eyebrows shot up when he saw me. Or it might have been Kim that piqued his curiosity. Whatever it was, he got over it quickly and invited me in.

"Fifteen minutes," I heard his burly guard grunt just before the door shut.

Alec rolled his eyes when he turned to me.

"Friendly guy?" I asked him.

"He's not the smartest pick of the litter. More brawn, less brain," Alec said. "He doesn't seem to think fifteen minutes is enough time for me—"

"Okay, Casanova," I interrupted. "Didn't come here to hear about all that you could do in fifteen minutes."

He shrugged as he muttered, "I could do a lot. Just saying."

I watched him as he took a seat on the edge of his bed. His room was identical to mine, except for a different color scheme. His was plain and boyish, while mine was tropical and girly.

"You okay?" I asked him.

His eyes wandered around the room, finally returning to mine. "Why wouldn't I be?"

I sat beside him, close enough that our shoulders touched. Whereas I'd always sought to keep my distance from Alec before, now I needed him close. My head nodded at the door. "The fact that we can't go anywhere without security, being surrounded by Kala, them apparently doing their best to keep us apart…need I go on?"

"I'm managing," he muttered. "I'm fine if I just stay in my

room."

I wondered if he felt like a prisoner, too. I took a deep breath, preparing to do what I had come here for. "They want me to resume working with Micah, practicing my skills with him. Gran will be there too, and Nathan sometimes. Just like before. The Kala think we'll be working on specialties, but we're going to be doing some incantation work too. I was wondering if you…"

"You want me to?"

I nodded eagerly. Despite the strained relationship between Alec and Micah—and the potential danger to Micah—I did want Alec there. Not only for moral support, but because I wanted to help him too.

And I missed being around him.

"Then I'll be there."

I beamed at him. When I heard his breath catch, my smile started to falter.

What was I doing? He was in love with me. I shouldn't be doing this, asking this of him.

"Kris," he started, his voice soft as he turned to face me. "Don't worry about me."

Oh, shit. Did I say that out loud?

"I'm happy for you. Really happy," he continued, then grinned. "I don't even really hate Nathan any more. He's not that bad."

My eyebrows shot up and Alec's grin widened.

"What? You that surprised?" he asked. "I'd rather you be with him than Micah."

I laughed. When Alec tilted his head at me, I only laughed

harder. Finally, after taking a few moments to pull myself together, I said, "Nathan said the same thing about you."

Now, Alec laughed, and it felt good, being with him like this. Because I'd missed him. And being around him always managed to lift my spirits. I spent my allotted fifteen minutes joking around with Alec. My good mood upon leaving his room gave me the boost I needed to face the next person on my list of people to visit today.

Micah.

He had security outside of his room, for a whole other reason than Alec and I did. At least I knew his guard. That didn't mean he returned my smile when he saw me.

Richie was one tough cookie.

Micah must have sensed me, because his door swung open before I said anything. With a look tossed at Richie, Micah invited me in.

"Or would you rather go for a walk?" Micah offered. "Get out for a little bit?"

"No, I'm not staying long." I had plans to meet Nathan a little later for lunch, and was not going to miss that. "I just…I haven't had the chance to thank you yet, for what you did. For all of it. So…thank you."

Micah shrugged. "No big deal, especially not after what you did for me."

The air in his room felt too dry, thinner, and I swallowed a couple of times to dislodge the lump that had formed in my throat. "I wasn't going to, you know?"

"Kill me? I know. I think that was the loudest your thoughts have ever been."

Right. He'd read me. Of course. "It was the one time I wanted you to read me."

We both smiled, but it felt all kinds of awkward. I wondered if we would ever have a normal friendship, one without the added stress of knowing our entwined destinies.

I often reminded myself of the message Lauren and Megan had given me: *Where there is free will, anything is possible.* I hoped that meant I would have some say in what became of me, of my future, and who I would spend it with.

Micah suddenly turned and walked away from me, opening the door to his balcony and stepping outside. The curtains billowed in the breeze. His voice carried to me, where I stood inside.

"You can fight it all you want, Kris," he said. "We both know where you're going to end up."

"Reading my mind again, Micah?" I pushed past the curtains and stepped out onto the balcony. Not far. Not close to him.

His back remained to me as he leaned on the railing. He didn't answer my question. "You know your heart might belong to Nathan right now, but your soul belongs to me." He finally turned, and his eyes bored into mine. "Eventually your soul will lead you back to me."

I stared at him a moment, biting my tongue a few times before I finally spoke. "Friends, Micah. That's all we'll be. And honestly, right now, that's a stretch."

"For now."

I nodded once and backpedaled into the room. "On that

note, I think I'll be going. Thank you, again."

I was surprised when I reached the door without Micah doing something to stop me. I glanced over my shoulder as I swung the door open, and saw him standing just inside the room, watching me. When my eyes met his, he smiled. And it was that smile I'd always hated, that one that made me think he was hiding something. Or like he knew something that he wasn't telling me.

I'd seen that smile one too many times already, and I wanted nothing to do with it now.

As the door shut behind me, I thought I heard him say something that sounded like, "I'll be waiting…"

I could have been wrong, but knowing Micah, I doubted it.

I wondered if the kid would ever give up. What it would take for him to give up.

I was with Nathan. Period.

I loved Nathan.

And as I left the boys' dormitory in search of him, for the first time in a long time, I felt hope.

My destiny awaited, but I no longer feared it. I had free will on my side, and I would bet on that over fate any day. Especially when my will led me to Nathan.

ACKNOWLEDGEMENTS

I'm humbled by the reception my debut novel, Ignited, has received, and by the requests for more by those that have read it. It's because of my fans that I'm doing this again…and again. So without you, this series would be nothing but thoughts in my head. Thank you for pushing me to put the words down.

My first fans were my wonderful family and friends, and I'd like to extend an extra thank you to them for their support through this entire crazy process. There are days I want to throw in the towel, days I don't think I can do it, days I don't want to do it, but their encouragement pushes me forward.

Special thanks to Georgina Brooks for designing my covers. You have a way of taking my poorly constructed ideas and turning them into a work of art, even in the midst of a record breaking heat wave. Looking forward to planning many more covers with you.

I'd like to thank the first readers, who took the time to dissect the first drafts of Sacrificed. Rachel and Lisa, thanks for pointing out what worked, what didn't worked, and helping me to piece together the gaps.

ABOUT THE AUTHOR

Desni Dantone resides in Greensburg, Pennsylvania with her husband, Stephen, son, Nicholas, and their dog and cat. She loves young adult paranormal romance books, and loves to write them even more. You can usually find her curled up on the couch with either a good book or her laptop, and a cup of tea nearby.

The third book of The Ignited Series, titled Salvaged Soul, is expected in late 2014, with the fourth and final book, Avenging Heart, coming in 2015.

You can follow her on her website: www.desnidantone.com or on Facebook at: www.facebook.com/ignitedbooks

Made in the USA
Middletown, DE
09 May 2017